Praise for

# SAVAGE T[...]

"A love story of the most fevered, brutal order.... The prose is propulsive, erotic, and darkly dreamlike, recalling the early novels of Marguerite Duras.... [*Savage Tongues*] interrogates the narratives we assign to the past and asks what we are allowed to expect of those who love us."

—Vulture

"Not many writers can convey both great beauty and horror at the same time, but in *Savage Tongues*, Azareen Van der Vliet Oloomi does so deftly.... She works through questions of sex, friendship, trauma, and the obliteration of the self, with an inventive approach to time, setting, and character.... Oloomi's sentences, whether evoking pain or pleasure, are electric, filled with life. If I'm honest, when I was reading, I often wished I had written them. The imagery is filmic, and sometimes piercing."

— Amina Cain, *Paris Review*

"A novel of ideas.... Though steeped in sex and haunted by fleshy frights ... their exorcism is mostly a matter of language."

—*Washington Post*

"Azareen Van der Vliet Oloomi's stunning new novel is a hauntingly beautiful depiction of the way past traumas grip at our insides, threatening to tear us apart years after we've experienced them.... *Savage Tongues* is rigorous in its exploration of the effects that violence and corruption have on our conception of ourselves."

—Refinery29

"This is a pulls-no-punches look at abandonment, ownership, trauma, and the convergence of political and personal pain. It is also a touching ode to friendship, a partial salve for these wounds."

— Literary Hub, Most Anticipated Books of 2021, Part Two

"Written with the intensity of early Duras and Ferrante's *Days of Abandonment*.... With the help of a dear friend, Arezu excavates and puts words to her past trauma in this novel about love, friendship, identity, and displacement."

—The Millions

"Azareen Van der Vliet Oloomi is no stranger to accolades . . . and, boy oh boy, does she deserve every one of them. I will be anticipating anything she writes. . . . *Savage Tongues* has drawn comparisons to Shirley Jackson and Samanta Schweblin for the way it keeps you suspended in a state of discomfort and hauntingly depicts a shattering of the self."

— Literary Hub, Most Anticipated Books of 2021

"By turns brilliant, erotic, and piercing, this third novel from PEN/Faulkner award winner Azareen Van der Vliet Oloomi shines new light into how historical oppression, both at a personal and societal level, continues to dominate our present-day thinking. Ostensibly a dissection of an exploitative relationship, the novel quickly broadens into a wide-ranging examination — and skewering — of master narratives around race, gender, sexuality, and religion which dictate the way we live now. . . . Van der Vliet Oloomi reflects the coexistence of pain and pleasure in lush descriptions of the southern Spanish landscape."

— *Asian Review of Books*

"The past bears with it a harrowing capacity to disrupt lives. . . . [*Savage Tongues*] follows one woman's reckoning with her own past, and the larger context that suffuses the history she's tried to leave behind."

— *Volume 1 Brooklyn*

"In *Savage Tongues*, Van der Vliet Oloomi establishes herself as a skilled cartographer of trauma. With a remarkably clear vision and dynamic, colorful prose, she takes us along on her journey into the deepest recesses of an embattled mind. This is a book for those who expect from the novel far more than a story."

— Amir Ahmadi Arian, author of *Then the Fish Swallowed Him*

"*Savage Tongues* breathes fresh life into ancient wounds, erasures, and annihilations. By mining transgressions — historical, sexual, bodily, and territorial — Van der Vliet Oloomi delivers a courageous book, as searing and terrifying as it is healing."

— Neda Maghbouleh, author of *The Limits of Whiteness*

BOOKS BY
AZAREEN VAN DER VLIET OLOOMI

*Call Me Zebra*

*Fra Keeler*

# SAVAGE
# TONGUES

◆

## AZAREEN
## VAN DER VLIET
## OLOOMI

MARINER BOOKS
*Boston   New York*

*To my queer family who lit the way all along*

Some moments in a life, and they needn't be very long or seem very important, can make up for so much in that life; can redeem, justify, that pain, that bewilderment, with which one lives, and invest one with the courage not only to endure it, but to profit from it; some moments teach one the price of the human connection: if one can live with one's own pain, then one respects the pain of others, and so, briefly, but transcendentally, we can release each other from pain.

—James Baldwin, *Tell Me How Long the Train's Been Gone*

Nowhere is the sadistic potential of a language built on agency so visible as in torture. While torture contains language, specific human words and sounds, it is itself a language, an objectification, an acting out.

—Elaine Scarry, *The Body in Pain:*
*The Making and Unmaking of the World*

Power not only acts on a subject but, in a transitive sense, enacts the subject into being.

—Judith Butler, *The Psychic Life of Power*

We were passing the time talking
about East and West
when death came to a peak of Albaicín.
So death reaches Granada too
with a message on the phone.
It came on its black horse
and took a friend
while the hooves wounded the sunset
over Alhambra, that summer palace.
I did not try to stop it—
we Arabs don't stop death,
we just want it to know the value
of the hand that slackens the reins.

—Najwan Darwish, "An Afternoon in Albaicín"
(trans. Kareem James Abu-Zeid)

# SAVAGE
# TONGUES

# 1

TWENTY YEARS HAD PASSED since I'd been to Marbella. *Twenty years,* I repeated to myself as the plane descended through the sky toward Spain. I leaned my head against the plexiglass. The cool surface felt good against my forehead. I could see the mountains in the distance covered in a forbidding veil of mist. We'd flown through the night; now dawn was breaking. An uncertain yellow light was coming through the pillowy masses of clouds. Wrapped in fog, the ring of mountains looked muted and dull; only their peaks glowed in the hushed smoky tones of the sky. Below, I could see airplanes lined up on the black belt of the runway waiting to take off; closer to the gates, there were tourists deplaning, leaning into the wind, their hair blown back, the turbines on the regional planes still spinning. The drone of the slowing engines echoed in my ears. I had the uneasy feeling that time had come to a standstill. That all of Marbella had existed in a state of suspension since I had last been there at seventeen—raw, restless, with a savage temperament that had led me into Omar's arms. Omar, my stepmother's nephew. Omar: my lover, my torturer, my confidant and enemy.

It had been one hell of a night. And now, here I was, returning to one of the ugliest episodes of my youth: that strange, wild summer I'd spent in this moonlit city of salt and gulls and palm trees, on this dark and playful coast, living in my father's vacant and abandoned apartment, learning to ride Omar in the blazing afternoon heat. I was supposed to spend the summer with my father, though I'd known full well that he would fail to show up, or that he would show up late, and that even if he did show up it would be with that wife of his, that fussy demimonde from Beirut, a woman of the old world who was raised on French colonial patisseries and who, at sixteen, was shuffled from her father's home to her first husband's, a cousin two decades her senior who had left her widowed in middle age. She is as naïve as she is possessive, manipulative, calculating.

I knew that my father would ignore me that summer, or that he would acknowledge my presence but deny his responsibility for me, his daughter, a human he'd created, whose health and happiness, if normal societal rules were applied, he should be tending to. But normal societal rules have never been a part of my life. They do not interest me. They provoke in me nothing but boredom.

I am a half-formed thing, neither this nor that. My mother is Iranian. My father, British. I am a split child of the gutters, raised in the shadowy streets of Tehran, where a few lonely hooded faces murmur with trembling lips, "Death to America." America, the country I moved to as an adolescent, a country that groans at the very thought of Iranians, calling us bloodthirsty tyrants, vowing to smoke us out of our holes, as if the whole Middle East were living under one big primordial rock, spinning the yarn of evil. I suppose from the white man's view we are so evil that we deserve to be eviscerated. Just look, for example, at how quickly after we set foot on American soil that my brother was subjugated by a hate crime that damaged him beyond repair, a cruel attack that I witnessed and that infused my already fragmented life with an unfocused rage and despair. I wonder now: If we had never moved to America, would my life still have collided with Omar's with such brutal force on the other side of the Atlantic in Spain? Would I still have been animated by self-loathing, self-immolation, a misdirected revenge? It never ceases to amaze and bewilder me how events that have germinated on one continent can be harvested in the shadows of another far, far away.

Yes, I have lived an itinerant life. I've lived here and there: in the sun-bleached streets of Los Angeles; the dull roads of Reno; the moody, superior streets of New York; the gritty, pulsating avenues of Chicago. My father, too, is a nomad; as children, we are, after all, an invention of our parents. My father had worked for years at sea with the British India Steam Navigation Company until he got tuberculosis. He hadn't been allowed to work on deck after that. That's the only concrete fact about his life that he ever shared with me. The rest is conjecture. But I know beyond a shadow of a doubt that he was devastated by the disease, that it distorted his whole sense of self, that he survived, but that he would have preferred not to; he'd never learned to conduct himself on dry land.

He'd softened the blow by finding new ways to insert himself into the vast and distant lands to which he'd grown accustomed: India, and later Iran, Lebanon, the Emirates. "Oh, the women of the Middle East!" he would say. "They're so sensual —dark and suggestive, loyal, obedient." He attached himself to what he called the "mysteries of the Orient," first through my mother, a girl from the upper echelons of Tehran society whose father had been killed during the revolution. When my father came along, she'd been confused, caught in the horrors of coups and confiscated property, of house-arrest orders and death executed in cold blood. My father would later abandon her for my stepmother, whom he'd married without finalizing his divorce to my mother; he'd converted to Islam purely to take advantage of its patriarchal leanings, which allowed him, a white British man, to be married to two Muslim women, one Shia, one Sunni, at the same time against their will. But as much as he fetishized them, he also echoed the words of violence so common in the West. He would often say, "I'm repulsed by how irrational your people are, their lack of logic, their bent toward murder, their self-destructiveness. It's why the Middle East can't survive without a benign dictator in place." His gaze was always forbidding, his tone declarative. Oh, how little regard we have for the power words have to wound!

A *benign dictator*, I'd thought to myself, examining the cruelty of my father's sentences. And that pair of words, *your people*. As if I weren't made of him, weren't a part of him. I was, in his eyes, part of the enemy camp no matter that my veins run with equal parts oil and the brackish waters of western seas.

My body—what an unlikely experiment. I'd always felt that I was fundamentally distorted, a reckless invention. That there was something deeply flawed about my being. Iranian American: victim and victimizer, colonized and colonizer. How I was meant to make my way through the world is beyond me. My own father, if someone so utterly absent from his children's life can be called that, had read my people with the same air of superiority with which we've long been read by Britain, France, America, modern nations that have defined themselves in opposition to us, that have split the world in two—Occident, Orient —that have defined us as morally impure, uncivilized fools with an unquenchable thirst for violence, barbarians who would only benefit from the levelheaded beneficence of the West, the Occidental man's even temper, his logician's mind.

And now, here I am: I've returned to Marbella, the only place where I'd ever tried to spend significant time with my father—a failed attempt, as he hadn't shown up until it was too late, until the dreadful events of that summer had unfolded, impressed themselves upon my already misshapen life. Instead of spending time with my father, I'd spent time in the hollow corridors of a life that belonged to him, a life from which he was absent, in the rooms of his barren apartment, a symbol of what he could have been to me but never was: a father not just in name, a protector, an unconditional source of love.

I'd come back to Marbella to examine the ways in which my own punishing destiny had intersected with Omar's, a man who was more or less family. He was my stepmother's favorite nephew. He'd been forty years old that summer, twenty-three years older than I was. Tall, handsome, seductive, he looked at me with big hungry eyes and a penetrating gaze, a gaze that— once it turned cruel, well into our affair, when I'd least expected it—had drained my body of its will to live.

I suppose I have what some might refer to as an investigative nature, a relentless edge, a charge to understand how it was that the crooked path of my life—a life that I'd wrongly thought Omar could save me from, a life lived in the shadows of parental neglect and informed by historical annihilation—had led me right to Omar. It had taken me twenty years to understand that the lens through which Omar had seen me was so wretched, so disgraceful, so disenfranchising, it had robbed me of my ability to see in return: I had lost the power to look. And because I had lost my ability to look, I had lost the ability to see myself clearly. Where then would I speak from? How would I retell my story? I had lost my descriptive capacities. He had reshaped my identity in his image, with his gaze. Going forward from that summer, who I am would always be, in part, because of what he did to me. I couldn't undo that. I no longer had any interest in denying myself the past. I needed to see and then unsee myself through Omar's eyes. Then, I wondered, would I be able to look at the world as myself for the first time?

I was returning to Marbella in order to face head-on the absolute pain and pleasure of our story. I needed to purge my body of his memory. To destroy all the sensual memories I had built up around him in my mind. To translate the bitterness and the heat of our relationship into a language of my own making. What, I wondered, had Omar asked me not to see, not to be? How had he both made and unmade me? I had no idea. He had worked my muscles with his tongue until his mouth had gone dry against my skin. He had left me raw and limp. That I was already wounded was clear from the lines on my face: at seventeen, my eyes shone with the heat of intense grief, my mouth curled downward, my nostrils flared easily. All Omar had to do was rework my bruises, expand their boundaries. And he did. He crafted an exquisite wound knowing full well that beneath that wound existed another, and beneath that, another still. My life had made his job easy.

Perhaps I should begin at the beginning. Like I said, I am not alone in my wretchedness though I have not seen my brother in years. In a decade. I have other brothers and sisters, too, half siblings, but I don't know them. I don't know how many of us there are. I only know my own brother, the one with whom I share a mother. Not long before I'd left for Marbella, just weeks after my mother, brother, and I arrived in the United States from Tehran, to Reno, my brother had been beaten to a pulp by a skinhead. His face had been shattered, his disfigured body left on the sidewalk, his hair matted with his own blood. I'd found him; I'd stepped off the school bus and onto his lifeless body, into a pool of our shared blood. For a moment, I thought I'd gone mad, that

I was in a nightmare. The pain of seeing my brother barely gulping for air, at the edge of death, deranged me. But then he moved. He must have felt me standing over him, looking down at his swollen eyes, as blue as the darkening sky above us, in disbelief. His school supplies were scattered around on the sidewalk, under the bushes, dirty with mud. He made a noise, let out a complaint, and I bent toward him; I kneeled on the ground beneath the trees and drew his head into my lap.

Thinking about it now, I felt my hands tingle. I was sweating. My palms were wet. I reached up and twisted the overhead fan on and breathed in the recycled air of the airplane. Then I looked out the window at the tarmac, at the mountains in the distance, at the green fields dotted with palm trees and *macchia mediterranea,* its wild red and purple flowers already in bloom. As we approached the glistening tarmac wet from the morning's rain, I saw my brother lying on the runway; there he was, his face still smashed, his bones shattered, his skin bruised and swollen and misshapen; he was looking up at me from the black ribbon of the runway, silently asking: *What are you doing back here?* I shut my eyes.

At seventeen, I'd come to Marbella numb with a rage I hadn't had the language to articulate. None of us—neither my mother, my brother, nor I—were able to speak to the others after his attack. We had always spoken to one another in Farsi, but now we heard the echo of his skull being shattered against concrete in every word of our mother tongue. And we couldn't speak to one another in English. No. That was the language of our first defeat. So we lived in an ever-widening silence. Once his face had healed enough for him to travel, my brother left for London to stay with my father, my father who seemed only to have affection for us when we were in danger; he'd sweep in and try to rescue us, make a grand gesture of love, then dispose of us once the novelty had passed. Back then my father lived near Hyde Park, spending what he could of his wife's money. My father who was always broke, who'd been raised as poor as a church mouse, kicking rocks around in the East End.

My mother had begged my brother not to go. She couldn't stand the thought of losing him. "Without you," she'd said to him, "it will be as if one-half of my life has disappeared. Each of you is like one of my lungs," she'd said. "How will I breathe with just one lung?" But he'd left anyway. And my father had promptly used his wife's money to send him away to a boarding school in the English countryside, I don't remember where. I barely saw him after that. His suffering had broken us down. The only kinship left between us was pain.

I became reckless, impulsive; I craved danger. I went to Marbella. My mother encouraged me to go. She was hopeful I would see my brother, that my father would bring him along for the summer. She wanted me to convince my brother to come back to her. He had stopped speaking to her. He had come to associate her with the beating he had taken. He'd said, "You didn't teach me how to be a man" and "What kind of man is incapable of defending himself?" He spoke as though my mother had castrated him. It was my job to remind him of our father's culpability, his cold, disaffected parenting, our mother's eternal sacrifice. But none of that came to be. I didn't see him in Marbella. I could never have anticipated what happened there. That summer will haunt me for the rest of my life.

I'd spent the first half of the summer living alone, tanning at the beach, smoking my Gauloises, reading Lorca, masturbating, ignoring my mother's phone calls. I couldn't stand hearing the disappointment in her voice. I couldn't stand her loneliness, the sense of disorientation that had weakened her resolve to live. Her pain seemed to tip me over the edge. The few times I'd picked up, I'd lied to her. I convinced her that my father was with me. She'd had no idea I'd been alone all along, alone until Omar showed up and declared himself my patron.

I remember the first time Omar and I met. One evening, he'd come to the apartment with money my father had sent me through his bank account. When I opened the door to let him in, he said, "You ordered money?" He was holding a white envelope in his hand, looking at me with a friendly intensity, his mouth ajar. He was wearing a gray T-shirt and a pair of black leather motorcycle pants with knee armor and red stitching on the sides that drew my eyes down the full length of his muscular thighs. When I met his gaze, his eyes widened and his expression, which had been light, even jocular, turned serious, as if, having caught sight of my desire, of my youth and foolishness, he'd recalibrated his thoughts. His brow was laced with sweat and he wiped his forehead with the back of his hand. His sweat dripped on the envelope, softening the paper, rendering it transparent, exposing the pinks and greens of the bills within. "I was out riding," he said, and stepped inside. He put the envelope on the console table where I kept my keys. "Don't spend it all in one place," he joked, sliding his fingers along the edge of the envelope, stroking it; I could have sworn that as his hand dropped to his side he let out a little moan. I remember that my heart was beating in a frightful way. I felt heat rising in my face. "Have you ever ridden a Ducati?" he said, turning to face me.

I swallowed, trying to extinguish the fire that had, quite suddenly and against my will, ignited inside me. "No," I managed to say, suppressing the tremor in my voice.

Omar walked into the kitchen. He took a cold drink, an orange soda, out of the fridge, then leaning against the door, he tilted his head back and laughed with a boyish charm that excited me. "Never?" he asked.

"Never," I said, laughing along with him. Our combined laughter swirled through the room, a whirlpool of pleasure laced with danger and darkness. It had been months since I'd heard an adult laugh. Months since anyone had broken the silence of my life with an intimation of joy.

Omar leaned away from the fridge and came toward me. "Feel here," he said, gently lifting my hand to his chest. "I think my heart is exploding," he said, rubbing my hand, squeezing it against his body. I felt the heat of his skin and the coarse hairs on his chest beneath his thin T-shirt, his heart pumping against my palm. "It's a lot of adrenaline," he said. "It feels great. I'm going to take you."

I removed my hand. He shrugged with what seemed to me feigned indifference, then finished his orange soda. Right before he left, we looked at each other with an intentionality and an intensity that had frightened and aroused me simultaneously. Our interlocked gaze pierced the silence; it was a form of communication unfamiliar to me, one that didn't rely on words but was extremely clear nevertheless. This was how I would come to feel in his presence—unnerved, even petrified at times, but still excited, exhilarated by the electric response that his body elicited in mine, something I'd never before experienced, an energy I didn't know how to control, didn't know how to create for myself.

"You," he said to me weeks later, said to me habitually then, his head tilted back, his throat exposed, "are my lover." He would draw me in and kiss me hungrily. I didn't always like it, perhaps wasn't even comfortable, but I let him. Maybe I even egged him on. I don't know. I'll never know. I was in acute pain, lonely in ways I was too young to grasp, and there was no one around to ask me to articulate my suffering, to help me fix it in language, so I raged on like a wounded animal who knows not what to do except soothe her pain with more pain, lust after the final blow of death that will put an end to it all. I became hooked on Omar. He was like a drug, a humiliation I craved, and I kept going back for more. I loved his voice, so deep, like a primordial cry ricocheting against the cold walls of a cave when he came.

It took me years to realize that Omar had had other youthful lovers, that I had shared his body with others, though I would never have the occasion to know them myself. Once unleashed, this knowledge, a caged beast that had long lurked in the shadows, gnawed on my nerves; it minced my heart. I felt I had gone mad. I wanted to rip my flesh off my bones and feed the beast before it had a chance to devour me whole. I could not understand how I could have been naïve to the fact that I had been just one of a whole repertoire of girls who had satiated Omar's appetites. But conscience can be slow to awaken. Especially when one is used to all manner of abuses.

And now here I was again, approaching Marbella. I needed to lift myself out of the tyranny of silence, the silence that had informed my life before and after Omar, the very silence he had sensed in me, had taken advantage of for his own secret desires. I needed to search the shadows. I needed to shine the light of language onto the dark vaults of my life. I had become a writer. I had devoted my life to language, to mapping the banality of suffering, to exposing hidden truths in everyday realities. A salubrious exercise, I supposed, to confront one's ghosts, but I had my doubts. There are things better put away in a box. That's what my father used to say; that's how he'd dealt with me.

When I think about his other children, my half siblings, my brother, I realize there's nothing unique about me. We're all in our own boxes, his children. We don't know one another, but we know of one another. We exist in silos just like Omar's lovers did. It's a carefully balanced economy, my father's. I suppose it's a lot for a man like him, a lot to give each of us our own box. We each get our own space; our own casket to grovel in, to pound against, to weep in. And now I'm standing at the cusp of reentering mine, the apartment he'd recently given me, that he'd purchased years ago with what little money he had as a way to pay back his wife for the financial sacrifices she'd made for him, to appease her; she had wanted to be closer to her twin sister, who lived in Marbella, and also, of course, to Omar, whom she'd helped care for during the bloodbath of the Lebanese civil war. He had been a teenager during the war, the same age I was when we met. They had lived together through raids and checkpoints, navigated alleyways severed by the rubble of fallen buildings, knowing every day could be their last. Their bond was unbreakable. They had survived death together, no small thing, and had come out the other end similarly selfish and cruel, with a scorching need to control others.

Ever since they met, my father has followed my stepmother's lead, her whims, her demands. He's never stood up for himself, for his children. He's the kind of man who exercises control by disappearing. When the pressure gets to be too much, he simply vanishes. No one knows where he goes. He'll call his wife to let her know that he's still alive, but that's it. And then, *when the moment has passed,* as he says, he comes home and settles back into his life as if he never left it. He has a gift, my father, for denying the discontinuities of his life. Take, for example, this apartment in Marbella; he bought it but never lived there. It remains an unoccupied container, a home empty of the warmth of bodies, an unfulfilled promise.

I could picture the building. Neutral. Forbidding. Austere. A beige block of medium height with rectangular windows and rows of terraces filled with plants and broken sun chairs. Over the course of the summer, the apartment had turned into a weapon, a trap, a dark and isolated enclosure that had witnessed and applauded my torture. I remembered the stale smell of its walls, their stained surfaces. I remembered the sleepless nights I'd spent walking its corridors. I felt exhausted at the thought of returning to that apartment, an exhaustion exacerbated by all the traveling I'd done in the past few months. I'd woken up at two that morning in a grim hotel room in Bristol to catch my flight to Marbella, having just finished the final leg of my book tour. I was spent. I was stiff from sitting on trains, buses, and airplanes after so many years hunched over my desk absorbed in the diabolical mania of writing. Before Bristol, I'd been in Oxford and London. I'd barely seen either place. I was moving through the world like a ghost, the ghost of literature, the ghost of my former book. I felt disembodied, as though I were floating across the rugged terrain of my life, which I had tried to come to terms with by writing. By the time I'd stood on the curb at three in the morning, the Bristol wind shearing my face, I felt like a fugitive, an old feeling that had, over the course of my itinerant life, built a home for itself in the center of my being.

I'd watched the cab approach, watched it follow along the curve of the road, its headlights rolling over the city's gray stone buildings. I got in and almost immediately caught my reflection in the window. I looked worn and a little lost. I didn't like to see myself that way. I had seen my face glide across the mirror as I was leaving my hotel room: my dark hair, my thin lips, my eyes large and brown, two wounded blue semicircles beneath them. Every time I saw my face that way, drawn and tired, I thought about how shallow my energy reserves were. I knew that Omar had robbed me of my youth. I imagined that energy, once destined to circulate in my veins, was poisoning him now; it didn't belong to him. It soothed me to think that way, to think of him diminishing as he aged, just as he had annihilated me in my youth. In reality, I didn't know if he was dead or alive.

I'd looked out the cab window, through my reflection, at the cold starless sky and watched my image dissolve into the impenetrable night. Soon we'd arrived at the airport parking lot, the whole structure flooded with bright lights. I got out and followed the crowd, a train of limbs advancing through the doors. We all lined up at security, removed our belts and shoes, carefully set our electronics in the bins, watched them move through the X-ray machine. People were either half-asleep or half-drunk. I'd been standing behind a crowd of young women; they were all wearing the same black cotton sleeveless shirts, the words BRIDE TRIBE printed in gold across their breasts. The bride herself was young, no more than twenty. She was wearing a makeshift wedding dress with a long veil that trailed down past her ankles and a bright-pink crown with fake diamonds that spelled out LOVE. They were drunk, the whole lot, and they'd kept on drinking as the plane glided into the night sky. At one point, I heard the bride yell out: "Costa del Sol, here we come!"

Throughout the flight, I'd turned to look at her through the gaps between the seats. Her veil was soiled. She'd removed it and bundled it up in her lap. Her head was tilted back, her mouth wide open, a single strand of her silky blond hair caught on her teeth. She looked like she had fangs. She looked as though her teeth had been allowed to grow—teeth, which allow us to feed and defend ourselves—at the expense of women like myself. I thought of my brother's teeth that had been knocked out of his mouth. Of the Farsi that had been trapped inside me, of the years I'd been unable to chew or speak. This bride didn't live in a state of skeptical inquiry, on guard, her ability to trust shattered by history, her sense of self ground to dust by the violence it had dispatched. She'd been left alone to thrive, to eat and drink and make love in peace.

I turned back to the window and leaned my head against the plexiglass. I could see the ribbon of asphalt below ready to greet us. I felt again like a fugitive. But as we hit the ground, as we taxied down the runway, that feeling gave way to terror, then to pangs of bitter solitude. I remembered when I'd told my father about my relationship with Omar years after it had happened, the threat and overt violence of it, he'd just looked at me, eyes narrowed, and said, "How will I tell my wife? He's her favorite nephew."

Until then, I'd kept the details of that summer to myself. It had seemed easier to pretend like nothing had happened. But over time, I'd grown quieter and more withdrawn, intensely secretive, private and mistrusting over the most basic things. It was as if the fact of my relationship with Omar was rotting inside of me.

When I finally told my mother, almost a decade after that summer, she'd said, in a fit of exasperated panic, as if she had been seething over my silence all those years: "You think I don't know what happened to you? I'm your mother!" Then she reached out and held my hand, and said, "I am a woman, too." I understood by inference that my silence had kept her at bay, that I'd denied myself the companionship of a mother, who was also a survivor, at the time when I'd needed her most.

And now my father had decided, in a solipsistic move, to gift me the very place where I'd incurred that pain, to put its cruel walls in my name—an apology, he'd claimed, for his absence from my life, which I'd interpreted as an implicit acknowledgment of the many ways he'd exposed me to Omar's sadism through neglect. I'd shared this conjecture with my best friend, Ellie, who was meeting me in Marbella, adding that, in my view, parenting requires the constant exercise of foresight, something my father had opted out of entirely.

I took comfort in the fact that Ellie was right behind me. Ellie who also had led an itinerant life, who had been homeless at times; her ties to the world in which she'd been raised were frayed. She had been raised in America in an Orthodox Jewish family but had been taken abruptly to Israel by her mother after her parents' divorce. Her people's survival had come to depend on their ability to lay claim to the lands of Palestine, to resurrect amid its soil and rocks and olive trees a language that had been muted by the violence of European pogroms, the Spanish Inquisition, the Holocaust. The land of Palestine and its people were used to absolve Europe of its guilt, to move bodies it had maimed and injured farther out of its line of sight.

On long nights when neither one of us could sleep in Amherst, where our friendship first began, where we both had attended graduate school, Ellie would talk to me freely about how being transplanted to Israel as a young girl had injured her burgeoning sense of integrity. As a queer woman, she'd been treated as an obstruction, a person who'd refused to be incorporated into the community. This sense of rejection had shaped her political views. She saw how absurd it was that she could move to Israel as if it were her natural home port while Palestinians were denied freedom of movement on their own land. She'd wanted to be as far away from Israel as possible. In return, I would tell her that seeing my brother battered on the concrete pavement just after our own arrival in America had depleted any sense of self-respect I'd had at that point and replaced it with a stinging shame that had left me defenseless.

We had, as all women in intense friendships do, fallen in love with each other. We were, we came to realize, most alike in our desire to question any master narrative's claim to truth, to make visible the lies these narratives concealed through language. And we were both willing to sacrifice our lives for it, to keel over in pain however sentimental or ridiculous this shared impulse seemed to others. We would remind each other that breaking silence was never ineffectual even if at times it felt as though we were trying to shatter a block of ice with the tips of our fingers.

Ellie's acknowledgment of the suffering of Palestinians had

led to accusations that she was an apologist for terrorists. She'd felt guilty all through her adolescence. Over time, though, she'd come to understand that it's an impossible but necessary line to walk, to recognize that one is implicated in injustice even if one is not a direct perpetrator. When she spoke that way, I often detected a stale taste in my mouth, which I understood to be the death of my mother tongue. I still spoke Farsi, but my words had gone rigid, stiff from disuse through the years following my brother's attack.

Ellie and I were both born into such deranged whirlpools of geopolitical conflict, with so many contradictory voices swirling through our minds, that locating our own could be a laborious, exhausting task. We'd learned to mitigate this exhaustion by accompanying each other on what we referred to as *recovery journeys;* we'd physically return to the sites of our traumas to map our stories in words, to reverse the language-destroying effects of unbearable pain. I had been with her to Israel and occupied Palestine. I'd held Ellie's hand when she was confronted by an onslaught of memories from her teenage years, when she'd struggled with the knowledge that the cost of her survival, the rehabilitation of her language and lifeworld, was the death and debilitation of others. She'd tried to mitigate Israel's structures of exclusion. She'd learned to speak Arabic. She'd translated the work of Palestinian writers into Hebrew and English without denying the asymmetrical networks of power she was operating in. She recognized her immense privilege and saw all around her people who ignored theirs, who led their lives with a sense of carefree entitlement.

Her open, inquisitive nature, combined with her anger at the political and religious constraints she was forced to operate in, had pushed her toward other forms of violence; she'd let herself be dominated by a string of angry men. The relationship between our political pain and our attraction to destructive men was not always clear; perhaps being with men who make us scream and gasp and moan takes us beyond the confines of language, back into our original pain; it allows us to explore and later confront the patriarchal and patriotic leanings of the colonial social project. "Arezu, I am not the main victim here," Ellie would say when she was grappling with the systemic denial of Palestinian personhood. "But I am still a victim of violence. I did not give my consent; I have been made a perpetrator of violence against my will."

I would say to her then that I had, at times, suspected myself of perpetuating violence against my own body. My relationship with Omar had bloomed in a place where Muslim life existed as a concealed reality, visible only in traces, in the landscape, the architecture, the food, the tonal inflections of the Spanish south. Muslim and Jewish life, I told her, had been purposefully suppressed by the Spanish national project. The very ground beneath my feet had been primed for centuries to annihilate my body. "That energy is real," I said to her. "Our bodies detect its negative charge. If we're not careful, it can overpower us, turn us against ourselves in a fit of rage." I told her that for that reason and many others, not least among them my brother's near death at the hands of a skinhead, I'd willingly participated in my own destruction.

As my plane sat on the tarmac waiting for a gate to be assigned to us, as I breathed in the cabin's stale air, I thought about the last conversation Ellie and I had had before I'd left home for England; we'd sat on opposite ends of the phone in silence, comforted only by the knowledge that we were on the line together, that we did not always need to speak to impart understanding to each other. And now she was accompanying me to Spain. She was catching a flight to Marbella that same morning from Oxford. We had spent a few days together there before I'd gone on to Bristol to finish my book tour. My Ellie. I pictured her understanding gaze. I thought of her easy laughter, how nimbly she guides conversation away from fear. My brilliant friend Ellie, the only woman in the world on the same wavelength as I was. She would have seen the bride's fangs, too. She would have seen them, and we would have died together right there, laughing, laughing out all of our pain.

I turned back to look at the bride-to-be one last time. Her crown was still on her head, shining under the overhead light. For a moment, I wondered if her partner knew the texture of her pain. If he knew her perversions. If he knew what turned her on, what made her wince, what shut her down. I thought of my husband, Xavi. He wouldn't have been the best companion on this trip, my first return to Marbella. We didn't always share the same moral convictions. I was interested in how desire is shaped by the destructive logic of empire, how at times sex facilitates the transmission of historical violence from one body to another. Xavi, however, possessed a purity I'd never be able to access. He experienced sex as a bridge, as union, as an explosive, an exhilarating coming together; I didn't deny that was so, but that didn't constitute the entire inventory of my experiences.

Xavi had paid the price for the bruises Omar had left me with. In the year leading up to my return to Marbella, I'd spent months sleepless, waking up in the middle of the night, sobbing, only to chase my grief with days spent remembering my affection for Omar. During those times, I would forget that what I'd experienced as union and tenderness had been, for Omar, a protracted disarmament; he'd lowered my defenses through seduction so he could have his way with me, consume my body, my youth, my fervor for his own satisfaction.

My contradictory, swinging emotions confused Xavi. They stoked his rage at the injustices Omar's lust had unleashed on my life. His love for me, his desire to protect me, made it difficult for him to sit by my side as I revisited the more pleasant memories of my time with Omar. There was no reasoning with him then. He turned into a wall of anger. He couldn't entertain any ambiguity in my account of Omar, would only accept a narrative in which he was entirely evil. I resisted the line of thought that Xavi was sure would salvage me from my pain: demonizing Omar in order to purify myself. I had no interest in obliterating the contradictions of the past. To the contrary, I wanted to savor them. Xavi was, I felt, asking me to ignore the nuances of my relationship with Omar, the historical and political terrain that had informed it. He didn't see that in doing so I would be sacrificing my own sense of self and my ability to articulate that self in language. He didn't understand, at least initially, how his attitude, pure to the extreme, dispossessed me of my own narrative, my sexuality, my appetite for inquiry, my openness to examining the darkest aspects of human nature, the things most people prefer to look away from. I was left to raise the frightening questions alone. In the process of vilifying Omar, Xavi had unwittingly placed an invisible restriction on my speech; what I needed was an eruption of language. He couldn't tolerate the idea that I was complicit in my own destruction, that I had weaponized what little agency I had and wielded it against myself.

I wanted to explore my grief, to lick my wounds, but to do so without erasing the burgeoning desire I'd felt at the time or sacrificing Omar to the Western gaze, a gaze eager to perceive him as yet another violent Arab man, a man incapable of reason and restraint, of employing the Victorian ideal handed down to him by his imperial keepers. Xavi's anger pushed me toward a reading of Omar's character that seemed only to affirm Western superiority and its repressive code of behavior, a code that served to disguise the rampant sexual violence in the West, the psychotic irrationality of colonialism, the savage brutality of progress.

It's odd that love so often acts as a barrier rather than a bridge. But so it goes. And yet, over the years, Xavi had come to know my pain. He'd learned it. It was never obvious to him, never legible. He'd studied it as if it were a map. He'd tried to figure out all the main roads, the detours, where they digressed and where they converged, where my pain met my pleasure. He'd tried to hold the most challenging facts of my life, had tried to tease out my conviction that violence and ecstasy often exist on the same terrible continuum. That pain, no matter how unfairly it's doled out, can be our biggest asset. That conflict can be the source of justice. But as much as we'd come to understand each other, there was always a gap between when I felt something and when he came to grips with it. Our experiences of life were, to put it mildly, extremely different; he'd been dealt his own dose of suffering, but his life had been built of continuities while mine has been a conglomeration of discontinuities, fault lines, chasms. I suppose that he, too, has had to be patient when I've been slow to understand his perspective. In those moments, those times when we work to see eye to eye, I try to remind myself that love is sustained attention and I think: I am so lucky; I am so incredibly lucky.

The thought was like a flash flood, quick and unexpected. It jolted me back to life. I felt a rush of pleasure filling my lungs with air. I realized that I was once again staring at the bride. She was gazing sadly at her soiled veil. I reached for my phone and secretly snapped a photo of her with that word—*love*—stamped to her forehead. I dropped it in a message to Ellie as soon as we deplaned. It would be the first thing she'd see upon landing. I wanted her to chuckle to herself as I had chuckled getting off the plane. I needed her to experience, as precisely as possible, what I was experiencing moment by moment—an impossible thing to do, but I knew that Ellie would get closer than anyone else would be able to; we were born of the same wounded clay, in the same ancient gutters of this fragile world.

**2**

WE DEPLANED AND THE HOT AIR, dense with moisture, hit me in the face with an urgency that made me feel claimed, spoken for. Here I am, I thought again. I've returned to Marbella to face its monstrosities.

The airport atmosphere filled me with a sense of disquiet. Everything appeared magnified in its yolky, oxidized light: the dirt on the marble floors, the vacant gazes of the other passengers, the screech of the conveyor belts, the luggage being thrown at them in even intervals. I felt oddly separate from myself as I walked across the nearly crumbling terminal to an ATM. I needed to take out cash.

I inserted my card into the machine's illuminated strip and entered my PIN, aware as I punched in the numbers that unlike the last time I was in Marbella I was about to retrieve money that belonged to me, cash that I'd earned through my own labor rather than bills my father had likely borrowed from my stepmother and handed off to a stranger, a relative whom I had never met, but who, soon after delivering the money to me, asserted his dominance over me; I remembered how strapped I'd been, how carefully I'd rationed my food that summer; and just as a procession of images began to run through my mind—the bruised peaches I bought at a discount at the end of the day from the corner store, the bunches of parsley the shop owner gifted me, the butterless bread rolls I ate in the mornings—I saw the face of a man emerge on the screen of the machine, a face that seemed to be attached to my own, that hovered over mine. In the glow of his countenance, I saw my own teenage face looking back at me. She had the gaze of a stranger, a person who was *not* me, but whose identity was encased within the boundaries of my body. A terrible chill went down my spine. I felt giddy, nauseated. And yet, despite the alienation, the dread and desire I'd experienced as a teenager rose up in me, those old discordant notes of terror and repulsion mixed with a burning hunger to be consumed by Omar, a perverse appetite born of defiance and the sting of my unmet needs. I was afraid Omar was standing behind me, looming over me as he had so many times before. I drew in a breath and was about to turn around to confront him when the ATM beeped and expelled my card with a click. His face disappeared, leaving in its place a message that my request had been denied. I couldn't get money out of the ATM. I had been refused. I had lapsed back into a state of need, my hand outstretched, a beggar.

I stared at the forbidding screen, my heart beating wildly against my chest. My blood pumped through my limbs with redoubled speed. How foolish I'd been to think that I could return to Marbella without resurrecting my adolescent fragility, the vulnerabilities of youth that I'd hidden for so long behind a facade of contrariness and provocation. I drew in a deep breath. I reinserted my card. Nothing. The machine refused it again.

Despondent, I walked toward the exit doors and into the assaulting heat. The sun had broken through the cloud cover, was beating harshly down onto the asphalt of the parking lot. The buses and cars seemed to be quivering, turning into liquid gas where their frames met the horizon. It occurred to me that what, as a teenager, I'd thought of as rebellion was in fact a deranged form of submission, a readiness to conform to the aberrant needs of others — specifically to Omar's. He'd had a fervent need to consume me, a need that I'd tragically interpreted as love when it had, I could see now, surged forth from an infinite well of sorrow and secrecy at the center of his life, an abyss that had drawn me to him with a magnetic force.

I had ten pounds left in my pocket. I walked to the money exchange kiosk next to the bar and changed them into euros. I needed to steady my nerves. The rugged elegance of Omar's face had impressed itself deep into my subconscious; I knew that if I wasn't careful it would reappear in the haunted stage of my mind every time I closed my eyes, just as it had on the screen. I thought about the fact that my teenage self existed in fossilized form within me and that I was loping around the world with her dead weight. I wondered if she returned to Omar's mind, too. I pictured him recalling the smell of my body, my unresolved adolescent gestures, my mercurial facial expressions that shifted from defiance to an almost infantile smile, a wide-open and stupid grin that made me wince with shame. He must have felt such pleasure at the thought of the two of us together, such self-satisfaction for having gotten away with the crime. But for all I knew, Omar was dead; he could have died years ago. Or if he hadn't died, if he was still alive and well, breathing in the brackish Mediterranean air, there was no knowing if we'd even recognize each other. I had no idea what he looked like these days, and my face, I considered—while thinking on a parallel plane of my mind that I could use a beer and a cigarette—had changed beyond recognition. I was no longer the open-faced girl I'd once been.

I crossed the sidewalk to the bar. I needed to distract myself, to pass the time while I waited for Ellie to land. It had been so long since I'd ordered a beer in Spain, since I'd looked at a bartender and said, "*Ponme una caña.*" I loved saying that word, *caña*, loved thinking of all of its literal meanings—cane, leg, bone. After all, there I was in Marbella again, twenty years later, waiting for Ellie to show up, Ellie who had said, "Arezu, you might need an extra limb to lean on while you're out there." It was true. I needed all the limbs I could get. I couldn't even get money out of the ATM. I'd been in Marbella for a quarter of an hour and already I was being stalled.

I took my place in the long line that had formed around the bar, behind tourists who were mispronouncing their orders, pointing at items tastefully laid out in the glass case, little ham sandwiches and *pan con chocolate,* willing the server to understand their demands. They nodded gleefully once they'd succeeded, satisfied at having communicated without employing language. It was a well-rehearsed guessing game; I enjoyed the exaggerated theatrics of the charade.

For me, it's Omar who robs me of words. What I experienced that summer may ultimately be resistant to language; the most terrible parts may forever remain unspeakable. I watched the bartender pour pints of cold blond beer into tipped glasses, the foam spilling over the edge. In a sense, the excess of pain and pleasure that I had accessed through Omar at such a premature time of life had obliterated me. How, I wondered, watching the bartender wipe the rim of the glass with a wet cloth, does one transcribe onto paper an experience of annihilation? Of erasure? Of having been forced to vanish, to evacuate oneself in order to survive the brutal event? How does one document in language an experience of pain so totalizing that it refuses the fixed nature of words altogether?

The line for the bar moved and I moved along with it. I thought to myself, I have returned to Marbella to conduct emotional fieldwork, to turn the soil with a plow and unearth the past, loosen its hold on the person I had become. My feelings in general and my feelings about Omar in particular had ossified. It had been years since I'd shed a tear over what had happened between us. The tremor I'd felt as I saw his reflection come forward on the screen—his long lashes, his black curls, his dark skin and large green eyes—was a reminder of the energy I'd felt with him, as menacing as it was hypnotic, the first indication of the emotional turbulence ahead and an affirmation that beneath the hard surface of denial I'd constructed around myself, my defense mechanism against the private catastrophes of my life, a subterranean network of toxic emotion continued to circulate.

"What will you do if all of the feelings you've been suppressing come out at once?" Ellie asked me as we'd prepared for the trip. "Who will remind you that your story with Omar already happened, that it isn't happening again?"

"My story with Omar," I'd said to her, "will always be happening; it will always be unfolding because it runs parallel to my life, a wild boar snapping at my heels" — and I remembered, in a terrible instant, the baby wild boar Omar had captured high up in the mountains. A second shiver went down my spine. Oh, that wild boar! I heard her high-pitched squeals of terror as though she were still trapped in the backpack Omar had shoved her into, the backpack he'd forced me to wear. I felt my back grow hot with her hurried breaths. Beneath her piercing screams I heard the echo of my moans in response to Omar's touch. I felt queasy. Those noises, mine and the wild boar's, had doubled Omar's power; we had used our voices to express his dominance over us. His internal life, his desires and needs, had extended beyond the boundaries of his body onto ours and outward again through our screams of pain and pleasure. I felt as though I were being strangled, as though an invisible hand were exerting pressure on my heart, filling my throat with blood, drowning my voice.

I needed a beer, some water, anything to counteract the heat that was rising through my esophagus. My turn at the bar finally came. I ordered the beer and some sliced watermelon for good measure. I sat in front of the television set hanging over the bar. A young man was being interviewed. He was sitting on a wooden chair in a dim room at a breakfast nook covered in an embroidered tablecloth; he kept leaning forward to speak. He had a tortured look on his face; he was trying to pry the words out of his chest, to cough them up. Eventually, the interviewer, who remained off screen, spoke over him. They had found his girlfriend dead, discarded behind a bush, her pants pulled down to her knees, her thighs and arms bruised, her fingers chopped off. I kept hearing the words *violent assault, dismemberment, rape.*

"How are you coping? What's helping you move on?" the interviewer asked. He repeated the first question a few times; his tone, initially urgent, went slack by the third time around.

Perhaps, I thought, the faceless interviewer, comfortably seated out of view, was beginning to see that there was no answer or that, given the circumstances, the questions he was asking were too pointed, too accusatory; that this young man's power had died with his girlfriend, had been converted into the instrument of another man's will. The interviewer's questions only served to assassinate whatever remained of the boyfriend's privacy, his sense of control over his own life. The boyfriend was being asked to resolve his grief efficiently and deliberately, to comfort us, to provide us with hope and insight despite the blinding darkness that had consumed him. He was being asked to tell us all how to survive the death of a loved one, a death caused by spontaneous, lurid violence, a death that kills the grievers as it does the grieved, maims and cripples. It was preposterous, callously insensitive. It takes time, I thought, a whole lifetime, to learn how to move forward with our lives after being thrown in such close proximity to mortality without degrading or ignoring the losses we've suffered.

Finally, the interviewer went silent. In that silence, the young man retrieved his words.

"She fought back," he said. It was clear that this gave him comfort. That he was proud of how his girlfriend had handled herself in those final moments of her life, that despite losing the battle she'd left him with the knowledge that she'd stood her ground, that she'd kicked and screamed and tried to strangle her attacker. Her belief in her dignity, her value and sense of self-worth in the face of a brutal, unjust death, gave him solace.

I hadn't known to fight back. I hadn't known enough to know to stand my ground. Or perhaps there was no ground beneath my feet in the first place; the ground had been dug, hollowed out, replaced by a trapdoor that led to further violence. Or maybe I'd only known the wrong things: betrayal, rejection, loss. After all, my own father had washed his hands of me. He'd sent another man to do his job for him, and that man, upon seeing that I was alone, without any protection, inserted himself into my life, forever changing its shape and the composition of my character. He'd obliterated what little trust I'd had in the world, altered the way I perceive other people; now I'm often overcome with a sense of disgust at the sight of other people; I see right through to the animal nature hiding just beneath our suits and makeup and ironed hair. We are, I consider, deeply disturbed and exquisitely deranged in those moments. We've tried so hard to transcend our basest instincts, to deny them, to pretend they aren't there, that we engage in a process of apparent refinement, a spectacle of our supposed progress. Progress, modernity, openness—that triumvirate of lies that guards the Western front against the absence of civilization that supposedly plagues the East.

I looked back up at the television screen to find the boyfriend crying, his voice trembling, his lips wet with spittle. "How could someone do something like this?" he sobbed, his words choppy. He was breathless; the interviewer clearly had no idea how to handle this breakdown. He said flatly, in a stern tone: "It's a tragedy; there are maniacs out there. In the interest of public safety, we caution women against walking alone, particularly at night, when they're most vulnerable to this sort of cruel attack."

The boyfriend steadied himself and looked fixedly at the interviewer. A perplexed and horrified expression hung on his face. He was clearly disgusted by the way this man was using his pain to perpetuate a state of terror, pretending not to be complicit in a system where women are savagely attacked, shut down, spied on, kept under wraps.

But women, I thought, aren't always attacked from behind

by strangers. Omar had been an insider. Our relationship was an inside job. He was family—whatever that meant—a relative even if I'd never met him before. My father had trusted him to act as his proxy. And despite not having much faith in my father, I'd gone along with his choice. How bad could Omar be, I'd thought, if my father sent him to check on me? He was, after all, my father. I was born of his body, and if the logic of parenting was sound, any harm done to me would be transferred over to him.

And Omar and I, we had laughed together. We had hiked the hills and mountains, swam in the high lakes, sunbathed on distant dunes facing the silver waters of the ocean. At that thought, a distant memory emerged as vivid as daylight. We were on the beach. We were playing badminton. I remembered the sensation of my feet sinking into the sand. The sky was pale blue and entirely clear but for a few strands of wispy clouds hovering over the horizon as thin as hairs. The sun was nowhere in sight, but the world was aflame with its heat, its limpid light, and beneath that wide-open sky, the sea drew in breath after breath, exhaling against the shore with the ease of a sleeping giant. The beach was small and enclosed by tall barren cliffs. Those rocks, puckered and blistery, appeared in my mind like claws silently preparing to pinch me. I could still hear the hollow wiry sound of the shuttle going back and forth between us, the tension in the cheap plastic grid of the racket, the dull snapping sound it made every time I hit the birdie.

After that summer in Marbella, I retreated into a solitude from which I never fully emerged; I clung to it the way I'd once clung to Omar's body despite knowing, on some deeply buried level of my consciousness, that he would hurt me, that he would extract what he needed from me, then dispose of me coldly, remorselessly, as soon as he was satisfied. But as devastating as the end of our relationship was, I still couldn't help but feel that our connection was anything but clear-cut. It hadn't been all good or all bad. It hadn't revolved exclusively around violence. There had been times when I'd wanted to dig my teeth into his neck, to bury my body in his. There were times when I'd gone after him, times when I'd yearned for him. I'd loved him, and while that love ultimately had wrapped itself around my neck like a noose and asphyxiated me, for a time it had nurtured me, too.

I took a bite of the watermelon and thought of all of the times Omar had lifted a forkful of blackened squid-ink rice or gently fried slices of calamari to my mouth. We ate and drank with such pleasure. We'd existed in a world apart, in isolation. I hadn't interacted with a single girl my own age that whole summer. What they were doing for pleasure I had no idea. I'd felt separate from other women my whole life; it was a feeling that had haunted me until I met Ellie.

The Bride Tribe walked past, their feet dragging across the concrete, their sunglasses shining with the light of the emboldened sun. It was high morning. They climbed onto a black bus with tinted windows in twos, arm in arm, steadying each other, until the last pair had been swallowed. I watched it drive off and imagined the whole lot of them passed out on the beach day after day, cooking their limbs under the Spanish sun.

The bartender changed the television channel. "Ay," he said, sighing and nodding his head at the state of the world.

I thought I might cry. I wanted to. I was sure I needed to. But I was all dried up.

I'd been dried up the year that I'd met Ellie, too, in Amherst, where I'd moved to write. As luck would have it, I, who could barely shed a tear then, was living with the easiest crier in the world, Sahar. She was born in America to Palestinian parents who returned to the occupied West Bank as an act of resistance, taking their three children, including Sahar, all of whom were American citizens by birth, to live with difficulty, without documentation, restricted from all mobility in the settler colonial regime of Israel. Sahar had come to Amherst to study; she'd tried to go back to the West Bank through Jordan several times to visit her parents and siblings but was continuously turned away by the Israel Defense Forces because, according to them, she'd been living there illegally in the first place. When they finally let her in, she refused to be separated from her family again and abandoned the small life she'd built for herself in America. What choice had she had?

When we'd lived together, she'd spent one-third of her time locked in the bathroom, sobbing uncontrollably. Her crying shattered me. I was poor, poorer than a street dog, and tired. Rent was cheap there and I'd wanted to bury myself in writing, but every time I sat down to face the page, Sahar would begin to weep and I would get up from my yellow wooden desk. There is nothing worse than hearing someone gagging on their own tears in the next room.

"Listen, Sahar," I would say, sitting in the dim corridor in front of the bathroom door, "breathe, like this," and I would draw in a loud, exaggerated breath. "I'm breathing with you. You're not alone."

Half an hour later she would open the door, her face red and swollen, and we would go our separate ways. We never talked about it. We didn't need to.

As I drank the last of my beer, I thought to myself, I've heard that weeping my whole life. It's the cry of the homeless. Not the kind that lives on the street; but the kind that lives in borrowed homes with documents and deeds and keys to houses that no longer exist because they've been confiscated, occupied, demolished; the kind that is warm enough and well-fed enough to yearn for what we've lost: land, loved ones, random objects. It's the wail of those who live under occupation, who know we're being watched, whose days are numbered and who are, nevertheless, free for the time being.

Free for the time being, I thought. What could be more confusing than to be free to get up and go to bed when we want, knowing that our days are numbered?

My thoughts circled back to Sahar. I remembered, smiling to myself, that she'd come home beaming one day. She'd been walking the aisles at the library and had met someone she'd connected with instantly, an Israeli woman who was a Palestinian ally. An hour later, Ellie was at our door, holding a six-pack of Miller Light, and she and Sahar sat at the kitchen table drinking and drawing maps of Israel and Palestine through the ages then comparing the imaginary geographies of their shared home with real maps they'd pulled off the library shelves, looking at each other with round horrified eyes each time they rediscovered how slim Palestine had become, how wide and tall Israel stood, how it appeared to be shaped like the blade of a serrated knife, a fact they both knew but that stung them every time they had to confront it anew. I'd never seen Sahar so happy.

I watched them from across the room, my dog at my heels. Ellie told me later that she'd been so sure that day that I disliked her. It's true. I'd thought she seemed oblivious. She'd walked in and made herself comfortable right away. She'd even brought her own beer. All of this offended my sensibilities. I, who had been raised in the horrifying panic-stricken atmosphere of Tehran in the aftermath of the revolution and the Iran-Iraq war, was trained never to make myself at home in another person's house unless they were a well-vetted family, a family from the same political camp, a family who wouldn't turn against me or my kind, wouldn't spit out my name even if they were being choked by the enemy. I was taught to censor myself, to say as little as possible because whatever I said could be misinterpreted by any number of opposing people. I understood that I was always under siege and I behaved accordingly.

Perhaps I envied Ellie, her ability to take up space unapologetically, a misconception informed by historical facts: Israel was a willing partner in the dirty business America seemed always to be conducting in our backyard. I wanted to ask her: *Have you come here to camp out for the evening?* But I'd just stood there instead, silently smoking my cigarettes—Gauloises—a dirty habit left over from Marbella.

As I waited for Ellie now, the bartender brought me an ashtray. I was still smoking Gauloises, but my feelings toward Ellie had changed entirely. Until I had met Xavi, I had loved her more than anyone. And even after, we would often joke with Xavi that she was my wife, my wifey, we would say, and he, whose networks of intimacy ran along more binary lines than ours, would look at us with a gaze that suggested he was charmed and confused in equal measure. My phone buzzed. Here she was. Ellie had landed.

*Arezu, where have you brought me?* she wrote.

So she had seen the picture, the photo of the sad bride with her soiled veil. *Welcome to the Costa del Sol,* I replied; *I'm outside, at the bar behind the bus stop.* I told her to get some money at the ATM, enough for the pair of us. I told her my card wasn't working. I told her that my heart was fat with joy that she was here.

*Mine, too,* she wrote back.

While we'd become inseparable, we barely spoke to Sahar now. Our contact had diminished significantly over the years. We missed her terribly and spoke of her often. She'd abandoned her poetry. She resented the time she'd spent in America, torturous months during which all of the fear and trauma she couldn't

allow herself to experience in the West Bank came rushing forward. She could never have expressed that kind of vulnerability
in the West Bank. Exposing oneself like that when you live under
occupation only makes you more defenseless; but of course, in a
painful twist, leaving that state opens you up to incredible pain.
In the end, the only way for Sahar to resist her own annihilation
had been to continue living under occupation. She'd returned to
Palestine, to Bil'in. Ellie and I had visited her once, almost eight
years ago now. She'd since stopped returning our phone calls,
our emails, our Facebook messages. She'd become a ghost. Eight
years can feel like a lifetime. So much had happened. She'd married and divorced. She's queer and she'd married a gay man, an
act that allowed them to carry on with their same-sex partners
under subterfuge. She'd existed in this way alongside other queer
Palestinians in the face of Israel's pinkwashing; their supposed
openness to gay life was still another form of colonial discourse,
another way of marking Palestine as backward, barbaric.

Ellie had gone through her fair share of relationships in those
eight years as well: a Colombian American woman, a Norwegian
man, then an Egyptian one. She moved around a lot. She went to
Cairo for a while to perfect her Arabic and work on a few trans-
lations. Then the Arab Spring had erupted. She'd stayed as long
as she could, but eventually she'd had to return to the States, to
Amherst.

When she came back to Amherst, I was living in Brooklyn,
with a chef who was fine enough at first, but who started coming home later and later at night, drunk, coked out, his mouth

smelling like another woman's vagina. He would often be going to bed just as I was getting up to write. We barely saw each other, and almost never had sex. We shared a bedroom and the cost of the rent, and continued that way for a long time because neither one of us could afford to move. And I had no interest in actually getting to know anyone anyway, no interest in letting anyone in, in asking or answering questions.

Now here Ellie and I were, I thought, putting out my cigarette, a decade later. I got up and moved through the crowd. There she was, laughing, laughing hysterically, coming toward me, pushing her glasses up her nose, her eyes wide, her mouth cracked open, her red curls bouncing as she lunged toward me. She threw her arms around me.

"Where are we?" she said.

"I don't know," I said.

But I knew exactly where we were. We were at the airport one hour outside of Marbella, that city of salt and sun, dust and death. I could point to it on a map with my eyes closed.

# 3

ELLIE AND I WOKE UP on the bus and found we'd gone astray. I was in a gloomy mood. The few times I'd opened my eyes to look out the window, at the foothills of the Sierra Blanca on one side of the *autopista* and the coastal dunes of the sea on the other, I'd had the nagging sensation that we were moving in the wrong direction. But I couldn't fully trust my judgment; I couldn't grasp my own mind. I'd slept badly in the weeks prior. I would sleep for an hour or two only to be startled awake, gripped by horror, my mind seized by a procession of images: the moonlit streets Omar and I had walked down, the rooms where I'd obediently spread my legs, the empty Chinese restaurants where we'd eaten under the red light of paper lanterns. Beneath my panic ran terrible rivers of latent lust that completely undid me. I'd lay awake thinking of the scent of basil and tobacco that wafted off Omar's skin. I thought of how I'd adored that smell, how I'd pressed my face against his armpits, his groin. I saw myself split in two, divided, my character composed of two antagonistic halves: one ruthless and perverse, predisposed toward a total abolition of rules, hungry for Omar's deviance; and the other consumed by feelings of terror and disgust at the very thought of our relationship.

Those long sleepless nights had left me in a somnambulant state. As I drifted between consciousness and sleep, the road Ellie and I were traveling on seemed to levitate; the thistle and grass growing at the foot of the firs and the pines sticking out of the white rock of the foothills shrunk beneath us. I felt a deep-seated sense of unreality surge forth, a light-headedness born of shame and exhilaration. I wondered for a moment if it was suicidal of me to return. I took in the glistening patch of azure through the rectangular window of the bus. A falcon darted across the sky. I followed its flight for as long as I could until my eyes started watering from the intense light, until the rugged cliffs beneath its wings appeared shrunken and wrinkled. I saw myself walking hand in hand with Omar across the arid landscape. My head was bent low, my gait slack and resigned. My hair was long, as straight as a dagger. I was tanned and thin.

He was muscular, tall, robust. I watched as a rising tide of rock and sand and bramble swallowed us up, as we disappeared into the landscape. The air seemed full of the ashes of the dead. I leaned my head back and closed my eyes. Omar, I thought to myself, had flattened my life. He'd turned it into a cautionary tale, and this Spanish landscape, with its jagged rocks and pale coasts, had been his accomplice. And no wonder. My Muslim ancestors had been purged from medieval Spain centuries earlier, as had Omar's, as had Ellie's Jewish ones. They'd all been eradicated in waves. As I looked out at the changing landscape, now more lush and sculpted, it seemed to me that the spirits of our ancestors were still moving through this space, microscopic fragments backlit by the harsh sun. How strange, I thought, how strange and devastating to think that Omar and I both had been emptied of our personhoods, our futures foreclosed before we'd ever been able to love or harm each other.

My eyes stung. I leaned my head back and closed them again. My thoughts were anxiously circling my mind. I wondered if Omar had felt more comfortable consigning me to my own extinction because he knew full well that we'd been subjected to a violence so severe and perseverant by the gears of history that the sheer magnitude of its force would conceal whatever brutality he might exercise against me. His compulsion to assault my body, however unforgivable, was minute compared to the disfigurement that had been engineered by the West against us both, and these losses, layered one on top of another, formed an entangled whole. How was I meant to take on the task of mourning a private violence that had historical valences of such magnitude? After all, you need autonomy in order to grieve. You need to feel worthy of the life you've been given. You need to be in charge of your own story, to feel ownership over your emotions, even the most despicable ones. But our lives had been modulated by the West. What did it matter if Omar asserted his power over me when my life was not worthy of being grieved? When my body had been designated a target for violence?

I felt dizzy, nauseated. My head began to spin. I felt as though space were folding over itself. I remembered posing these very questions to Ellie over one of our long phone calls. Take care, someone had said to me, a colleague or an acquaintance, perhaps a reader who had attended one of my events while I'd been on the book tour; the words had stuck in my mind—*take care*—a shot and its echo. The two words, side by side, had sounded to me like a warning. What does it mean for us to take care when the odds are stacked against us? I'd asked Ellie in that last phone call of ours. How are we meant to believe that we're deserving of care when we're repeatedly told that we're a problem?

"I don't know," she'd said. "I don't know." Silence settled between us. We listened to each other breathing on opposite ends of the line. Then, finally, she'd added: "You won't be mourning alone." She believed in the power of communal grieving, in sharing our sharpest reservoirs of personal pain as a means of recovering our political agency. "The task," she'd said, breathing into the phone, "will leave you undone and that undoing will transform you." Perhaps, we'd agreed, mourning isn't really possible when you're alone. If the transmission of violence requires the collision of bodies so too does grieving require community; they are two sides of the same coin. I looked over at Ellie. I was so grateful she had come to Marbella with me. Our bodies, I considered, exist in relation to each other; there's no such thing as "I" without "you." Ellie stirred awake and turned toward me. She had felt my gaze on her in her sleep.

"Are we there yet?" she asked.

"No," I said. "We still have a ways to go."

She went back to sleep. The sky was flooded with a limpid light. I saw my younger self—hair tangled, knees covered in dirt —resurface on the horizon. My face was streaked with tears. The falcon, too, reappeared. I watched myself lift my gaze to take in its elegant circumnavigation. There I am, I thought, taking in my slight figure, simultaneously dead and alive. It occurred to me that the borders of my life would forever be stitched to hers: her death would be my death; her life, mine. An obvious thought and yet, as I took in her frail figure, I was of two minds: I experienced her as both myself and *not* me. I suddenly felt terribly uneasy in my body. The bus seat felt too constricting, the ride interminably long. I needed fresh air. I needed to move my limbs. I looked down at my thighs. They were strong, muscular. I had filled in. I was healthy, and yet I felt I could see through them to the legs of that other me, stick thin, my knees a knobby pair of bones. I remembered Ellie feeling unsettled in similar ways when we had gone together to her childhood home in Jerusalem, the site of her primordial wounds.

I squeezed Ellie's hand and she drew a deep, relaxed breath. I thought again of the journey we'd made together through Israel and Palestine: the long bus rides, the intermittent power outages in the West Bank, the militarized control of Palestinian civilians, the dizzying heat of the sun, the scent of exhaust and body odor, the hours spent standing in the labyrinthine cages at the checkpoints in Jerusalem and Bethlehem and Jenin.

The bus began to exit the highway, and the feelings of unreality that had grabbed hold of me suddenly magnified. I felt a rising sense of panic. Throughout the ride, it had occurred to me at intervals that we were moving in the wrong direction, that we were going to Málaga instead of Marbella. In fact, the bus driver had said as much, but I hadn't heard him, hadn't wanted to hear him, hadn't wanted to register the fact that we were about to arrive in Málaga when we were meant to be going to Marbella, a place I had avoided returning to for twenty years. Even now, two decades later, with Ellie by my side, I felt atomized remembering how carefully Omar had wielded terror and tenderness as tools of domination. He'd made me aware of my body for the first time, aware of the wild whirlpools of pain and pleasure that can run through my veins. He'd pulled my head back, pinned my hands to the floor against my will, and I'd felt a frightening clash of sensations: a riveting tremor running across my skin, a base-level instinct to lie immobile until he was through with me, dread at the thought of what else he might do when he was done, and a thrill at the transgression I was being subjected to, a transgression I'd learned to crave. I could hardly stand my thoughts, the onslaught of memories. I reached over to Ellie and stirred her awake.

I told her to wake up.

"We're here?" she asked groggily.

"Not exactly," I said. "But we need to get off the bus."

"What do you mean?" she asked, searching the landscape with a confused gaze. "The light is so bright," she said, squinting. "Do you have any water? I'm really thirsty."

I told her I didn't. I explained to her that we'd gotten on the wrong bus and were headed away rather than toward Marbella, and that while I'd suspected as much, I'd felt too anxious at the thought, too disoriented to ask the driver which way we were headed. She let out a loud laugh. Of course, that laugh was saying, *We've been disoriented for so long, getting lost is a foregone conclusion.* We pressed our heads together and giggled like hyenas, tears streaming down our faces.

The bus pulled into the station and the driver shut the engine, pumped open the doors. We got a waft of dense, hot air. We got up and stood in the aisle. I told her that I'd seen my child-self through the bus window, walking across the landscape, and that I'd realized that by enabling his own desire Omar had succeeded in suppressing mine deep into the future. "The thought split me in half." I sighed. "I couldn't come to grips with the fact that we were moving in the wrong direction."

"Don't worry," Ellie said, leaning against me sleepily. "Every time I return to Israel I feel completely fragmented, like parts of me are dying." She said that she always gets on the wrong bus when she lands at Ben Gurion Airport, that she unconsciously travels away from her home even when she knows her mother and stepfather were waiting to receive her, even though someone had changed the sheets on her bed and put warm food on the table.

I reminded her that the apartment in Marbella had been vacant for two decades. I told her that it's possible that, like her apartment in Jerusalem, the apartment in Marbella had had every intention of being a home, a sacred abode where the most beautiful aspects of the external world were reproduced to create a balanced, harmonious microcosm, but that the walls had turned evil, that their natural disposition had shifted, likely due to what had passed between Omar and me. I told her that I'd had the feeling while living there that the apartment was campaigning against me, as though it had acquired a vigilant and vengeful nature. I thought again of the bruised version of myself that I'd seen walking across the arid landscape among the striated rocks that stuck out of the dry earth like swords. I said that at times I'd had the impression that the apartment's walls were moving in on me; that the walls were attempting to squash me, to evacuate all depth from my life, to convert me into a surface designated for attack. I told her that when I'd looked in the mirror I'd occasionally seen reflected a different expression on my face than what I felt I was expressing. I'd seen terror, remorse, fright. I'd seen my mouth open wide, my lips drawn back, my teeth exposed, my tongue flat against the base of my jaw. I was screaming and yet there was no sound. I felt nothing.

Ellie shivered. "You're giving me chills!"

I turned awkwardly in the narrow aisle and put my hands on her shoulders. It was taking those ahead of us in line forever to gather their belongings and descend from the bus.

"So, Málaga?" she asked, throwing her head back against my chest.

"Málaga," I confirmed.

When we finally deboarded, we stood on the street in the long shadow cast by the station. As we scanned the roads, the taxis lined up against the curb, the square pink buildings, the unassuming bars on the corners, Ellie told me that for years she'd felt that it was almost impossible to record the passage of her pain into speech. That her identity as a Jew whose ancestors had been persecuted through the ages in Europe, whose grandmother had come to Israel in the late twenties when the war was still a rumor, made it difficult, if not impossible, to record the layered geography of her nation's pain, a nation born of violence, a national project executed out of fear and the memory of unthinkable violence, complete annihilation. She had inherited pain through stories her neighbors and distant family members told about surviving the Holocaust, and from her grandmother's stories about the Arabs' killing sprees in Mandatory Palestine, the maiming of Jews during the 1929 Hebron massacre — "They chopped off our doctor's fingers," her grandmother would say, a conversation, Ellie told me, that repeated itself, that more often than not collapsed into a senseless argument between her and her family about who had outinjured whom in the Israeli-Palestinian conflict. To archive the region's pain, she told me, and the events associated with that pain — its trigger episodes — was extremely difficult because, coupled with pain's own resistance to language, there were silencing political forces that kept certain key realities out of the realm of public discourse. "It was forbidden," she had said, "to acknowledge the suffering of Palestinians, to accept the glaring fact that the insurmountable and gruesome affair of the Holocaust, caused by Aryans, conducted with the silence of the Christians, was directly influencing the fate of Palestinians, legitimizing the project of their extinction on what had been their land, land they were forbidden from returning to." The names of their villages had been wiped from the map; their reality, their history made invisible, and with it, their right to exist on that land. Ellie said that, as an Israeli citizen and a Jewish person of Sephardic and Lithuanian descent, her empathy for the plight of the Palestinians—her belief that they had a right to self-determination—was considered an unforgivable transgression by her family and community. "You care more about the Arabs who are trying to kill us than you do about your own family," she'd been told. In order for her to practice her humanity, she told me, she had to betray the unacknowledged gag order that was thought to be necessary for the survival of the Israeli state. And that meant that she was alone in the world, trapped in an absurd paradox: she was complicit in the violence enacted against Palestinians at the same time that she was disowned by her family for denouncing the crimes of the state and the hypocrisy of the people who denied Palestinians their dignity, their humanity, their basic civil rights, who treated Black and Mizrahi Jews as second-class citizens.

I told her that I understood the feeling of being forced to decide between one's own sense of integrity and the assumed modes of well-being expressed by one's community, that when the two are at odds with each other it feels as though one-half of us is dying. I told her that despite the pressure to do so I had never been able to bring myself to hate Omar. What would bother me for the rest of my life, I told her as we stood on the corner search-ing for a place to eat, is that I hadn't come to know the nature of Omar's pain. The question haunted me. What had happened to him? What had been done to him? How had *he* been made to feel invisible, unreal? I had no way of knowing now, but I wished that I did. I wished I had known the hidden geography of his grief, because that knowledge would have liberated our story from the simplistic tale of good and evil.

"It's an impossible position to be in," she said, "to process your own loss of dignity without demonizing him or subject-ing him to the dominant narrative of the Arab man." Then she pointed at a bar across the street, and said, "In the meantime, we're back to what we do best: killing time over beers!"

*Killing time*, as if time weren't killing us, I thought, as we stepped off the sidewalk into the sun. But we were happy, con-tent to be together wherever that bus had taken us. We were born to kill time together. That was the pleasure of our friend-ship. Drinking beers, eating fish, smoking cigarettes, talking while we waited for this or that bus, train, airplane, elevator— whatever it was that was going to transport us from A to B.

"Málaga!" Ellie exclaimed as we approached the bar. "As in the birthplace of Picasso?"

"The very one," I replied.

The wind had picked up. The low-hanging clouds that had bloomed in the sky were moving overhead at breakneck speed. The bar where we took refuge was offering a *menú del día*. It was dark and narrow, with a high ceiling, cracked wooden chairs, an old register, a slot machine tucked in the back under a staircase that led to a quieter upstairs where people could sit and eat their food undisturbed. The waiter, a sweaty man with stubble and hollowed-out cheeks, told us to sit anywhere we wanted before he dashed off to the back. We sat next to two couples who were speaking in Hebrew.

"What are they saying?" I asked Ellie.

I had the strange feeling that I could somehow decode all the years that had passed since I'd last been to Andalusia if I could only understand where this pair of couples was coming from, what they were doing in Málaga, this place that holds the ghosts of all of our ancestors, ancestors who fled or disappeared or were tortured to death, who were present in so far as they were absent on this land, who had left behind their belongings and temples of worship. I wondered if this pair of couples, whose flat glances moved over us quickly, had come to Spain to reinhabit the past, to salute the dust of our ancestors, to conduct a ritual of collective mourning. I felt time folding and unfolding as if in a dream. I hoped someday our people might return to this land arm in arm and convert the tyrannical laws of the universe into the steady laws of poetry; I felt a mild, passing happiness bloom in my chest where the trapdoor had been.

"What are they saying?" I insisted.

But Ellie wouldn't yield to my request. "I'd rather not know," she said, and leaned away from them.

I wanted to tell her not to be so self-loathing, but then again, my request wasn't exactly innocent. I was trying to understand something about myself through them—and who were they anyway, just a pair of couples we happened to be sitting next to because we'd taken the wrong bus and ended up in Málaga instead of Marbella. They sat there indifferent to us, disengaged, concerned only with the quality of their meal. They were not susceptible to the devious assaults of the past.

I tried to get the waiter's attention. *"Te escucho, te escucho,"* he kept saying from behind the bar, but every time I started to communicate our order to him, he turned and walked into the kitchen, where a rotund, middle-aged woman with a hairnet and a blue apron was frying the fish of the day—my favorite, bacalao. So I got up and followed him to the back. I heard Ellie yell after me.

"Can you ask for a beer and some bread?" she said.

She didn't speak any Spanish. I was our translator, our sole ambassador. It was up to me to get our point across, and what we wanted in that moment was a ration of bacalao to share, some *patatas bravas*, a couple of *cañas*, and bread.

I got our order in and sat back down. The food came flying over our heads ten minutes later. It was delicious. The fish and the potatoes perfectly fried, covered with the sweet bitterness of freshly pressed olives. We ate to our heart's content. The two hours until the next bus to Marbella sped by.

As soon as we got on the bus, Ellie fell asleep again. She'd passed out before the bus had even left the station. She'd pulled her sweater over her head, a black cotton one. She couldn't cope with the sun. She was too fair. She was better off in Oxford—the sun barely showed its face there—though she resisted it because the place resisted her: a lapsed Orthodox Jew, a queer postcolonial scholar dating a woman.

I closed my eyes and tried to sleep, but I couldn't. I was so sick of being on buses and trains. I'd been on the road for months. It hadn't been easy touring my second novel. I'd gotten sick several times while traveling, had acquired a terrible cold that seemed incapable of healing. It would retreat for a few weeks and I'd feel exhilarated, victorious, until the congestion began blocking my airways again, leaving me defeated, invaded, sultry.

I'd spent my last few hours in Oxford sitting with Ellie in a sauna, trying to inhale moisture back into my lungs. She'd talked to me for hours about how alienated she felt there, how the very stones of the city seemed to refute her right to exist because they'd been walked on for so long by a very specific brand of human: wealthy, elite, with a reserved discourse that she felt certain was capable of strangling her direct nature like a boa constrictor. All business, she told me, was conducted politely, even the business of discrimination; it was conducted with the intention of leaving no trace.

My own days in England had been filled with a series of minor incidents that acquired an inconspicuous quality by virtue of their frequency. It was a hot, clammy May, one of the warmest springs in decades. In Oxford people were spread out on blankets in the parks, wearing sun hats and drinking champagne, idling, indulging their bodies, allowing themselves to feel momentarily aimless. Every morning I walked along the river. I took pleasure in watching the cows pile up against one another on the grassy banks, in the shade of willows. The swans, regal birds of the queen, glided by in the cool water. I laughed each time I saw a swan, each time I thought of the queen. I could not help but think of her possession of those birds as a deliberate strategy for inserting her image, the scope of her power and influence, into the insipid repertoire of the everyday. The swans, too, were a symbol of nationalism, a polite intimation of England's timeless colonial agenda. And they were everywhere, those birds, in the parks and on the sidewalks, in the museum gardens and the universities, a quiet but steady reminder that whiteness was in charge.

I thought about how once I'd left behind the pastoral air of Oxford, and the closer I'd come to my departure for Marbella, I'd felt curiously distant from myself. I'd begun to experience the world with a detached lucidity, with an uncanny sense of unreality. Bristol, with its damp, milk-colored sky, its port and reinforcing boulders, its warehouses-turned-restaurants, felt oddly familiar to me despite the fact that I'd never been there before. I felt as though I'd seen the city in a dream. I became convinced that I wasn't actually seeing Bristol but remembering having seen it. In the hotel, the desk manager, a young Italian man who spoke broken English, who was hard at work covering up the gaps in his grammar with a flirtatious act that only further revealed the faults he was trying to conceal with his false confidence, asked me to pronounce my name several times. Each time he insisted that I was mispronouncing my own name, a statement he maintained despite my protests. It was an outrageously absurd claim, grating in a way that called to mind the whining of the hotel fridge, the horrible squealing sound the faucet made every time I turned it; none of it disastrous on its own, but together they unmoored me.

I carried on. I showered—there was no tub, no proper shower, just a retractable shower head screwed into the wall above a tiled floor with a large drain—and put on fresh clothes: a pink silk shirt and gray jeans. I pulled on my boots and left the hotel to attend what I'd been told would be a live interview about my book at the BBC headquarters in Bristol. This was my second interview with the BBC. The first, in London, had been conducted at a speed that left me startled and confused. I was on with another guest, an American film critic, and we were asked a quick succession of questions on subjects ranging from Childish Gambino's *This Is America* to gender reassignment surgeries in Iran; we had less than one minute to respond to each one. One minute, I'd thought to myself, when Donald Glover had studied —had inhabited—the history of violence and the image of the Black body in white America from the days of slavery and Jim Crow straight through to the twenty-first century to compose his music video. It was possible he'd spent years thinking about the composition of each frame, the seconds he would allocate to each gesture. It troubled me, as it always had, to know that what artists spent years synthesizing and elucidating for the public would be dissected in a nanosecond; our attention span, narrow and impatient, resists prolonged engagement, eschews the transformative power of art, the task of collective mourning and rit-ual celebration that art is capable of undertaking.

I arrived at the BBC in Bristol for my scheduled interview only to discover that no one knew who I was. I heard the security guard announce my name over the telephone several times with a doubtful tone that quickly turned to confusion. I heard several versions of my name, all of them genuine but failed attempts at pronouncing it correctly. I thought of the desk manager at the hotel. Perhaps, I thought, smiling to myself, the pair should con-sult with each other; maybe then they'd get it right.

"Yes," the guard had said. "That's the name." His tone sud-denly became hushed. "It's very long, I know." At that point, he began referring to me as either "young woman" or "young lady."

There's nothing I despise more than being referred to as a young lady. I am in my late thirties. There's nothing young about me, though I have a baby face. It's the face of my father, a man-child in his eighties who still has a full head of hair and all his teeth. The same man who once told me that my face would be my biggest asset precisely because it is so deceptive.

"No one," he'd said, "would suspect your age or your level of maturity; it's the best form of camouflage. It's always best," he'd said to me time and again, "to be underestimated."

All these years later, I still don't know what he meant. Did he mean I would be better off in the world if I appeared to be naïve? How could I appear to be naïve and feel dignified at the same time? It seemed he was telling me that in order to survive

I needed to act weak, stupid, like an empty receptacle. That I should hide my strengths in order to avoid making others—men, most likely—uncomfortable. For a time, I took the advice to heart; I avoided appearing too self-possessed. And somewhere along the line, I began to feel a gap grow inside of me between my thoughts and emotions and my behavior. I began to make choices that undermined my own instincts, my own judgments. I became suspicious of myself, afraid of exposing who I really was. This pattern of turning against myself became habitual. It took me years to understand that what my father was telling me was never to raise my voice in protest, never to articulate my demands or assert whatever I thought would be more just, equitable, respectful than the status quo. He'd infantilized me; maybe acting as if I were still a child was a way of excusing himself, of letting himself believe that there might still be time to parent me. But, of course, *tomorrow* never arrived. Omar, too, had wanted a child—not an adolescent and certainly not an adult; he'd wanted a child, a child with an unsuspecting heart and a smooth, pure face. I had known exactly how to play the part.

I heard "a young lady" again as I was finally escorted back to the BBC studio through a series of revolving glass doors—but only after I'd spent a good forty minutes waiting in the lobby. I'd sat on a red couch eating peanuts from a bowl set on a laminated white coffee table and watching on a large-screen television a spectacular drama between a husband and a wife who'd lost her mind after a terrible accident and now felt persecuted by large shadowy figures that weren't, in actuality, there. I couldn't figure out what the originating trauma had been. Her words were barely audible through her sobs. Her voice was muffled, her lines indistinguishable from her delirious screams.

I walked behind the producer through rows and rows of poorly lit cubicles, listening to the warble produced by a considerable mass of people working alongside one another, answering phones, sending emails, confirming appointments, checking facts, all of them packed into a small space underground, a windowless room that kept the distant drone of traffic at bay.

"So what's your name again?" the producer asked once we were in the recording studio, her eyes scanning three large screens that had been placed adjacent to one another on a large steel desk. I dreaded telling her. I couldn't bear to hear my name turned into a butchered, fragmented sequence of words while she looked at me with a pleading gaze.

Her hand reached for the phone. She was about to pass the baton to someone else. By then, the time of my appointment had come and gone. There was no point in lingering there any longer; I was beginning to lose patience, defeated by the notion that even if my voice aired on the radio there was no telling that anyone would be listening at the other end anyway. I was drowning in a deep sense of futility, exhausted from repeating my name and hearing it repeated back to me as if the world couldn't quite wrap its mind around the basic fact of my existence; frankly, neither could I. I put my hand over hers and asked her to let it go, told her I wanted to leave, that I needed to go out for a cigarette and a walk. "Maybe next time," I said.

"But you're here," she said. "Let's make something of it."

Backup arrived in the form of a tall overweight man wearing a greasy shirt. He was the man who had committed to and swiftly forgotten our appointment. He offered to get me on air so I could introduce myself and my book, said he would give me a few minutes of his time to do so. He kept waving his bloated hand around, saying, "Why not just introduce yourself?"

*To whom?* I wanted to bark back, but I held the words in and instead said no, kindly at first, then firmly. I had sworn off doing other people's jobs for them, or that was my objective—an impossible project tied to a ridiculous hope of being reborn. A foolish wish to be free from the demands of other people, untouched by our human shortcomings, our imperfections.

Then I turned on my heels and left. Dusk had fallen. The sky was an electric-blue dome lit from below by the streetlights. The city looked like a jewel. I walked back to the hotel, down the hills of Bristol, with the river, steely and cold, always within view.

I looked through the rectangular window of the bus at the azure sky that glowed with the light of a stubborn Mediterranean sun. The sun looked to me like a hole that had been punched in the sky through which a bright light that exposed our collective despair, our thirst and hunger, shone. I woke Ellie up again. I told her we were there, that we had actually arrived at the correct destination. I could hardly believe it. I had returned. Soon I would have to climb up the stairs to the apartment, Ellie trailing behind me, my heart in my mouth, beating in an awful way. I felt feverish, terrified that Omar would be there, still forty and handsome and tall, smiling seductively, ready to whisper in my ear, to say again and again—I can still hear his voice, low but firm, carrying a controlled anger palpable to me only now—"I want you naked as the day you were born."

# 4

IT WAS STILL EARLY IN THE SEASON. After lying empty and exposed to the tides of winter, the streets were renewed by the arrival of foreign tourists, Arab sheiks, Spaniards who kept summer apartments by the sea. The local shopkeepers had stocked and decorated their shelves, thrown their polished windows open to let in the warm air, which trembled with the prospect of money. The early summer light was brilliant, luminous, incandescent. The palms and aloes with their green arching leaves thick with water, the white stucco walls of the homes set squarely against one another, the thick, papery bougainvillea that crawled across the city's surfaces like mouths painted rouge, like kisses turned toward the vivid blue of the sky—all of it screamed yes to life. We made our way through the crowd. We maneuvered our suitcases around elderly women dressed in modest pale peaches and purples and sequined flat shoes, around children playfully walking their dogs. Parents trailed languorously behind, occasionally yelling words of caution at their children, who were full of zest for the lazy pleasures of summer. We walked alongside the old straw-colored walls of the city, puckered with cavernous holes that resisted the bright, eager light. We stopped a few times, breathless, and set down our suitcases to listen to the cawing of the crows, the whining of the seagulls.

Eventually, all that remained of our journey was to cross the promenade that ran parallel to the old Arab walls, walk across the cut-granite pavement, the pink and gray stone shimmering in the gleam of the sun. I felt heavy. Across the way, the light seemed to have been sucked from the sky; darkness abided over our building. It sat on a narrow, crooked street in cold shade. As I took in its smog-stained walls, its blistering paint and cracked terraces artlessly stacked on top of one another, I felt a dreadful stirring. An acidic terror stung my throat. It was a feeling that had stirred in me then, too, during that most terrible summer of my life, its darkest dawn, when the hours had passed under the Spanish sky with no one watching over me.

On we went. We walked up the steep, curved road flanked on either side by cars parked nose to tail, their wheels pulled up on the sidewalk to leave room for passing traffic. All at once, we made our way through the heavy doors of the building into its cool dim interior. The light in the lobby was wounded, bleak. There was a deadly silence. It was midafternoon. The neighbors were likely napping or sprawled out on the sand at the beach. The only footfalls were ours, and yet I felt certain that I was being followed, tracked at a distance. I kept turning to look behind us. When I pressed the elevator button, I felt Omar's hand reaching through mine as if our bodies were superimposed; for a moment, my limbs filled with lead. All of the energy and vitality and strength I'd cultivated over the years drained out of me. I felt the pressure of his finger against the illuminated call button and a cold shiver rushed down my spine. I could hear Ellie breathing behind me. I wasn't alone, I reminded myself. No, not this time. I stubbornly held up my head in the face of rising horror. I thought, I've come this far; I'm not going to turn around now, to reverse my steps as I should have done then.

The elevator arrived with a disconcerting thump and its old doors jerked open. The structure was rusty; the hinges squeaked as we rose through the floors, an uncertain, hollow sound, an eerie drone that unleashed a feeling of vertigo within me. I closed my eyes.

"Everything is okay," Ellie reassured. "I'm here with you."

I heard her words echo against the metal walls of that narrow vault. The elevator halted and bounced on the traction cords before the doors lunged open again. We pushed our way through and stood quietly on the landing, our belongings in tow.

"Which one is it?" Ellie asked, as her eyes glided down the hall.

"This one," I said. "Door H." I moved closer to its wooden frame and examined the golden *H* that had been drilled into the wood. When I'd come here before, when I'd first seen that letter, which appeared to me now like two *I*s joined together by a knife or a dagger, I'd lost my way in the world. Returning to it now, I was tense, fearful. It's just a door, I told myself, a door like any other, made of wood, adorned with a knocker. It had a peephole installed at eye level. I remembered looking through it and seeing Omar for the first time. The concave glass distended his face and curved the corridor. I should have known what he was capable of there and then. I should have sensed the brutality simmering in the depths of his soul from the expression on his face, distorted as it appeared through the peephole, from the way he'd moaned when he let go of the envelope with my allowance, meager as it was, always late, arriving only after I'd been thoroughly gripped by the despair of not having enough.

Ellie stood beside me. "We're in this together," she said. It was her second attempt at ushering me in. I could hear the consolation in her voice.

I took the key out of my pocket, inserted it in the lock, and turned. The door swung open with a strange force, as if its hinges were loose; or maybe it had a will of its own, had been wanting to open for a long time, to welcome my body back into its hideous entrails so it could feed on fresh blood again.

An odious air of mold and sewage and dirt rushed out at us. "I promise no one died here," I said to Ellie, forcing a smile.

"Death comes in many forms," she said. "What you went through was a kind of death."

I said that I supposed she was right, that I'd died a death in that apartment. I couldn't bring myself to move. My feet were firmly planted in the foyer. The longer I stood there, the more convinced I became that no time had passed since I'd last arrived at this point. Or that time had passed—it had acquired new dimensions, I'd lived new experiences—but everything that had happened between Omar and me was still in the process of *becoming*, as though that summer had never found its due place in the grand flow of my life. The events of that summer—that summer of lust and trepidation in the Costa del Sol—were continuous. They were stubbornly rupturing the sallow crust of time to call me back to this apartment, this apartment where I'd been ravished by Omar, strategically consumed—groomed, some might say—this same apartment with its low ceiling and stained walls, the faint smell of sewage that rose from the floors every time I flushed the toilet.

I could hardly believe that I was there. The apartment had been waiting for two decades, neglected and yet more or less intact. As I stood in the entryway, I realized that the apartment was a map of my wound. The apartment, I thought, looking around in disbelief, with its emptiness, its dirt, its false appearance as a home. This apartment where I'd arranged my body, exposed it to Omar's terrible desire to drink from my mouth, to stroke my limbs.

My eye caught the answering machine, a white plastic box covered with grime and dust, its surface, I could see even from across the room, sticky from disuse. I remembered unplugging it because I was sick of its little red light flashing every day. I was avoiding my mother even though she was all alone in the world. She'd left message after message for me, the despair in her voice rising to panic, pleading for me to call her, to pick up, to stop torturing her. The memory of those words, the knowledge that I'd hardened in Omar's company, acted cruelly toward myself and my mother, the woman who made me, was a stab to my heart. I was disgusted with myself.

I watched Ellie forge ahead through the silent hallways and rooms, and considered how incapable I'd been, how incapable I remained, of fully grasping my adolescent impulses. For years I hadn't talked to anyone about what had happened. I could barely admit the facts to myself. They settled in the bottom of my mind like sediment, and I did my utmost not to disturb them. But the air of my life was murky, full of dirt and dust and fog. For years, I deceived myself with a story I could live with; instead of acknowledging that Omar had taken advantage of my naïveté and innocence, I wove together a hard-edged story that celebrated my perversions and recklessness. Perhaps, I considered, both stories were true. Perhaps my aberrations existed alongside my vulnerabilities; perhaps they appeared as dichotomous traits when in reality they informed one another.

I remembered how Omar had leaned against the refrigerator, how he'd stared at me with his brazen gaze; he was a man preparing for conquest, a fact I could see so clearly now but had not known to look for then. I heard the deep, heaving gurgle of the sea. The sound droned in my ear, and for a moment, I was convinced that the apartment would soon be underwater, that a great big tidal wave was going to crash over its unmopped floors and wash the whole thing away. I heard a heavy clambering behind me; heat spread across my back. It was Omar. I was sure of it. This apartment was his waystation. A part of him had died here, too. He was still in the apartment, dead and yet walking, clambering down the hall, living out his death alongside my former self, the part of me that had died servicing his needs. I shivered at the thought of it. I closed my eyes. I felt his hot breath against my back, his hand wrapping around the nape of my neck. I could hardly breathe. I wanted to scream but couldn't. He spoke to me through his teeth. He was breathless, his tone insinuating. "Don't lie," I heard him say. "You're not a virgin." I gasped with horror. He'd said those words to me so often that I'd believed him. I felt a bitter pain spread in my chest. It was the sediment of the past rising to the surface. I had to force myself to step farther into the apartment, to breathe. My throat ached. I called Ellie, but she didn't hear me. She was moving about the apartment. When she reemerged, she looked at me, astonished, and said: "What happened? All the color's gone from your face."

"Nothing," I said. "I'm just tired."

For a moment, I didn't know what to do, what more to say. The sound of the ocean had retreated. The heat that had pressed against my back had given way to a chill. The apartment was empty of life again, a hollow container; nothing stirred, not even death.

"Why don't you sit for a minute," Ellie said, and she walked me over to the sofa, the tired old sofa with its worn geometric patterns; I'd hated how dated it was even then. I searched the cushions for impressions of our bodies, Omar's and mine, indentations where we'd sat or lain down, before taking my place on the edge and resting my head in my hands. Ellie left to grab me some water. I heard her open the cabinet and reach for a glass.

The problem, I thought, as I waited for her to return, is that I'll never know how much of that summer was my fault, how complicit I was in my own destruction—was I more reckless or more vulnerable? It was the not knowing that continued to erode my trust in myself. I was trapped in a circuitous mental loop. In Western society, I kept thinking, in the part of the world where I've spent my adult years, the accepted narrative is that rape retroactively strips its victims of agency. In order for society to acknowledge that a woman has been raped, she has to be able to prove that she was not complicit in any way, that her will was not divided. You have to give in to the notion that, as a survivor, healing is only possible once you acknowledge your own lack of agency. But I hadn't been a passive body. No. Not entirely. I had pursued Omar. I had gone after him. I was unaware of the danger I was in. Of his power over me. Each time he'd dropped me off, I'd made sure that he was going to return the next day. I never wondered where he went during the hours he didn't spend with me—whom he slept with, what he ate or wore, or how he combed his hair. I only cared that he would come back to me soon. I felt desired, wanted. What a fool I'd been.

I was so deeply ashamed of myself. I couldn't stop thinking that I'd been old enough to know that I was placing myself in danger. That was what I'd wanted. It was what I'd needed. An unconscious impulse to be hurt. The fact that I hadn't been able to see the full extent of the damage Omar was unleashing in my life didn't absolve me of responsibility, didn't erase my desire, nor would I want it to. My desire was real; it was a source of life, of energy that could propel me through my grief. And my right to that desire—pure and straightforward—did not absolve Omar of responsibility or diminish the scale of his assault. Of course, I hadn't known that the pain would unravel and grow and change with me forever, become a bitter companion for the rest of my life.

Ellie returned and handed me a murky glass of water; there was sediment swirling in the dark green glass. She told me that it was the best she could get, that she had run the water for a few minutes and it still hadn't turned transparent. I took the glass from her and she disappeared down the hallway.

Ellie was the only person I'd met who was willing to let me consider all of the pieces and parts of that summer. Take Xavi, for example. My willingness to forgive Omar, to look at the issue within its larger social context, terrified him. Each time the subject arose, he turned tense, rigid. His gaze would harden and he'd insist that the only correct emotional response would be to loathe Omar for damaging me beyond repair, not to integrate that damage into who I had become, into how Omar had shaped me. "But he did shape me," I would insist. "What's the point in wanting to return to who I was before? What's the point in wishing I'd never crossed paths with him? I have to live with what is," I would say to Xavi, "not with what could or should have been." And he would fall silent, draw me into his embrace, and say, "I know, I know. I just wish I'd been there to protect you." He would hold me, tenderly stroking my hair and my arms and my back, admitting through the gentleness of his touch that he knew that wanting to shift my narrative to match his emotional response was a transgression he shouldn't permit himself, not if I'm to rise out of the ashes of my past. And it wasn't only Xavi. The long line of therapists I'd consulted over the years. My mother. They all wanted me to adhere to the traditional narrative of victimhood. It was only with Ellie that I could acknowledge my yearning for Omar openly without being confronted with a totalizing narrative of the unequal power dynamic that had existed between us.

"Look!" Ellie commanded now, pointing at the floors. She was standing beside me again.

I looked. The white tiles of the floors had turned black. She kneeled down to wipe one with her hand and brought a sooty finger up to my face. I acknowledged that we would have to scrub them. But I wasn't in the mood to clean. I wasn't in the mood to instruct anyone, myself included, and least of all Ellie, who can be lazy when it comes to chores, on how to buff the floors until our faces were reflected in the glow of the tiles. I wondered if I'd be able to see the red print of Omar's fingers on my neck then. I thought, in quiet distress: How am I to know whose face will come forward in those tiles once we polish them? Mine? Omar's? The person I'd been that summer? I didn't want to see the decomposed face of my former self, my mouth contorted in a painful grin. And what of the person I would have become had

I stayed on, an adult who had misspent her youth being Omar's lover? I imagined her face, pale and bloodless. I imagined her disintegrating flesh. Her sunken eyes. Her wrinkled forehead. Her anxious, unsettling gaze. I felt repulsed, horrified at the thought of her.

"I'm going to take a shower," Ellie said. Her voice came at me like a soothing breeze.

"Okay," I said. Then I warned her that it would likely take some time for the hot water to kick in, that the pipes would likely burp and squeal at first and maybe even spout rust-colored water. "Or worse," I said, with an irony that failed to land. "Blood."

"Oh god!" she said, and laughed forcibly from between her teeth. She walked off, leaving me alone with my thoughts.

I moved into the kitchen and leaned against the stove. I felt Omar sliding alongside me, as though he were ready to begin our story again, to lean his elegant brown body against the fridge, to hang his head back, to laugh sardonically, to drink an orange soda, to lick his fine lips tasting of basil and tobacco and honey. I felt unsettled by his presence, and yet I found myself submitting to it as though by habit. His presence, I thought, opening the cabinets and reaching for a glass to drink more water, will be with me until the day I die. I will forever carry with me the stormy timbre of his voice. The smell of his body will forever rise from the very earth on which I tread. I grabbed the glass. It was sticky, thick with grime. It had sat unused for so long that it had turned opaque.

I remembered a conversation that I'd had in therapy, a conversation in which my therapist, whose depth of understanding I usually considered extraordinary, had claimed that, most likely, I'd felt flattered by Omar's attention, that I'd likely just been charmed by the fact that of all the young girls in the world he'd settled his attentions on me. I'd felt numb in the face of that comment, but right before I shut down, I'd felt an upsurge of doubt, a swell that manifested itself as a tightening in my chest, a constriction of my throat. I remembered feeling as though I were choking on her comment, just as I'd felt a few minutes earlier. Her comment had seemed too simple, too vain, but still likely, still plausible, despite the fact that I had no recollection of ever having felt that way in the least.

What had bothered me about the comment, I considered, returning the dirty glass to the cabinet, thinking that I'd retrieve the one Ellie had already washed, was not so much what the therapist had said but how she'd said it, as if it were a singular truth, a fact that contained revelatory powers. As if her comment alone would forever clarify for me what had happened between Omar and me. I had interpreted her tone—which had been austere, direct, unadorned—to mean that she was offering me the missing link that would allow me to settle, once and for all, the question of what my motivations had been, why I had pursued a relationship with Omar in the first place, a question that plagued me just as much as it plagued me to undermine the desire, pure and healthy, that had catapulted me toward him.

I felt my face prime for tears. I closed the cabinet door and stood there a while with my arm on the handle and my head rest-

ing against it. I felt heavy and a little shattered. I looked around.
I took in the walls and windows and floors. There were cracks in
the kitchen floor tiles and the grout had turned black with dirt.
The walls were yellow, the color of abandoned teeth. And I could
hardly see through the streaks of grease and the grainy specks
of dust that had gotten caught on the window's surface. It was
uncanny, this apartment, this waylaid enclosure. It was at once
alive and dead, full of ghosts and yet as empty as a tunnel leading
to nowhere at the end of the earth.

This apartment, a vacation home no one in my family fre-
quented—certainly not my father, nor his wife, the main insti-
gator of its purchase. In my mind's eye, I could see her walking
from room to room in her negligee, airing out her limbs in the
Mediterranean breeze for two summers, maybe three, before
she'd tired of it and directed her attention elsewhere. With hers
went my father's; she pulled the reins of their lives left and right
and left again, so they were forever doing circles around themselves, unable to advance. The same way my father had children spread around the world, I thought, as I left the kitchen to
search for my cigarettes—children who had internalized his
remoteness and who, as adults, consciously or not, considered
it our duty to perpetuate the legacy of estrangement that he'd
set into motion—he also had apartments gathering dust. He
had so many empty homes that he struggled to pay the taxes,
was always borrowing against one to pay for another; and yet
he refused to liquidate his assets even if it meant living hand to
mouth, dying impoverished.

I had never understood my father. He is the most perplexing person I know, and since I am an extension of him, I am equally perplexed by the parts of me that reflect his detachment and laissez-faire attitude, traits that, upon further consideration, were likely the very ones that encouraged me to open myself up to Omar's secretive, shameful pleasures, to give way to the darkness between us, to applaud and enable his aberrant will.

I found my bag and retrieved my cigarettes. Perhaps, I considered, taking in the hideous walls of the apartment yet again — their crusted seams, their cracks, their sliced and slashed plaster — my father had accumulated children and homes in the hope that each time a new child or apartment came along he would do better; make up for his past errors; keep, once and for all, his feet to the fire. But I did not believe my father capable of change. There had been a time when I had. But I no longer did.

I lit a cigarette and brought it to my lips. The smoke relaxed my throat. I could breathe again. It was a simple gesture, that of lifting a cigarette to my lips, but one that gave me immense pleasure: drawing in the hot smoke, feeling the sting of nicotine against my lungs. Smoking gave me a sense of control over my fate, a destiny that I knew had been shaped in large part by self-contempt. How many times had I lit a cigarette in this apartment? I wondered. Hundreds if not more. And the act, repeated, unchanging, wounding and gratifying at the same time, had the odd effect of reminding me of all of the years that had passed. My hands were rougher now. I had freckles on my skin where there had never been spots before. I was wearing a ring, a simple gold band engraved with Xavi's name. As I deposited the ash on an old piece of torn glossy paper—a brochure describing the flora and fauna of the region—as I watched the ash tumble onto the brochure, a thin plume of smoke rising from its laminated surface, I felt Omar's hand sliding off the nape of my neck. For a moment, I breathed easily. I felt that what had passed between us had passed in another lifetime long ago. I resolved to air out the apartment, to open up all of the windows. After that, I thought to myself, I will open the door to my old room. I've come here to lay my eyes on whatever monstrosity is there waiting to assault me. It was always like that, my mood: retreating then rising to the occasion.

Ellie stepped out of the shower. Her cheeks were red from the steam. She'd dried herself with a stiff towel she'd found in the bathroom.

"How was it?" I asked.

"Tepid." She smiled. "But I could feel the hot water coming on at the end."

I asked her if she would help me draw back the curtains, roll up the shutters, open up all of the windows.

"We need to air this place out," I said with a forced enthusiasm that betrayed the fact that, deep down, I was feeling restless, unsure, uneasy. I was struggling.

Ellie disappeared into her room to change. I looked down the hall at my bedroom door and felt the sting of fear again. I was gripped by the terror of finding myself—who I had been—still there, sitting on the edge of my old bed, an aged version of me, of who I would have become had I stayed, blue and bloated, her skin hanging off her bones like wet rags. My legs grew weak and wobbly beneath me; I thought they might give out. But I kept on moving.

I opened the window in the living room and the light of the day leaked in. Blond rays pooled at my feet. I wanted to lavish in them, to draw from them my rightful share of life. Ellie re-emerged wearing a green cotton dress that came down to her knees. She barely ever wore pants, a habit from having been raised in an Orthodox household. Her hair was wet and it was dripping onto her back and chest, leaving dark marks that spread as she moved around the house taking it in. She'd already digressed from the task at hand. Instead of unlatching the windows, she was going through the closets and cabinets in the bathroom and the corridor with a bemused look on her face, pulling out every object she came across: a large red pair of sunglasses, a cropped yellow top I'd worn almost daily that summer, the two-piece purple Speedo I'd trained in for years. I stood in the living room watching her. She seemed so remote, her figure distant and diminished. A cavernous hole opened in my mind as I stared at that swimsuit, Omar's voice emerging from inside that drafty cave.

"A fish," he said. "My little fish." I had always been a strong swimmer.

"Is this yours?" Ellie asked with a drawn tone that betrayed her dismay, the Speedo hanging from her finger like a wounded piece of meat from a hook.

I didn't answer at first. Used to my silences, she continued her search. I watched her hand plunge in and out of the corridor as if it were disconnected from her body. Her hand looked so white against the metallic light of that tunnel. I felt the swell building again. I heard the deep echo of a roaring ocean. I was about to be submerged, as though the sea were rising to swallow the apartment, or as though the lakes high up in the mountains where Omar and I had gone swimming were hovering over me, about to tip over and flood me with their warm waters. Who would have known, I thought, that the same skill required to do laps across a pool would serve me in going down on him? I managed to move, to take a step into the feeble light of the corridor and snatch the suit from Ellie's hand.

"Stop touching everything," I said angrily.

She backed away from the closet and went into her room and closed the door.

I felt terrible. She'd always been ahead of me in health and healing, in knowing what to do in the face of insurmountable loss. She'd made it her life's work to study her own grief, to catalogue the invisible pain of others. I could barely deal with my own lot in life. While this asymmetry between us was integral to our friendship, to the care and respect we had for each other, in my weakest moments it also made me feel small, selfish, inadequate, an incomplete citizen of the world. I stood there and lifted the swimsuit to my nose. It smelled like moss and fresh water. It was stiff, the elastic bands rotted, likely because I'd put it away while it was still wet, though I couldn't remember doing so, couldn't remember the last time I'd worn it, if it had been on an outing with Omar or if I had, as I tended to do, lain out all day, alone in the scorching sun, occasionally taking a dip into the water, reading Lorca. I remembered reciting lines from *The Gypsy Ballads*—*the wind leaves in the mouth a rare and generous savor.* I had sung them quietly to myself. The same savage animal lust I felt for Omar, I also felt, already then, for language.

As I stood there speechless, deferring my apology to Ellie, I felt my hand burning; it cramped up. I felt a scalding, searing pain, an inhibiting pressure, as though my Speedo had acquired a crushing weight in the years since I'd last seen it. I wanted to toss it out the window, burn it in a fire, bury it in mud. It dawned on me again that there were memories from that summer I could not access. I could not plot the sequence of events on a line. The sediment at the base of my mind had solidified, turned to cement, a dead weight I carried around but for which I had no language. I wanted to tell Ellie that she should be careful not to disturb the contents of the apartment, that every object contained information about how I had lived in this space. That I was afraid of losing control, of the chaos I suspected would ensue once I began touching things, moving them around, dislodging them from the past where they were securely moored. It was already happening. As I held that suit, I saw Omar peeling it off my small body at the end of a long day hiking to the high tranquil lakes that lay hidden in the mountains.

I retreated to the living-room window and leaned my head out to take in the fresh air. Below, I saw the vendors preparing to close their shops, retrieving the leeks and oranges and celery that stood in piles on the sidewalk, and thought to myself, Omar knew all of the mountain roads. He knew the mountains like a guerrilla fighter. He lived off those mountains, taking people on excursions, hunting birds and rabbits and wild boars. He knew every rock and tree. I had been so skinny then, so tiny, like that wild boar he'd captured, with her spotted back and coarse hair and blinking eyes, her small raw hooves. I felt an unbearable ache in my heart at the thought of her.

A dog came bounding down the promenade, answering to a whistle that seemed to come from one of the vendors beneath the building. I heard the metal shutters of stores opening and closing. A young woman was making her way up the promenade, her tanned muscular legs shining in the copper light of the descending sun. I had also been strong then, I considered, wiry, perfectly capable of keeping up despite my incessant smoking habit. I'd swim across the lakes, leaving Omar heaving behind on the rocky shores. I remembered him placing his hand on my hip bones, his gorgeous hands. I remembered him lifting hot sand from the beach and pouring it onto my belly, saying all the while that I needed to eat more. I couldn't help but feel a pang of nostalgia for him, a feeling that disturbed me greatly because it suggested that I missed him on some deep physiological level I could neither justify nor control. The girl disappeared from view, and for a moment, the promenade lay empty, silent.

The cut-granite stones of the promenade looked dazzling beneath the incandescent sky. I watched three old men come up the road dressed in brown slacks and button-down shirts, wearing espadrilles, leaning into their canes. I pictured my father alone at fourteen, his features swollen as they were preparing to find their final shape, his face red from the cold ocean winds, his small gray eyes raw from the searing salt of the stormy water, the damp air, his back to Great Britain, his neck and shoulders tense from the absence of his own parents, his stomach turning on the high seas. And then I thought of myself at seventeen, alone in this seaside apartment. My father must have thought, What a luxury, what a life this child of mine has.

Ellie reappeared in the corridor. "I'm sorry," she said.

"I'm sorry, too," I told her. "It was my fault. I shouldn't have been so abrasive."

"You don't need to apologize," she conceded. "It's just hard to guess what you're feeling sometimes."

I gave Ellie a knowing look then walked past her into the bathroom. I needed to wash my face. The bathroom, narrow, rectangular, windowless, smelled damp with mold. The mirror had lost its shine. I looked at myself. I looked eaten with exhaustion. I remembered seeing my face staring back at me helplessly from that mirror before, my mouth stretched into a painful grimace. I'd been hungry. I thought of all of the figs Omar and I had eaten that summer, of all the times we'd pulled to the side of the mountain roads on his Ducati and removed our helmets to pluck fruit from the trees. We'd fed them to each other. We'd been happy, happy at the expense of my future self.

I wondered if that younger version of myself had known the power she'd ultimately wield, if she'd known then that I'd be accountable to her for the rest of my life, pushing myself to my limits trying to retrieve her from the abysmal well she'd found herself in. I wanted to tell Ellie that after the first terrible time when Omar had forced himself on me, trapped me the way he'd trapped that wild boar and had his way, I'd gone back for more until it became the most natural thing in the world. I wanted to tell her that my memories of the time I'd spent with Omar outside of the bedroom felt nebulous and disjointed, that I needed to remember more than the earthy taste of Omar's cock, the sour smell of his sperm, the way it spilled onto his belly when he came, soaking his pubes, making his skin glow in the dim light of all of the rooms we'd ever exchanged fluids in. But I couldn't find my voice, and besides, Ellie was already intimately familiar with my story. And in any case, she had stories of her own.

She had witnessed firsthand the power sex has to destroy, to decimate, to stifle. She'd left home at fifteen, unable to withstand the severity of her parents, the surveillance culture of the wider Orthodox community, the oppression bearing down on her body, the covenants policing her sex, curbing her desires. She'd lived on the streets for a year, sleeping under bridges huddled together with other runaways, relying on strangers' leftovers, which she stole off the tables at sidewalk cafés. She moved in with a man halfway through the year. An older man in his twenties who was far more sexually experienced than she was; he'd insisted that in exchange for a warm bed and shelter she had to sleep with all of his friends and she'd done it. She had removed herself from her body. She had floated above herself or stood beside herself and watched this other curly-haired girl twist her body to conform to the needs of others. She told me that a few times this girl, this other girl, had lifted her face as if she were searching for Ellie but that her gaze had been vacant, that she'd stared emptily at something behind Ellie, that after that Ellie had removed herself altogether from the room. "I'd been remorseless toward myself, unforgiving," she'd said to me once. She'd spent years in therapy sewing together all of her dissonant parts. She'd become convinced that the Israelis' unacknowledged violence against the Palestinians—the repressed fear and guilt and grief of protecting one's life at the expense of another's—was erroneously expressed through sexual aggression. Sex, she believed, had become a way for the lost youth of that dense, troubled land to work through the cycle of violence and inherited fear that had shaped their lives, entrapped them. As Ellie walked into the bathroom and stood behind me, her plastic peach-colored makeup bag in hand, I remembered that we'd walked past the cafés that she'd stolen cold French fries and half-eaten falafel from and that we'd realized then that anything that has the ability to create life has the capacity to exterminate it in equal or greater measure. We had talked about the fact that sex could simultaneously create life and extinguish it, that people were either in denial of its power or terrified of it, that the closest Western society had come to acknowledging its influence was its romanticization of motherhood and procreation, a facet of femininity neither one of us was particularly interested in.

I took in Ellie's face in the mirror. I tried to speak, but the words wouldn't rise up through my chest. There was something in my throat holding them down. I could feel the accumulated pressure of all of the tears I hadn't shed. Some understanding was taking shape: that the constriction in my throat was likely a result of my silence, a silence that had become habitual, that had shut me down, cut me off from myself.

I had tried my whole life to recover my relationship to language. I had tried through writing to arrive at the totalizing quality of torture, its capacity to destroy speech, to exterminate the contents of one's consciousness, to turn reality itself—all of the concrete objects of one's life (walls, underwear, couches) into participants in one's destruction. But I wasn't sure that I'd found adequate language for my pain. I wasn't even sure that a structure built of words was capable of containing it.

Ellie was now busy applying her lipstick. She was leaning so far into the mirror that I could see her pores. Behind her, I saw myself, and I saw my child's face come forward alongside my reflection. She regarded me from the space of the mirror with a remote, contemptuous gaze that terrified me. Her anger and her shame were palpable. My heart began to beat furiously. In the lineaments of her face, I saw, for a brief moment, the flickering image of who I would have become had I stayed in this apartment. I saw a ravaged, wounded face, her eyes leaking and as blue as bruises, her hair thin and brittle, her teeth yellowed and chipped. She was all grief, all remorse, all helplessness. Then the frozen rictus of that face slid away and my child's face returned, a helpless, pleading expression on her face.

"You don't look good," Ellie said. "Why don't you rest. You need to lie down."

It was true. I looked as white as chalk. I thought of my younger self. I couldn't believe how much darker my skin had been then, how much lighter my eyes appeared. I'd looked so much more like my mother. My mother to whom I'd barely spoken that summer.

I left the bathroom quietly. I told Ellie I needed to be alone. I still didn't dare open the door to my old room, so I returned to the window in the living room and lit a cigarette. My hand was shaking. The couch with its geometric patterns looked to me even more aged than it had moments before. I noticed that the legs of the wicker coffee table had come undone, and there were bits of straw missing, likely due to the humidity or the salt coming off the sea or some rodent that had run freely through our family wreckage. I stood at the window. I took a few long drags and held the smoke in my chest. The nicotine steadied my nerves. As I smoked, I considered the fact that my adolescent years had been dulled by the same sinking silence that still grabbed hold of me. The rest of my adolescence, the years that came after Omar had had his way with me—after he'd made it impossible for me to know who I would have become without his leaning into me with all of his weight—were muted by my encounter with him. I'd spent those years unsure which parts of me had come from me and which had come from him. There was no way of measuring my sense of self without also accounting for Omar, for his darkness, for the ways in which he'd been tarnished by the demands others had imposed on him—to be a friend and a father to his mother, who'd been widowed during the Lebanese civil war, to show courage despite his own growing trepidation at such a young age—demands that had escalated when he'd graduated into adulthood, which he'd likely been too weak to either fulfill or refute. And so, in his cowardice, he'd turned around and placed those demands on me.

I heard Ellie call after me in a benevolent, admiring tone.

"I'm fine," I told her, lifting the cigarette to my lips. I remembered that throughout high school, I'd watched other students as they slung their backpacks over their shoulders and walked the corridors, as they changed confidently in the locker rooms and leapt into the chlorinated waters of the pool for training. I'd watched them as they pulled their cars into the school parking lot, as they applied their lipstick during lunch, as they struggled to recover from a weekend of binge drinking. I could feel them asking themselves, *Who am I?* I could see them shaping an identity for others to adore. They were crafting a life, carefully curating their habits, exhibiting their most desirable traits, a privilege that had been stolen from me, my ability to compose my own identity eclipsed by Omar.

Or perhaps, I considered, inhaling the sweet warm scent of

tobacco, I hadn't so much as lost the ability to ask who I was as I had lost the ability to decide what the answer would be. Who I was in the process of becoming had been interrupted by Omar. My life had collided with his. Only his life, by virtue of being larger, had steered mine; it had influenced the course of my barely formed life more forcefully than mine had influenced his. I had misjudged him terribly, his motivations, his ruthless desire to satisfy his personal needs, to allow me to believe he was in love with me; I'd been so wrong about him that the rest of my life became incomprehensible to me. I didn't trust my sense of anyone, of what other people wanted from me, or from others, or from themselves.

I smoked my cigarette and enumerated certain facts that I'd begun to understand as integral to my relationship with Omar —my father's absence, his emotional debt to my melodramatic stepmother, Omar's own disappeared father (his body was never found), the civil war in Lebanon, my father's Orientalism, the poverty in which he'd been raised in the East End of London, my mother's hatred toward my stepmother. All of that, I was realizing with greater lucidity, was central to our story; we were caught in a series of powerful social dynamics, our bodies conduits for all of the toxic energies flowing through the fabric of our blended families. Omar and I were merely the denouement, the final act of a generations-long psychic play. I was the sacrificial lamb in a humiliating stage set not only by my parents but also by the two supposedly absolute hemispheres of good and evil from which they originated. So Omar, I considered, as I finished my cigarette, had acted on me in private but had certainly not acted on me alone.

My gaze shifted flatly across the surfaces of the apartment. Everything was caked in dirt. Nothing had been spared. I looked at the television set, its concave glass thick with dust, the antenna bent and hanging between the console and the wall. I glanced again at the answering machine, imagined my mother's voice trapped inside. I could hear people walking outside; cars, motorcycles, and buses navigating the narrow streets; shops closing their doors, drawing their metal shutters, turning their locks. I could hear the ebb and flow of the city, the even, familiar tempo of noise rising and retreating. But it was as if I were listening to it all from afar.

I put my cigarette out and returned to the window. Dusk was beginning to flood the sky, to unload the day's burdens. A soft auburn glow hung over the silvery roads of Marbella. I watched the wind shear the palm fronds that lined the tiled boulevard from the city center down to the sea. I closed my eyes and listened to the wind moving through the leaves. It was a sound I loved. I opened the windows even wider. The wind we'd felt in Málaga was lifting again, a damp, brackish air that carried with it the scent of jasmine, oranges, four o'clock flowers.

I could hear Ellie moving about the kitchen. I heard her open the refrigerator door.

"It smells like mold in here," she announced.

"What did you think it would smell like?" I asked as jovially as I could.

I stuck my face in the wind and let the air wash over me. There I was in Marbella, I reiterated, as if in disbelief. Marbella, *beautiful sea*. There I was, caught once again in its savage beauty.

"Should we go get some groceries?" Ellie asked.

"In a minute," I said.

It suddenly dawned on me that Omar might still be in Marbella, living up near the lakes in the Sierra Blanca where his first transgressions had taken place; that he was more than likely still there, fishing, laying down traps for the birds, catching baby wild boars with his bare hands. Or perhaps, I suddenly considered, he was dead and it was his ghost that lingered behind. I considered hiking up those hills, going in search of him, confronting him once and for all, levying him to the same turbulence and rage to which he'd subjected me.

I couldn't understand why I had so rarely considered the possibility of his death. His actual death. How rarely I'd considered that he might have exited this world. Somewhere along the line, I thought, I must have come to believe that, were he to die, I would know, that I would have intuited it, that some part of me would have died with him. His death would open a space inside me for the winds of the cosmos to rush into, and the air would burn, burn the way a wound burns when it's prematurely exposed to the elements. But I had no idea if Omar was dead or alive. I only assumed he was alive because I hadn't heard otherwise. I'd heard other news of him here and there. He'd had an accident, a terrible accident, an accident the details of which I can barely consider even now because it had happened so soon after that summer, on a windy fall day, and I'd still loved him then. I pined for him and he refused to pick up the phone, to hear me, to have anything to do with me; the pain of being cut off from him was searing. Everything else I knew of him I knew from my stepmother, from details she would share in passing, a sarcastic, mocking smile on her face. I knew that he'd gone to South America, that he'd grown a beard, a long, wild beard, and been arrested at the US-Mexico border in the immediate aftermath of 9/11 because his profile too closely resembled that of an Islamist terrorist's. That was when I learned that Omar was a pilot. That he'd gone to school in Germany, the same school that the terrorists who'd piloted their way into the Twin Towers had attended.

Ellie's voice came at me from behind. She was saying something about there not being any coffee in the house, insisting that we leave the apartment immediately before all of the shops closed because if there's one thing she hated it was waking up in a house with no coffee.

I told her to go ahead without me. She left suddenly, anxiously, in a manner that suggested she was irritated with my smoking and perhaps even, if only momentarily, with my shell-shocked face.

"Don't forget the keys," I said.

"Just buzz me in," she said, closing the door behind her.

I heard her say the door was rotten, then I heard her footsteps as she made her way down the marble corridor, the steps that opened up to the lobby and the dark crooked street beyond. I walked through the apartment flipping light switches. Most of the bulbs were out, but every second room seemed to have one that still worked. I noticed the stains on the walls had darkened. It looked as though blood had pooled throughout the apartment: near the baseboards, on the ceiling, beneath the frames of the windows. Blood seemed to be running down the walls like ink on paper; I felt the trace of it trickling down my limbs and nearly gasped in horror. I tried to regain my focus. I couldn't be sure the buzzer worked, so I returned to the window to watch for Ellie. I gazed at the old stone walls of Marbella, at the hyacinth bushes and the palms, the aloes and the interlaced trunks of the palms, the serrated edges of the Arabic fortress, the shadows of the seagulls that flew over the chipped wheat-colored stone. I considered again that I needed to enter my old room. I'd watched Omar bury his broad face and drink from between my legs in that room. The first time it happened, I'd stood there, just as Ellie described, dumb, mute, a little astonished. He'd spoken to me violently, his face hard, severe. He'd closed the door behind him, had blocked it off with his body; he was large enough to crush me. I understood then what was about to happen. My legs gave out and I fell back on the bed. "Good," he'd said. "Good. That's exactly where you should be."

I remembered his powerful chest, his broad shoulders. I remembered considering the texture of the curtains as he worked his way up to my breasts. I'd torn those curtains off the rails the next morning. I no longer recalled what they looked like or what I'd done with them. Were they made of cotton, satin, velvet? The baby wild boar was there then, in the bathroom. I remembered hearing her squealing on the other side of the wall, the wild boar he'd captured with his bare hands. She'd been separated from her mother, and as he chased her, she'd run hysterically into the dried bramble at the edge of the dirt road. I'd stood next to the Ducati, watching, stunned, as Omar chased her. I'd protested, telling him to stop, to leave the poor animal alone, but by then he'd caught her and stuffed her into an empty backpack he kept in the compartment beneath the motorcycle seat.

He'd forced me to wear that backpack as we rode back down the hills. I remembered the wild boar's warmth against my back, her heavy breathing. She squealed and kicked her legs, but there was no way out. Omar had fastened the zipper with a rope. I'd breathed against her, trying to calm her down, to show her that she wasn't alone. I'd tried to comfort her once we were back in the apartment, but Omar had thrown her in the bath. I'd watched mutely as he washed her, as she struggled against the slippery edges of the tub. Omar was going to fatten her up and sell her. That was one of the ways he made a living. He thought the whole world was at his disposal, his to manipulate, waste, consume.

I examined the curtains on the living-room window. They were pale blue, the same color as the sky, now as flat as a bed as it prepared for nightfall. The auburn glow had faded. I searched the street for Ellie. No sign of her yet. The wind sucked the curtains out of the window. I watched them billow and fall limp. I took in the city: the Arab ruins, the old Roman walls, the forsaken Visigoth rubble. The pillars of oblivion. The day was on the cusp of being sealed. I watched the seagulls dash through the sky. I traced their flight—a spiral, then a straight line, the approach of a calculated descent—and thought, rather hesitatingly, about the path I was attempting to trace as I tried to recover all of the parts of myself that I'd previously amputated from memory.

I remembered that when I'd been in Oxford with Ellie, we'd sat in the university's steam room, and I'd told her that while I could remember the incidents, the sinister transactions, that took place between Omar and me, I couldn't recall *how* or in what order I'd experienced them. I told her that each time I'd tried to assign words to the experience I felt as if someone had reached into my brain and scrambled the alphabet, so I could no longer recall the correct progression of letters: what came first, what it led to, what I was meant to discover at the end.

"But that's writing," she'd countered, "an attempt to keep pace with life that, while doomed, was not useless." She told me that I had to lean into the pain with all my weight because truth resides in the darkest corners, hidden from view.

I conceded that she was right, that when it comes to writing there are no guarantees, no guarantees that I—or, for that matter, anyone who takes pen to paper—will make it out the other end. There's even no guarantee that there is an end or that, hitched to that end, there's another beginning waiting for me to arrive.

But that, I reminded myself, as I watched the sun recede and the faint predusk light fill the sky, is not what writing is. Writing is not an insurance policy; it is not about drawing conclusions that will cordon us off from our pain. It is, I thought, an invitation to live with our pain and pleasure together, to honor them as equals.

I saw Ellie coming back up the promenade. She was carrying a plastic bag full of groceries. She'd likely bought a moka pot, coffee, dates, oil, and cheese and olives. Her face, ordinarily pale, was flushed with the effort of walking down the steep road to the corner store and back up, a distance still more strenuous after a sleepless night and an unnecessary bus trip in the baking sun. I watched her turn then pause to study the building on the corner, an expression of doubt on her face as she searched for the plaque that indicated the street name. Once found, she boldly set forth again. The buzzer worked. I let her in. I heard the door click shut and her footsteps, heavy with fatigue, coming up the steps. I considered my options again, or perhaps to be more accurate, my expectations of language vis-à-vis life's most indigestible experiences. I worried that my attempts to document in words an experience that had always been, for me, inexpressible might be entirely futile. I worried that I would run out of language before I could get to my teenage self, to resuscitate her. What, I often wondered, was the point of giving expression to this lost version of myself twenty years later? Of exposing myself to the violence of the retelling? And what would I do with her if I succeeded in drawing her out into the world through language?

Perhaps, I mused, as I opened the door to let Ellie in, writing is a record of the unspeakable. Perhaps language is mutable, ghostly, ephemeral; it's not meant to be conclusive, to deliver us from our pain, to heal us. But it can bring us closer to ourselves, to the parts we hide even from ourselves. It allows us to dramatize the hidden geographies of our souls, to reach beyond the boundaries of our bodies. Our voices can change with us, because language is infinitely wise, unstable, as mercurial as life. I hugged Ellie as she came in. I told her I couldn't wait to have coffee with her in the morning, that I was grateful to her for going out to buy us food. Then I returned to the window to watch the night gather in the sky like a bruise; the city, for a moment, lay wasted, ravaged, consumed beneath it.

# 5

DARK. THE SKY WAS an unbroken tapestry of black. An overwhelming darkness gnawed at the edges of the two lights in the apartment that turned on at all — one in the kitchen, the other in Ellie's bedroom. She'd left the door open so some of the light could spill out into the corridor, and she was now busy airing out the fridge, putting the groceries away. She was walking back and forth across the apartment, spreading her stuff in the bedroom and the bathroom, taking up space, claiming ownership.

"Close the window," she ordered. "I'm cold."

She appeared to be floating in the feeble light of the kitchen, her features slightly blurred, blended together so all I could see was her outline and her lips, painted dark pink. The intense rose of her lipstick reminded me of the bougainvillea growing gently over the city's stucco walls.

"In a minute," I told her, and lit another cigarette.

"The last of the day?" she asked.

I promised.

"Did you hear me before?" she asked. "When I said there was no coffee or when I said we need to get groceries?"

I told her I had.

She reminded me that I'd responded to most of her demands, all of them reasonable, by telling her that I would get to them in a minute and that she recognized this strategy as one I often used when I wanted to pass the buck, so to speak.

I reassured her that I'd heard her, that I'd do better by morning, and I again thought to myself, as I had when she'd mentioned that there was no coffee, that I had been raped. Oh, how I loathed that word. It felt so heavy. It shut everything down, descended on me like a boulder; I felt annihilated beneath its weight. *Rape*, such a small and simple word. And yet I feared it was capable of fixing things in place, as if it alone were capable of carrying this story forward, as if it alone could decide everything in advance, communicate all that there is to communicate, retroactively assign a lucid understanding to a set of tenebrous transactions. *Rape*. I felt steamrolled by the word. I wanted something to rise up in me, something equally strong, equally powerful, so I could push back against the pressure the word inflicted on me—but I was unable to form a response.

I told Ellie that I was sorry, that I felt as though I were walking through mud, that when it came to Omar what disturbed me the most was that there were things I remembered and things I didn't. Some incidents stood in stark relief in my mind, all of their contours clear, while others were muted by an impenetrable darkness. I told her that it was painful to realize that I'd hidden certain facts of my own life from view so expertly that I could no longer retrieve them. My inability to remember, I considered, made me shudder all the more at the sound of that word —*rape*—as if the word itself were as murderous as the act, insufferably potent. I felt a surge of anxiety. I was afraid that there was nothing left for me to recover from those dark corners, nothing with even a tremble of life left inside it. I began, once again, to feel the futility of returning here, the uselessness of this exercise in memory. I descended further down the steep planes of my existence. I began to doubt that anything had happened at all, that I had ever met Omar. And if nothing had happened, what were Ellie and I doing here now?

I thought again of the injured face of the person I would have become if I'd dropped out of high school and stayed on as Omar's lover—his object, I reminded myself, because that's what I was, all I had turned out to be, an object that provided him with a shameful release. Her face came forward in my mind —blue, wounded, eyes stretched and raw—as it had come forward momentarily in the mirror. I thought of her blemished face and realized that nested within that face were my brother's pulverized cheekbones, his smashed nose. I winced with pain at the memory of his assaulted features, of the blow of those punches, so potent that they'd gone through him and landed on me. His attacker had battered my soul. I believed that I'd stayed in Marbella, despite the fact that my father hadn't joined me, because I'd *wanted* to be there. I'd gone there in the first place to get away from my mother, her oppressive, tyrannical obsession with protecting me following my brother's departure. And I'd stayed because I was *in love* with Omar. That soiled narrative of love had offered me respite; I'd thought that love would render the word *rape* meaningless. But that, too, had been an error of judgment; the word *rape* waxed again as I waned.

Ellie looked at me tearfully, and said, "I know, I know you're suffering."

That was all she could say. That was all anyone could say.

I put out my cigarette, shut the window, and boldly, furiously marched toward the door of my old room. The gloomy air of the corridor clung to my bones. I reached for the handle. I heard Ellie say something to me from the living room, but I couldn't make out her words. All I could hear was the sound of my blood coursing through my ears, my veins pulsing with the rush. I leaned my ear against the door. I was convinced that I could hear the moans of two people in the throes of love. A simpering that escalated into breathless cries. I could hear Omar's panting, the contraction of his muscles followed by a generous, groundless release.

My hand grew warm again, burning just as it had when I'd held my old Speedo. I wondered again what cries Omar had vocalized in his life. What screams of anguish he'd suppressed. I felt my hand acting on its own accord, joining with Omar's hand to turn the knob. The door clicked open with a subtlety and ease that filled me with horror. I turned the light on. It worked.

There was no one there. The shutters were drawn, the walls

mute. I looked at my old bed. I needed to cry, to scream, to heave out tears of grief, but all I could feel was a searing sensation in my chest and gut, that old constriction of my throat. I closed the door behind me and sat on the edge of the bed.

I'd had so many dreams about Omar in that bed. I remembered how thin I'd been that summer, how tan, how I'd draw my hair back into a tight ponytail, how the winter prior I'd worn the same pair of jeans for months, jeans that, come summer, I'd cut into shorts. They were my only pair of pants. I'd wanted it that way, wanted that feeling of scarcity, of wearing something down, of putting it to use until it had nothing left to give. I was, I believed, exercising a politics of austerity. I was, I believed, resisting extravagance.

I had always been this way; I had always carefully monitored my needs. I was teaching myself to be self-reliant, which, due to my age and lack of resources, meant little more than learning to live with the absolute minimum. Now I could see how terrible that was, how dangerous, that all it taught me was to take up as little space as possible. It left me wide open to Omar's wickedness. All he'd had to do was nudge me over the edge, twist the weakness he'd seen in me, the weakness that I'd deluded myself into believing was a strength, a roughness at the edges, an eroded innocence. I had, I suppose, a consumed look that turned him on, a hardened gaze. I was careful not to smile too much. Not to invite warmth, intimacy, conversation. I didn't want to appear in need. Lacking. Pitiful. I took on the look of a fatalistic child, a bold child, an adult in jest.

I opened the shutters. The light from the moon and the street lamps slid through the gaps between the shutters into the room. The clouds must have parted. I could hear the drone of the cars in the distance. I leaned back on my bed. It was so small, so narrow. I closed my eyes, felt my heart pound wildly against my chest. I brought a hand to my stomach. It was still flat. I barely ate. I ate a proper meal once a day. The rest of the time, I grazed. I grazed even though life had administered its lessons, had taught me again and again that one should eat and take up space while one can. I was allegedly free.

I heard life reproaching me. *What are you making of your freedom?* it asked.

"I'm here, aren't I?" I whispered back.

"Are you talking to yourself?" Ellie asked from the other side of the door. She'd been standing there just in case.

"Yes," I said. I told her that I was having a Socratic dialogue with life. I told her to let me be.

"Don't be a sour plum," she admonished. This was her best attempt at cheering me up; it always worked.

"Someone has to be the sour plum," I said, aware that I owed her a joke, a smile. "We can't all be sweet plums all the time." I told her that this would be boring, dishonest. "What could be more tiresome than a monolith of happiness?" I insisted.

"A monolith of happiness," she repeated from beyond the door, giggling.

Neither one of us knew what any of this meant — sour plum,

sweet plum—this naming of each other, this assignation of language, but it always gave us a lift.

I drifted off again. The image of a plum—egg shaped and silver—came to mind followed by that of a shriveled prune: black, shiny, wrinkled. How long, I wondered, does it take for a plum to turn into a prune? For it to collapse, become dehydrated, shrunken. Irreversibly transformed. I remembered dreaming night after night that I was pregnant, that another life was growing inside of me, that Omar had made way inside of me for a baby, a second life, a being who would haunt me, who would herd me about the house, a remorseless being who would snap at my heels and demand repeatedly, *Come back from the dead and mother me!* I used to shiver with fear until Omar entered the dream. He always appeared. He would sit—his body stately, elegant—at the foot of my bed, bend over me lovingly, reassure me that I couldn't be pregnant, that we hadn't had unprotected sex. But it was a lie. We always had unprotected sex. And yet the dreams felt so real, they frightened me. For days, I confused them with reality. In that moment before waking, I'd convince myself that he really was there at the foot of my bed telling me not to worry, that there was no way I could be carrying his child. Our child. And I'd open my eyes expecting to see him only to be startled by his absence.

Even then, after all these years, that word—*our*—caused me such torment. I was gutted by it. We hadn't shared anything. We had never been equals. I had been plundered, exploited, then refused, cast aside, discarded like an empty bottle. I got up and stood over my bed. I took the bed in again. It looked so sterile. Unused. The sheets were gray, the mattress lumpy. There was no pillow, no place to lay my head.

I retrieved my luggage then promptly returned to my room and closed the door again. I opened my suitcase and removed my favorite sweater from the carefully folded pile: a black wrap-around with a thin silk belt that I like to tie into a side knot. I caught my face in the mirror right before I left the room—my teenage face—and thought: it's no accident that the backdrop to our affair was spectacularly breathtaking. And there was that word again: *our*. And right next to it the word *affair*—a second stroke. I was trying to extract meaning from this triangle of words: *rape*, then *our*—which is supposed to connote together-ness, unity, clarity of vision, but which instead drained me of any sense of direction and engendered a sense of foolish idleness, causing me to halt in my tracks, to stand motionless over the bed—and finally, the whispered third word, *affair*. I said it softly to myself, thinking that I must dissect it, that I must treat it to the autopsy it deserves. *Affair*. A word so light and atmospheric that it contains the word *air*. So deceptive. I was seized by the strange sensation that this sneaky triumvirate of words—*rape, our, affair*—had multiplied, that the words were all floating before me as a multiheaded beast, tempting me with the spirit of unruliness that had commandeered my life as an adolescent, a girl-child, a woman-girl, a heedless, curious girl whose lust and craving for danger overpowered her fear of being wickedly violated. A girl becoming—becoming what?

I gazed at the neglected walls. I tried to backtrack, to return to an earlier thought that I hadn't quite finished collecting: that *our affair* was made possible by the beauty of the Andalusian landscape, because beauty, I had come to understand, engendered a false sense of trust; it calmed the nervous system. The land—this land—I considered, had claimed my body with all its eroded cliffs and stone; its dunes of sand; its native plants; its suckling, spitting sea. The landscape had acted as foreplay; it had helped Omar's plans along. The mercurial moon, the jasmine bush, the orange blossoms. The piles of pomegranates—orbs of blood, life—stacked high outside the grocery stores. The influence of our forebears was visible all around us in the architecture, the old walls, the food, the flowers. The city seduced us with the magic of familiarity, the anthem of belonging, the forgotten memories of our ancestors who had resisted and survived persecution through subterfuge.

I felt a strong urge to air out the apartment. I walked down the corridor to the bathroom and paused to look at Ellie. She was trying to clean with a sponge she'd purchased at the corner store.

"What did life say?" she asked absentmindedly. Then she pointed out the grime that had settled on the tub, the loose seal around its edges, the rusted drains. She'd moved on before I had a chance to answer. "Isn't this supposed to be the Costa del Sol? Why is it so chilly?" she asked. She smacked her lips.

I didn't respond. I was afraid I would start crying, but it was a false fear; what I felt more than anything was numb.

I returned to the living-room window. I opened it again, a thoughtless act given how cold Ellie was. I looked out across the promenade at the arabesque windows of the homes on the hill. The sky had darkened enough that people had turned on their lights. I lit another cigarette. *Last one,* I said to myself.

The tranquil streets, bathed in the funereal stillness of the fast-approaching night, seemed to suggest that nothing of consequence ever happened here. In the darkening sky, I tried to imagine the unique features of Omar's face. But the sky was unsympathetic to my desires. *I am not a canvas,* it seemed to say. *I am air, air, air.*

As I listened to its murmuring, I saw through the telescope of my mind the bright lights of the carnivals I'd gone to with Omar and smelled again the sweet spice of the liquors we drank as we strolled between the booths, drinking, smoking, eating cheese to our heart's content. I saw the donkey ride in Mijas, and for a brief, flickering moment, I felt my leg rubbing against the whitewashed walls of the village precariously perched on the rocky cliffs, the winding roads carved into the mountain's side. I saw the grassy dunes of the beach where we lay kissing, the moonlit streets of Granada, the pomegranates we'd split on the rocks and fed to each other, the figs, the avocados, those tranquil lakes high up in the mountains, their glassy reflective surface. He the tireless strategist, I the whimsical fool. How expertly I had concealed my unease. How easily I'd justified his brutality. How easily I'd come to believe that we were in love. That we were equals.

Just as I felt the sky giving in, as I began to see the contours of his face form in the nebulous night air, Ellie said, "Did you open the window again?"

I shut it. I put out my cigarette. I grabbed the sweater I had removed from my luggage and returned to the bathroom. "Here, wear this; it's thin but it does the job."

She looked at me in the mirror. I stood there and watched her put the sweater on. She tilted her head to one side as she took in her image. She seemed satisfied. She moved on to setting her curls. She had gorgeous red hair, perfect curls.

"Should I braid my hair?" she asked.

I let out a twisted laugh. Ellie laughed, too, even though she had no idea what I was laughing about.

I told her yes, braid your hair. I told her that I was laughing at the fact that I'd been trying to picture Omar's face, but all that had been rising from the swamps of memory were words, words that rejected me, words like *rape* and *our affair*. "They're ghosts, resurrected and come to confess."

At this, she laughed again; she laughed harder. She knew that I'd been trying to harvest the energy of these words for two decades, for two-thirds of my life. I'd been trying for so long to transubstantiate what had come to be, what was still becoming, into a story of failed love, an illicit liaison, trying to turn a protracted encounter with deadly peaks and tender valleys into a completed action when I knew, of course, that it would always

be unfolding. The treacherous underside of passion, its bottom-
lessness.

*Affair,* I thought to myself as I retreated from the bathroom
and resumed my perch near the living-room window. I briefly
heard the roar of the sea again. But if it hadn't been an affair,
then what was it? He hadn't made it easy to understand; he
hadn't forcibly spread my legs and raped me. Not at first. We'd
spent time together, days, weeks, before we ever slept together,
before that first time when he assaulted me. He'd waited until
he'd earned my trust. I'd been caught off guard, in disbelief, terrified, and yet in denial despite having heard the intimations of
violence in his voice. I'd thought stupidly that this must be how
it's done or that this is just a game we're playing. I'd drunk the
elixir of his dominion over me. It had taken me years to have the
courage to look at the truth. It was only then, as I viewed my adolescence through the kaleidoscopic prism of time, that I could
see clearly. I had been lied to so often that I'd become an expert
at lying to myself.

More lights came on in the windows on the hill. I lit another cigarette and again told myself that it would be the last of
the day. I was disgusted by how many cigarettes I'd smoked. I
wanted to open the window and flick it over the ledge, watch its
lit arch float through the inky sky that had drawn over the city
like a dome, cutting us off from the silky golden light of the sun.
But I didn't. I always tried not to chain-smoke. I tried not to light
one cigarette with the butt of another, a habit I'd first acquired in
this very apartment. A habit I'd taken up as part of my perfor-

mance of adulthood. Smoking had helped me to seal my fate as a feral child of the streets. Smoking had been part of my armed response to boredom and neglect.

These days, I'm rarely bored. In fact, there are times when I beg for boredom, when I track it down with the appetite of a hunter. No one ever told me that boredom becomes a scarce commodity as we age. But then again, people are rarely direct. They prefer to insinuate, to drop hints; they make such great efforts to imply and suggest their feelings. I considered this grandiose theater of evasion one of the primary causes of my discontent. Hardly surprising given my father's disposition. I heard his voice—that's what my father was to me, a disembodied, roving voice I'd occasionally hear over the telephone—saying, *The hard lessons in life are best learned early; the early bird gets the worm; you can't turn back the clock; it's not over till the fat lady sings.*

"Be warned," I yelled to Ellie. "I'm letting in some air."

The sky had darkened another few degrees, turned as black as tar. In the glass, I could see my hand lying directly over the reflection of my mouth, the bleak sky a halo surrounding my head. I looked closer. Omar's hand was there, lying over my own. That hand of his that had ushered me into my own pleasure. That hand that had crushed me, gagged me. I laughed. A wild, unbuckled laugh. That, too, I learned early: to laugh my way back to reality even when I felt it had been lost to me forever, cracked, punctured beyond repair.

And what was my reality to be now that I'd returned to this sublime coast of sun and light, this place where Omar had silenced and strangled me? Where his hand had reached over the glazed surface of the lake time and again to peel off my bathing suit as I lay on my back on the paddleboard he'd procured? He kept a fishing rod, a canoe, a few boards chained to a tree near the shore. No one went there. No one except one or two other recluses. We would occasionally find an empty can of beer tossed behind a pile of rocks; the remains of a fire; a worn, soiled condom tossed aside, heavy with sperm. I felt the water of those lakes spilling over me, submerging me in their warmth. By returning to Marbella, had I caused my whole life to turn on its axis? I pushed the window open. My face disappeared. I saw our hands, asymmetrical, one smaller than the other, fly together into the night: two wings of a lopsided bird fluttering in the wind. I thought to myself, There's no *ours* to speak of, but my pain is tied irrevocably to his ecstasy. He had, quite literally, extracted his power from my fragility.

A great damp breeze came blowing back through. It filled my lungs. It filled the apartment, the apartment that was and always had been antilife, antimatter. It was a blissful, decided breeze. Indeed, I thought, my life had turned on its axis. Finally, I thought. Because for so long I had been trapped inside a revolving door. I believed the door to have been constructed out of language, out of other people's interpretations of the facts, the facts of my rape, my *chronic rape*, I should say, or *my affair with Omar during the course of which I was raped*. I'd been going around and around in this revolving door for so long that I couldn't distinguish anymore between my own thoughts and the thoughts that were assigned to me, imparted to me not only by Omar but also by therapists, my father, and Xavi, who had always tried to stand between me and the dark. I am here, alone, I thought—and then I remembered Ellie, who was likely strapping on her heels, who would soon drag me out into the dim light of the night for a drink and a quiet, restorative stroll. How I loved her spirit, her soulfulness. How I needed it like I needed air, water, food.

I heard the sound of a motorcycle pulling up outside the apartment. I leaned out of the window to see who it was. The motorcycle pulled up onto the curb directly beneath the window. The driver unsaddled the bike and leaned against it. He left the motor running and the lights on. I felt my heart begin to race. I stood there and watched silently, frozen in place, terrified that the man could see me, that he could feel me watching him. I turned the apartment lights off then returned to the window. Was it Omar? I could see that the man was putting his helmet back on, getting ready to saddle his motorcycle again. My legs felt weak. I couldn't see his face, couldn't make out his features. Then he got back on his bike and squeezed the handgrip. The engine ripped through the air. He put his feet down, backed the motorcycle out of the spot he'd parked in, and took off into the night, disappearing into the horizon, a searchlight gliding down the street. I sat on the edge of the sofa.

"Did you have a good summer?" I heard my father asking.

"Of course she did," my stepmother answered.

I was sitting in the backseat of my father's old Mercedes as he drove me to the airport to return me to my mother—my fa-

ther who had appeared at the tail end of the summer as myste-
riously as he'd failed to appear at its beginning. I remembered
quite suddenly that Omar had been following closely behind on
his Ducati; he wasn't wearing his helmet so I could see his face
one last time, and he mine. I looked at him through the rear window and saw that he was accelerating with the pace of a madman, that he was about to drive his motorcycle into the car, right
through the rear windshield, right into me. There was something implacable in his gaze, obstinate; he'd had his eyes fixed on
me. That was the last time I saw him. A man with the eyes of a
tiger perched on the back of a Ducati.

"Should we leave in a bit?" I heard and turned around. It was
Ellie with her rosy cheeks, pale skin, and red curls, her black
eyes, smiling widely, unblinking, beckoning me out for a drink.

I conceded. I needed to shake Omar from my memory. The
image of his driving like a madman, hot in pursuit, without a
helmet, as I sat in the backseat of my father's battered Mercedes
attracted and repulsed me in equal measure. It was clear to me
that in some recondite corners of my soul I still desired Omar.
I still believed that all I had to do to reach him was turn around,
that he would be there, making me feel wanted with his gaze,
with his indefatigable appetite for observing me, a hunger that
hung over me like a dead weight. He had shaped my desire. My
perversions would always bear the imprint of his touch, of his
particular tastes; it was painful, embarrassing, and left me with
a tinge of guilt.

For a whole summer, I'd done nothing but wait for him to

come around to the apartment. It was only now, as an adult in her prime child-rearing years, that it dawned on me that it had been easier to wait for Omar than it was to wait for my father. My father who was nothing but a roving, nomadic voice at the edges of my life. His absence had made me vulnerable to Omar, a man who had only taken things from me. He'd wanted my sex. He'd wanted desperately to drink from between my legs, to bend me over or sit me up, his doll, his pupil in all matters of lovemaking. I knew he would come around to the apartment to pick me up with his Ducati—he always did. And I wanted him to. We would go out to a deserted beach or run errands at a post office or a mechanic's at the edges of town, to places where no one would recognize him. I hadn't realized that then. I'd thought, We are in public; there must not be anything shameful here, nothing to hide.

The wait for Omar had superimposed itself onto the wait for my father. I'd walk up and down the promenade, pretending to admire the sea. I bought pomegranates, dates, and walnuts from a fruit vendor. I sustained myself on what I could afford to buy with the money Omar would give me each time I saw him, money he claimed my father had sent him to give to me, to tide me over until he arrived. Whether the money belonged to my father or to my stepmother or to Omar I did not know or care to know; what I cared about was the realization come too late that I was offering sex in exchange for the money Omar delivered. The thought left me stone-cold.

I bought what I could afford to buy and what I felt convinced I could swallow. My throat had closed up, my stomach had shrunk. I was always struggling with a sense of nausea. As though I were, on some level, rejecting life. And yet, I remembered how whole words, sentences, requests had formed on my lips against my will. Once, after freshly shaving my legs, I told Omar, "Feel how smooth they are."

He was delighted at first, then annoyed, taken aback. He cast a hostile, impatient gaze in my direction. I registered the message immediately. I wasn't supposed to express agency; it cut through his desire like a knife.

I remembered one day when I took the bus to Granada by myself and went to the Alhambra to luxuriate in the palace's extravagance, in its majestic walls and eroded glory. I had felt beautiful then. The sun gleamed off my olive skin, made it shine like the leaves of the high trees and the surface of the rocks in the shallows of the sea. The Alhambra had restored to me a sense of dignity that I felt had been forever drained from my body. I marveled at its smooth arches and thin columns of pale marble, its tiles covered with Quranic verses, the words like a thousand hummingbirds come together. There were courtyards lined with roses, their faces greeting the broad blue sky, and diamond-shaped fountains, water flowing forth with the sound of life. Those waters were intended to replicate the sky, to remind us that heaven is as much above us as it is beneath the earth. I had felt safe, whole, unencumbered. I no longer felt like a problem. The world, for those few hours, seemed to be saying, *You belong*. Its shape mirrored the shapes of my inner landscapes and I felt that I fit, that there existed a space for me next to my ancestors. I had loved the doorways carved like locks, the magical terra-cotta passageways, the palms and aloes and cedars that lined the garden walls. I felt wide open to life's mystery, to its strange way of shaping our fate. I didn't feel repulsed by the exaggerated importance Omar had taken in my life. Perhaps I should have. Perhaps I should have felt embarrassed. But once I had matched and outdone his desire for me, once I had begun to crave him, there was no going back. I was intoxicated. In love.

I returned to my bedroom and sat on the bed. But I couldn't just sit there, mute, obsolete, on the edge of the bed where Omar had ravished me. I could feel his odor coming off the sheets, faint but familiar enough to stir in me an old restlessness. I asked Ellie, who had followed me into the bedroom, to give me a moment; she walked out silently and closed the door behind her.

I got up and leaned against that door. I stared at the bed. I heard the roar of the ocean again. I saw the space shift, the present give way to the past as though they were adjoined, partitioned off by walls that could slide open or give way. The sheets were undone; my underwear, black, decorated with tiny hyacinths, lay on the floor beside his. He was lying back with his head propped up on the pillows. A faint light was coming through the window from the moon and had fallen across his thighs and torso, illuminating his bronze skin, his thick black chest hair, his long muscular legs. I felt my heart begin to race.

"Arezu," he said tenderly, his voice beckoning me to return to bed. He was smiling at me, a secret smile I had come to believe that he reserved exclusively for me, a smile no other girl had seen on his youthful, sweet mouth. My name fell again from his lips.

I felt at war with myself. I wanted nothing more than to go toward him, to cry in his arms about what he had done to me, to hear him say that he was sorry, that he'd been wrong. But my body was as heavy as lead—it was smarter than I was; it was holding me back, telling me to avoid the humiliation he would always be capable of inflicting on me.

I breathed deeply, sliding air into my stomach to calm myself. I observed his long thick eyelashes, his green eyes, his arched eyebrows and the look of boyish surprise they gave him, the zestful air that contrasted so beautifully with his hair, already turning to gray. I stood there in the echo of my name. He repeated it, this time more firmly.

I moved away from the door and walked to my suitcase to pick out a dress to wear, to shake off his presence in my room. I turned away from the bed, but still I felt I was not alone. I heard his voice as I bent over my suitcase and retrieved a long black dress, simple but elegant, a boat-neck dress I had purchased in London during my tour, a distraction from my increasing fatigue. He was still there no matter what I did; his voice pursued me around the room, turning more resolute, more vulgar, with every passing second. I opened the window to drown him out with the commotion of cars, motorcycles, and people from the street below.

What an idiot I'd been to believe that I was special to him, that he'd loved me as he'd never loved any other girl. He'd pushed me prematurely over the ravine into womanhood; I'd crossed over with a lame leg, limping, unsure. There had been a moment at the start of our long encounter when I'd felt so powerful, a moment that had lasted only a few weeks, when I'd foolishly felt that I was his lover. Before he'd uttered those cutting words: *I want you naked as the day you were born.*

I undressed now and smiled at myself in the mirror, looked through it at the empty bed, the clear floors. I pulled on the long black dress. It was elegant, dignified, a little playful. I admired its fine lines, its structure. As I was pulling up the zipper and removing the tags, I remembered having said to Ellie, right before she purchased her ticket from Oxford to Marbella, "I feel such contempt for who I was as a teenager." I told her I was worried that old self-loathing would return the second I set foot in Spain. That I would come face-to-face with that adolescent who had tried, albeit indirectly, to kill herself, me.

It was true. As I removed the tags, I considered that I'd been complicit in my own murder, an accomplice in my own death. This, I acknowledged as I reached for the door handle to exit my room and head out into the night with Ellie, was another one of my reoccurring thoughts. It was and would likely forever remain one of the most painful to hold, and yet I refused to release it, refused to let it go, because I feared that if I did I would also have to let go of the notion that I'd had any agency in the relationship, that my desire had been valid, had been mine, a sign that I was a living, breathing human.

AZAREEN VAN DER VLIET OLOOMI

"I'm despicable!" I repeated breathlessly, just as I'd repeated to Ellie that day on the phone.

"No," she had said on the phone. "You're not."

I could hear her breathing on the other end just as I could feel her coming down the cavernous hallway now to beckon me along. "Have you changed your mind?" she asked.

"No," I told her. "I haven't. Let's go." I, too, was in the mood to put on some lipstick, to strap on a pair of heels, to go out to a bar where we could listen to music, where I could trace the rim of my wineglass with my finger. I was in the mood to drink some blood, to become intoxicated. Perhaps I am a vampire, the child of vampires. Meant to feed and be fed on.

The last remnants of that phone call came back to me as we walked out the door into the night together. "A deviant and not in a good way!" I'd said on the phone after a long heavy pause and we'd both laughed. Neither one of us believed in deviancy. How could we when our whole lives had been one side step stacked atop another? I was still in the United States with Xavi then, and Ellie was in her Victorian office overlooking the rose gardens of Oxford. I had pictured those flowers as we spoke. Pink, perfectly manicured. The same color as the lipstick she'd put on and that I was about to borrow, applying it in the dark corridor of the building.

She had remained silent and I had loved her for it. She knew better than to bark back, *But you were seventeen! A pawn.* She knew that I would have much rather heard her say, *Little nymph, haven't you read Nabokov?*

## 6

THAT NIGHT I SLEPT on and off for a few hours. At first, my sleep was empty of dreams, but the last stretch assaulted me with a gruesome, uncanny vision of the woman with the wounded face who'd come to me earlier in the mirror. In the dream, she'd grown out of a tree. The bark had peeled away so you could see her sitting inside the trunk, her hands covering her face. But then they opened; I saw that they weren't really hands at all but insects, dark and winged, crawling over her nose, her eyes as dark as bruises, every last bit of light punched out of them. I gasped and her hands dropped from her face. I felt my throat constrict with terror. Her features were so battered, so grotesquely ravished, that I could barely stand to look at her. She had the face of someone who's forgotten how to love, how to be loved. The face of someone long dead.

I woke up breathing forcefully, wheezing and wincing, a disturbingly acute smell of rot, sewage, mold, and dirt all around me. The room smelled rancid. The odor was overpowering.

It stung my nose. It seemed to be released from the walls, the floors, and the ceiling, which appeared lower than it had before I'd gone to sleep, as though it were descending on me with cunning subtlety, moving in nearly imperceptible degrees. I could feel the walls sliding, shifting, drawing back to reveal my private ruins, the barren foundation of my youth, the parentless desert of my adolescence. I lay there in a frozen state, unable to tell if the dream had contaminated what small modicum of reality I held on to or if the smell was real and had seeped into my dream. Perhaps, I thought, it doesn't matter. Perhaps there is no clear line to be drawn between waking life and sleep, between reality and perception.

It was dawn. I forced myself to sit up in bed and look out the window. The darkness was reluctantly giving way to morning. A rose-colored hue clung to the edges of the sky, nudging the screen of night apart. Soon we would all be vertical again, the streets packed with the machinery of moving limbs. I caught my reflection in the windowpane. My features were stiff with bewilderment, my mouth open in an O. I looked through myself to the trees. They looked as they always had: little scaled and silky tufts of golden hair sticking out of the bark, the fronds suspended in the air, flapping tenderly in the wind. The lanterns in the street were cupping the sky with their soft light. Soon, I thought, trying to distract myself from the assaulting images of my dream, the trees will be loaded with singing birds.

I opened the window to air out the room and returned to bed.

I reached for my cigarettes. I'd left them on the nightstand along with my lighter and an ashtray Ellie had found in the kitchen, the same pale-green ashtray I'd used at seventeen. I lay there smoking in a nicotine-induced anesthetic fog. The smoke dissipated the smell, cutting through to the apartment's musty air, the smell that had settled into the seams and the walls throughout the years the place had been empty, bereft of inhabitants. There hadn't even been a stray visitor, a distant friend or cousin who'd requested the keys for a family vacation. The apartment seemed to have a will of its own, an energy that coursed through its stained walls, repelling anyone who might enter. Only I had remained trapped here. The apartment, I considered, drawing in the warm smoke, watching it float in rivulets up to that menacing ceiling, had threatened to annihilate me with the most tender trick of all: love's oblivion.

I had tried to masturbate on and off through the night. Each time I awoke, I reached down to touch myself in the hopes that an orgasm would ease my breathing and help me glide back to sleep. But I felt nothing. I was numb and indifferent to my own touch, so I gave up and instead lay there in a state of disorientation thinking of all the times I had fantasized about Omar, his broad chest, his hands guiding me onto his hips, his encouraging voice as I rode him in the afternoons. I wondered what our days of lovemaking had meant to him. Did he rewind the tape of his life to relive those encounters while he was masturbating? Did he fantasize about me, too? The thought disturbed me.

Yet, at the same time, it had a soothing effect: it cut through the gnawing pain of being discarded. But only for a moment, a brief flicker of a second.

I felt my blood bubble up at the base of my heart. I felt the old rage return at the thought that he'd consumed me only to dispose of me. That he'd thought of me as refuse. I placed the ashtray on my stomach and flicked the burned end of my cigarette into it. I sucked in all the smoke I could hold in my lungs in a single inhale and felt its warmth spread across my chest. I remembered lying on the carpeted floor of my college dorm room with my friend, a soft-spoken man from Thailand who'd been disowned by his family for being gay; we'd gone into the clinic together to get tested for HIV. The night before we were to receive the results, we'd lain there, side by side, wide awake, staring mutely at the ceiling. I'd been seized by a delirious terror, convinced that I'd contracted HIV from Omar. I'd gotten away without getting pregnant. There's no way, I'd thought then, that I could have escaped from him physically unscathed. I was searching for a tangible consequence of our affair. I needed my body, which felt so dirty to me then, so despicable, to be my witness. I was tired of standing at the edge of an abyss, of the hollow well that had opened at the center of my life because I knew, even then, that emptiness cannot be combated; you have to learn to live with its sting, to bare the raw surfaces of your buried wounds. But I didn't have the strength. I'd wanted visible evidence. *See*, I'd say, stupidly, thoughtlessly waving my test results, *Omar and I are linked in the negative. Here*, I would say, *is con-*

*firmation that he had entered my body and changed it forever, left it in disrepair.* What a fool I had been.

But then again, I considered now, just as I had considered then, on the few occasions when I'd dared talk about Omar even I couldn't believe my own story. It seemed untrue, made up. The words seemed false. Suddenly, upon hearing them, I would feel cut off from myself, oddly detached, a single thought repeating endlessly in my head: that I had been both repulsed and compliant, a participant in Omar's ruthless behavior; that I'd helped that exceptionally handsome man take advantage of the fact that I was only partially conscious of my sexual power, to contaminate me with his actions, his motives, his aberrant desire, so I would be the one to spend the rest of my waking life considering these pitiable flashbacks and wondering if it was then, during that strange lonesome summer when I'd had no one to consult, when I'd pushed even my own mother away, if it was then that my life had been cleaved in two, each horn forking and reforking until my future resembled nothing more than a maze.

I ran my hands through my hair. I lifted a few strands and let them drop back down onto the pillow. My hair had been a source of drama in my life, covered in Tehran with a scarf, always pulled back and tucked away. I had come to consider it a sexual organ of sorts. Why else would one need to hide it from men? I thought of Omar grabbing my hair from behind, twisting it around his fist to draw my head back. I remembered shaving my hair off in college. I had wanted to begin again, to erase the convoluted labyrinth that had taken over my life. I had wanted a smooth, round surface ready to have new lines drawn across it. I'd driven to Supercuts and asked the hairdresser to shave my head. She'd refused. She was Iranian.

"What will your mother say?" she'd asked, bewildered.

"Should I ask someone else?" I said tersely.

She'd finally agreed, reluctantly. I watched her face in the mirror. As my hair dropped in thick strands to the floor, her eyes grew darker, the lines around her mouth deeper. Her brow was furrowed from the distress she imagined my bald head would cause my mother. And it had. She'd buried her face in her hands and sobbed at the sight of my shaved head.

"Why? Why? Why?" she'd asked, as she gasped for air, even though she had known why before I had ever mentioned a word about it. She had intuited what Omar had done to me while it was happening, and her premonition had been confirmed by my remoteness, my despondence, the embittered silence with which I had greeted her upon my return that summer.

But her question had hung unanswered between us. I didn't know why I'd shaved my hair. Or I did, but I had lost my grip on language, was unable to articulate my needs, to build a coherent story to justify my impulses. It was only now that understanding was sliding into place.

I put out my cigarette. Beyond the window, the black canvas of the night sky had faded into a dull pinkish gray. There were a few birds chirping in the trees, announcing the imminent arrival of daylight. I could hear the shopkeepers opening their stores, lifting the metal shutters, stacking their piles of leeks and onions and apples, the red globular pomegranates, the bright bushels of herbs arranged in plastic bins on the sidewalks. I thought about how lonely I'd been in college. I'd refused to have sex while I was at university. I couldn't have verbalized this then, but I'd become fearful of the frontiers sex offered me, of the yawning emptiness it opened inside of me. Perhaps, I thought, the sex I'd had with Omar had burned up my full reserve of teenage desire. Perhaps I was punishing myself for having misused my sexual energy. I'd watched my friends brag about sex while I shaved my hair and took shower after shower. During my sophomore year, I'd showered constantly. Sometimes three or four times a day. I'd sit in the tub and let the water run over me until it turned cold, then I'd get out shivering, my toenails and lips blue. I felt perpetually dirty. I was often constipated. Once, I remembered, I had to stick my finger up my ass and pull the shit out myself. It was so painful, I almost fainted. It hadn't occurred to me to go to the pharmacy to buy laxatives or make an appointment with a doctor. I hadn't wanted to deal with anybody. I'd recoiled at the thought of being touched by a stranger. I suffered quietly.

I got up. I felt restless, likely from the nicotine surging through my veins I thought as I got dressed. I grabbed my cigarettes and wallet, and headed out. I closed the door lightly so as not to wake up Ellie. Neither of us were ever sharp in the mornings, never eager for conversation. We had that in common. We tended to let each other be until noon.

It was seven in the morning now. I stood near the neighbor's door. I no longer knew who lived there. Likely an older woman with whiskers, a lady in the habit of wearing oil-stained aprons, a woman who fries food—potatoes and breaded cod—for her grandchildren all day.

I felt as though I'd been stopped in my tracks. I was being assaulted with memories that seemed to be surging forth of their own volition. When I was living in Brooklyn, I thought, deep into my relationship with the chef, I mostly stopped eating. We were both lean, not an ounce of fat on our bodies. But whenever he developed a new plate—chocolate foie gras, venison with plum sorbet and eucalyptus air, lobster decorated with lemon verbena bubbles—he would have me come into the restaurant to try it. He worked at a three-Michelin-star restaurant in Manhattan, and it was easy enough for me to get there from Brooklyn. There were always famous people loitering at the bar, drunk actors who came in followed by a herd of young women in short sequined dresses, their hair ironed and shining like a leopard's skin, high heels like weapons, mouths painted bright, fake lashes they expertly batted. They were so loud, they often ruined everyone's meal, but they brought in the cash, stashes of money spent on the finest food and wine. No one dared say a word to them. That's how we lionize the wealthy, I thought.

I would eat like a queen on those nights then wait for my boyfriend to finish his shift at three or four in the morning, at which point we would ride the subway all the way down the spine of the island and back across the bridge. The only words we'd exchange would be about the showmanship of his food or the moon hanging over the river, sometimes as round and bright as a peach; the sky in New York always seemed to keep one eye open. We would walk quietly to our rat-infested apartment. Sometimes, just to take the temperature of our relationship, I would try to seduce him, and he would go stiff, likely from exhaustion but also because he'd probably had sex in the dry pantry—like I said, his mouth often smelled like another woman's vagina. I didn't care much. I was too busy writing, trying to make my own way; in that regard, we were a good match. When it came to art, we held ourselves to the highest standard and weren't afraid of a life of discipline and resolve. We pushed each other to succeed, which is, I suppose, its own kind of high.

I remembered that the chef had gone through a phase of dreadful nightmares; a faceless man would rape him and he would wake up whimpering, defenseless. He'd lean into me and sob. But then suddenly, with a terrifying resolve, he would get up and go to work and come home with a distant, self-protective air that, if I tried to puncture it, would only lead to a confoundingly cruel exchange. The sexual transgressions he had likely suffered would remain beyond my reach. I could neither soothe him nor relate to him to ease my own suffering. I could only listen during the rare moments he allowed himself vulnerability. One time, he told me, he'd dreamt that he had two penises and that he was fucking me with both his dicks and that it felt amazing, that he could have stayed in that dream forever. I joked that I was sure he would eventually run out of steam. I didn't know what to say. It had been months since he'd approached me with the singular penis of his waking hours; I couldn't understand the chasm between the reality of our sexless relationship and his erotic flights of the night. I suppose any psychologist would say that I'd stayed with him to avoid having sex, a simple enough conjecture I couldn't entirely refute even if at times I felt so tortured by the lack of desire in our relationship that I considered cheating on him. But I'd had my fill of lies. I didn't want to live a double life. It's incredible, the capacity we have for living with someone for years, for rearing children with them, without ever letting them in or extending ourselves to know them, without ever truly understanding the source of their grief. I suppose the tangled web of our future is imprinted upon us long before we learn to speak; it's no easy task to trace our behavior, all of our impulses, to the network of disturbances in which we were raised. I suppose that's not even the answer, or is only partially the answer, to our inner turbulence.

A loud noise—a broken plate or a fallen glass—startled me out of my reverie and I realized that I'd been standing there, stupidly staring at the neighbor's door for quite a while. I decided it was time to get some coffee and head down to the beach. Once I was on the street, I turned left onto the main road that descended sharply toward the water. Light had broken, but the sky was overcast. A mild fog hung at the lit windows of the shops. The hills in the distance looked blue in the opaque light; the palms appeared to be made of steel; the air, still and dense, was firmly set against their fronds so they appeared to have been covered with silver varnish. I could hear the fierce howling of dogs in the distance. There were seagulls perched on the serrated edges of the old city's fortified walls. The gunmetal sky seemed to exhaust everything, to mute the colors of the roads, the native plants, to drain the blood from the faces of the few people who were out on the streets.

I stopped to have a coffee and a *pan con tomate* at the first bar that had sidewalk tables where I could smoke in peace. I was one of the only customers at that hour except for a few elderly men sitting morosely at the bar inside, busily reading their newspapers and dunking their croissants into their *café con leches* in semiautomatic movements. The intense smell of coffee wafted outdoors, and even from the sidewalk, I could hear the braying sound of the espresso machine. I sat in a red plastic chair with the Estrella Damm beer logo plastered onto it—those chairs were a hallmark of my adolescence—and faced the mountains. They looked beautiful in the subtle light of the morning. Their backs, carpeted in greenery, lent them an air of solitary grandeur. I could see the sky opening up in the distance, a ribbed sky that suggested the wind was picking up over the craggy rocks and would soon shear the fog that had settled overnight.

Finally, a heavyset woman walked over to my table to take my order. She stared rigidly ahead and was gesturing at a pair of chattering women who were walking their dogs across the street. Without turning to face me, she asked, "*¿Qué te pongo, guapa?*"

I had forgotten that in Spain, women often called each other *guapa*, a habit I treated with disdain because it suggested that our existence began and ended with our bodies, that we were undifferentiated, pretty face after pretty face, our personalities flattened.

Once I'd finished my coffee and toast, I headed to the beach. I crossed the main avenue and made my way down to the wide seaside promenade. A few steps led down to the beach, which was stark and empty at this hour, bereft of humans. Massive clouds were coasting above the sea. Little had changed since I'd last been there in the '90s. There were putrid remnants of fruits and vegetables abandoned by the previous day's beachgoers in the sand—tomatoes, orange rinds, sliced watermelon, pears left to rot. I observed the coconut-hair umbrellas staked into the blond sand, the sun beds with their white cushions lined up to receive the lazy bodies of tanners, tourists from Britain and the Nordic countries desperate for sun. They would spend their days lying on the beach, ordering expensive drinks poured into carved pineapples. Beyond the beach, along the promenade, beneath the shade of the awnings, shopkeepers were hanging bikinis and summer dresses out on racks next to stacks of sun hats and tanning lotions and bright extra-large beach towels.

The sounds of the city were still so faint that I could hear the birds cawing overhead. The sea, which I'd heard roaring from the apartment, as if water were on the verge of coming up through the floorboards, was silent now, still. I felt my chest tighten; my stomach began to ache. I heard the frenetic sound of a motorcycle in the distance and remembered the feeling of the hot leather seat pressing against my jeans as I clung to Omar on the Ducati while we whizzed through traffic. I was astonished that I hadn't died. That we hadn't wiped out or flown off a cliff. There were times when he'd gone up to two hundred kilometers an hour. The sheer force of the wind had opened my backpack once and my CDs had gone flying out; they'd scattered across the highway and gotten shredded to bits. The only thing left in my backpack was my passport, and that had survived only because I'd been cautious enough to tuck it into an inside pocket. I couldn't understand how we'd never been pulled over, nor would I ever know why Omar lived so recklessly. What, I wondered, my stomach twisting itself into a knot, had his father been like? He'd disappeared during the war, but I couldn't trace the effects of his absence on Omar. Had Omar's father treated him like a feral animal before he'd died, prematurely weaned and left to survive on his own, as mine had? Had his mother become undone, left to raise her children alone during the bloodshed of the civil war? I had, at times, intimated the searing ache that moved like a great flood through him, but I had never asked him any questions about it. When the subject of family came up, his neck and shoulders would tense, his jaw would lock, and his gaze would turn simultaneously sad and vindictive. His whole body seemed to become armed in those moments, to turn into a weapon; and I, in order to avoid provoking him, instinctively kept quiet. While he discovered my body, revealed its limitless capabilities to me, shaped my desire and my peculiar perversions and longings, I had neither knowledge of nor influence over the dark passages of his life.

I thought again of my brother, of his vulnerability. I went over the incident in my head. He'd been viciously charged at from behind while walking home from school, first with vulgar racist remarks then with punches that pounded his skull against the sidewalk. His attacker had crawled on top of him even after he'd passed out and continued smashing his brain against the concrete. I thought about how my brother had left us as soon as he'd physically recovered. How now, years later, he'd taken to disappearing, vanishing for weeks or months at a time. His absence cleaved my mother in two. She barely spoke while he was gone. Throughout my high school years, when I still lived with her, she wept in bed for hours every morning. When she finally did get up, I'd make her bed. I'd dry out her pillowcase, which was always wet with tears. I tried to fill the dent her head had left in the pillow. We spent our days waiting for my brother in a silent state of dread, unsure if he was dead or alive.

It hadn't taken long before my mother had fallen into a deep depression, a monolith of confusion and grief punctuated by moments of intense panic. She'd become so fearful of losing me, the only proof left in the world that she was a mother, that she'd ripped children from her womb and nursed them with her own milk, that she never let me out of her sight, not even to cross the street to CVS to buy nail polish with my friends. She would drop me off at school and pick me up promptly after swim practice. It was a life of tyranny, a dry life, empty of love or laughter, a life in which pleasure had turned into a distant memory.

When my brother eventually reappeared months later, he

was a different person. He had wild eyes and a suspicious gaze; he hallucinated, had turned violent. It took my mother nearly a decade to rehabilitate him. By then, I had faded into the margins. I was strong-willed, stubborn, impatient, quick on my feet. My mother believed that she could afford to look away from me while she focused on my brother's pain, pain that had taken just a few moments of a skinhead's life to cause but that we would spend the rest of our lives contending with. My brother (and I by extension) had horrified that skinhead. Our presence in school and around town terrorized him because, even though we had white skin just like he did, we also had Persian accents and wore clothes made in Turkey or Iran: flowered vests, neatly pressed shirts, shoes with beads or bells on them. We were not "quite white," or we were too white, or not white in the right ways.

Until he had laid his hands on my brother, I considered, his was a nuanced, concealed racism. Difficult to prove until the moment he'd raised his fist but nonetheless palpable to those of us on the receiving end of its toxic waste. I know now how to recognize this grade of racism. I can feel the air pressure change. It's a racism that persists, that leans into the stereotype that Iranians, whose history is intertwined with Russia, Turkey, Mongolia, Greece, the Arabian Peninsula, and elsewhere, are either too dark or not dark enough; our brand of whiteness, if we can even call it that, has nothing in common with the entitled whiteness of America. What this kind of racism claims, I considered, is an exclusive and proprietary right to whiteness; it considers whiteness as a privileged status that belongs to Europeans exclusively, and to their American descendants, who have flung themselves so far from the annals of history that they've deliberately repressed the truth of their own immigration, their own otherness. Whiteness, the skinhead taught my brother and me just weeks after we'd landed on US soil, is a performance the standards of which we failed to meet. *We*, with our near-white skin and our un-American manners, gestures, clothes, and gait, were tainting *his* whiteness, reducing its stock value, lowering the profitability of his biggest asset.

I took off my clothes and got in the ocean. I'd made sure to wear my swimsuit in case the water called me to it. It was cold, colder than I'd expected; for a moment, I couldn't breathe. I felt as though my lungs were being squeezed. I swam to warm up. I was still a strong swimmer, capable of doing a thousand yards without stopping to take a break. I was always most at home in the water.

When I finally stopped, I turned around, treaded water, and stared back at the empty shore. The air turned heavy. I heard a rumble in the distance. A heavy mass of compressed air was rolling down the cordillera, a gloomy avalanche that expanded as it approached. I was cold. My lungs stung. I could barely feel my fingers; they were as stiff as twigs. A darkness descended upon me; I watched the metallic light of the sky disappear from the sea. All I could see was night. I was alone in a world apart.

My life, I thought in a surge of panic, runs parallel to the lives of others. I felt a rising sense of trepidation, the sense that I was about to be carried out to sea never to be seen or heard from again. My heart ached with loneliness.

But I wasn't alone. I was bathing under Omar's gaze. I could feel him hovering over me. I felt something move over my skin, crawl up my limbs. I started to gasp for air. I thought to myself, Calm down, search the water. But the darkness was complete, impenetrable. I dipped my head under, reemerged, wiped my face and eyes. I took in a deep breath. My heart was beating furiously. I heard Omar's voice; I heard my name. "Arezu, Arezu." He was searching for me, calling my name as if it were a question, an existential plea he was making to the universe only to be greeted with silence. So he, too, was lost. I steadied my nerves. I thought, He has come to me because I have searched for him, for who we had been, for all of the ways we'd bent each other's will. He'd bent mine to a much larger extent than I had his, and yet we'd each of us been susceptible to the other, willing to transgress any sense of propriety that our families and society had instilled in us in order to be near each other.

I closed my eyes and felt something swim over me. It was his hand, and it was crawling up my back to my neck, turning me over. He pulled me toward him. My hair tangled like soft rope in his fingers. His breath was hot against my face. That boyish smile of his sent a shiver down my spine. I looked up. It was a different sky altogether: a pure electric-blue sky with just a few wispy clouds careening down to the sea. We were high up in the lakes again; the water that was dripping off his chin into my mouth was sweet. The air was sublime. The world, I felt, was aflame with pleasure and the danger of deceit.

Who knows what would have become of me if I hadn't met Omar? We'd laughed together and played in the mountains like they belonged to us and us alone. I was willing to give him my sex in exchange for that. Or so I'd thought then. I'd thought that Omar had shocked me back to life. Until I met him, I'd been standing on the great hungry lips of death, prepared to sacrifice myself to its insatiable appetite. Omar, while bringing into center stage the knowledge of my mortality, had also jolted me back into existence, into being. It was a delicate trade: a return to life as a teenager that would drain me of vital energy in the future. He had deposited such a surplus of fear in me that I would need the rest of my life to parse through it. The fear hadn't been palpable to me then. Or perhaps it had been so all consuming, so much larger than I was, that I couldn't see or recognize or name it. What I did know was that he'd made me laugh my way back to the world of the living that summer. And for that I was eternally grateful to him.

I got out of the water and pulled my jeans on and peeled my swimsuit top off. I didn't care. Most of the women tanning on the beach were already topless. I let my breasts dry off in the wind and then put my shirt back on and began to make my way back to the apartment. Ellie would be up by now, and I wanted to bring her down to the beach with me. I felt exhausted, drained.

It was my turn to rent a sun bed, to luxuriate, to order bottle after bottle of rosé, to eat shrimp out of an impossibly tall martini glass, to pluck olives out of a dish with a toothpick. I wanted to get drunk. I wanted to spend the day fantasizing about having unprotected sex with a stranger. For a brief moment, I forgot that I was married, that I had left Xavi with a lump in his throat that was only somewhat assuaged by the fact that I had agreed not to go to Marbella alone, to allow Ellie to come with me, because according to him, and to her, too, returning would be more difficult than I could ever predict. I couldn't say that they'd turned out to be wrong. I could never have guessed that Omar's ghost would be here waiting to greet me, that I'd be retracing my footsteps under his gaze.

Halfway to the apartment, I decided to cut through the blind alleys of the old city, to climb up through its shaded streets and stout houses, their windows gazing at one another coyly, to the Plaza de los Naranjos. I remembered an old woman who ran a shop in the far corner of that plaza; we'd chatted once or twice. I wondered if she was still alive. She was thin and had a wrinkled face, a humped back, but nevertheless she was elegant, attractive, a woman with a poised demeanor, pearls in her ears, and hair meticulously combed into a chignon pinned together with silk flowers.

I walked resignedly through the streets now, jostled by crowds of chattering tourists, by young men in leather jackets, their motorcycle helmets hanging off their forearms, the odor of alcohol wafting from their armpits as they staggered home from the clubs. As I looked at them, I felt an intense, searing heat crawl up my throat. It was Omar's name rising to my lips. My eyes grew moist. I felt as though steam were rising from the center of my being, forcing its way up and out of my eyes, ears, nose. It was time. The hour of sobbing had arrived. I didn't want to submit to my tears. I didn't want to succumb. I feared I would collapse, turn to liquid, be unable to put myself back together. So I swallowed his name. I willed it to drown. And for a moment —a brief minute—I experienced relief. Perhaps, I considered, I could hardly bear the thought that Omar was still there, in that recondite twist of alleys, hiking through the brush and bramble of the mountains, drying herbs on his terrace, because I feared that, if given the chance, he would work his way through my body again. I shook away the thought. I pushed his name down.

I entered the shop and asked for the woman. Rosario. Her name had come back to me the second I crossed the threshold. I said it over and over to myself—*Rosario*—a prayer bead, an incantation, shoving Omar's name further down with each repetition. Rosario. The man who was minding the shop looked at me with expert eyes, then looked down at his desk, which was crowded with objects—saltshakers shaped like tuna fruit, tiny olive and almond and salt platters with flowers painted on their glazed yellow surfaces. Slowly, without raising his gaze from his desk, he told me that Rosario was his mother, that she'd passed away nearly ten years prior, that the shop was his now. There was a grandfather clock standing against the wall behind him. The clock was wheezing like a pair of lungs. I stared at its swinging pendulum. It seemed to be whispering something to me. I felt a hot breath on my neck. Omar. There it was: his name trembling on my lips, more powerful than I was.

"I want you naked," I heard, "as the day you were born."

"Excuse me?" I asked Rosario's son. He had a concerned look on his face.

"I was just asking," he said, "if you were looking to buy something."

"Yes," I said. "Yes." Nervously moving about the store, I picked out a candleholder, a beautiful centerpiece delicately carved and painted a regal blue. I told him that I was looking to light some candles, paid him, and quietly left.

Outside, I sat on a bench. The ache in my stomach had worsened; the pain had become unbearable. I felt as though someone had turned up the pressure in my gut. I felt ready to burst. I needed to take a moment to breathe before walking the rest of the way to the apartment. There were two men standing a few meters behind me. I directed my attention to them in order to distract myself from the tears working their way out of my body, tears I was afraid would be toxic. I swallowed hard. I shoved everything that was rising up in me as far down as I could. Listen to their conversation, I told myself, and my old habit of obedience kicked in; I resigned myself to listening. They were talking about women, marriage. I heard one of them say that he preferred his women to be ugly because the ugly ones made more competent housewives. They're better cooks and don't complain when it's time to mop the floors and deweb the ceiling. Besides, he added, he could always go down to the beach and stare at the foreign women, their bodies overflowing with sexual offerings, their habits and tastes indiscriminate. "Obscene women," he said. "Women who spread their legs for anybody."

The other man laughed and clapped encouragingly.

"What happened to women cutting their hair short when they got married and letting their waists thicken and being happy in their house slippers and aprons?" the first man asked. "They used to go down to the butcher looking like that, and now they all want to be appreciated; they want us to cup their breasts as if they were pears carved from gold by the hands of Jesus," he exclaimed happily. "Forget it. Give me an ugly wife or nothing."

His friend went on clapping, applauding what he kept referring to as a timely sermon.

It dawned on me then why all the women called one another *guapa* here. It was a code of solidarity, a rallying against the abusive language catapulted at them by certain men. It was a collective affirmation of their dignity.

I'd closed my eyes. When I opened them, I saw that Rosario's son was standing before me. He was holding out his arm. He said, "You forgot your change." He opened his palm to show me a five-euro bill.

I took the bill and thanked him.

He walked away, dragging his feet, head hanging, his eyes on the ground. A man who was afraid, who had likely always been afraid, of making eye contact with women. There are all kinds of men in this world, I thought. All kinds.

As soon as he was out of sight, I began shaking. I tried to push the surge of tears back down. I swallowed. I begged. I negotiated with the heavens. But nothing worked, and soon I had given in to a long bereft fit of weeping. It hurt. My throat and the backs of my lids hurt. I cried until my head throbbed. My lungs were exhausted and sore, my lips raw, but I couldn't stop. It was as if a great flood were moving through me. A terrible earthquake. A shifting of the fault lines in the oceanic depths of my life. I thought of Ellie, reminded myself that I wasn't alone. I just had to get myself to the apartment. I just had to make my way to Ellie. I got up and walked downhill through the old quarter. I could hardly see straight. My vision was blurred with tears that were collecting faster than I could unload them. I walked down a narrow street flanked by the puckered walls of the Arab ruins; great tufts of lavender and capers were growing out of the cracks and seams. I stopped halfway down the road and clung to one of those bushes. I nearly yanked it out of that great ancient wall, those stones that were as rough as sandpaper. The street was deserted. There was no one in sight. I heard my mother's voice. I heard her utter that saying she had so often repeated: "God is our only witness." I didn't even know if I believed there was a God hovering in the heavens, crowning our heads.

I couldn't wait to get home to Ellie. I thought of the healing power of friendship as I made my way down that empty street, a street as old as time. Friendship, I thought, is a form of witness. She had received my testimony. She had held it with tenderness and love. She had taken care with my story. If it hadn't been for her, I would have never been able to receive Xavi. I could feel myself—my whole body—rushing toward Ellie. I thought of her contagious laughter, how we'd doubled over laughing in the middle of an empty maze of streets behind the Damascus Gate in Jerusalem, the air thick with the smell of incense and the sound of murmured prayers because I, who did not even know if I believed in God, had been turned away from the Al-Aqsa Mosque that morning by two Israeli soldiers in green fatigues and combat boots, bullet belts strapped to their chests. They were holding machine guns. "You are not Muslim," they'd said in unison, as if channeling God herself. I was wearing a full hijab. I'd wanted to go into the mosque, to pray, to press my forehead against its well-worn floors as a way to be near my mother and her parents, to salute their deep religiosity despite my own confused ambivalence. I had been raised, after all, to greet God every morning, to thank God every evening. "Recite the Ash-Shura," the soldiers commanded, stroking their guns. And I had. I stood there with a fire in my eyes, holding back my pain, hardening my face so it wouldn't show my sorrow or anger. I recited the verses. I recited them for myself. I recited them for the soldiers, for the collective humiliation that we had been forced to perform. For the Palestinians whose relationship to the divine was eclipsed by the Occupation, a form of psychological and spiritual torture, not to be allowed to access the sacred sites of one's culture. And as I recited the Ash-Shura, in that moment, against all odds, I had suddenly believed there was a God. I had felt heard, accompanied by an invisible fleet of bodies that had gathered at my back to support me. I was sure my ancestors were standing behind me, placing each verse of the Quran in my mouth to be uttered. Halfway through the prayer, the soldiers grew impatient and let me in. And my privilege in comparison to the Palestinians to whom this land and its sites belonged was not lost on me. What business did I have entering the mosque while they, who were devoted to the mosque, were cut off from its holy walls? I almost turned away, but the soldiers waved me through the arched passageway with their guns and a nod of their heads, and I walked, aware that I was a target, that all my life there had been a gun pointed at my back. I walked through the courtyard of olive trees, beneath a blue sun so bright that it appeared to have been lit from below, past men and women dressed in simple robes, toward the golden dome of the mosque, and left my shoes at the door. I'd needed to cry but hadn't been able to.

I met Ellie at the Damascus Gate after that. I told her what happened, and we'd begun to laugh. *You are not a Muslim*, we kept repeating to each other, laughing our hearts out at the preposterous request that I justify my humanity. It was an absurd utterance, a statement that ushered hatred into the world —a statement designed to remind me that I was under surveillance, that I, a potential purveyor of future violence, needed to be monitored, controlled. How, Ellie and I had wondered, laughing out our pained hearts, were we expected to carve out lives for ourselves amid all of that suspicion and hatred? How were we meant to believe in God? And what would that belief absolve us of? We had treated our friendship as sacred, as a kind of religion. Was that not, then, a manifestation of devotion? Was love and laughter not devotional? "Laugh," my mother had often said to me as a young child. "Laugh as a way of being close to the grace of God." That was long before this story had unfolded. As I emerged from the street and looked up at our building, I remembered how Ellie and I had stood in the shade of those ancient walls and given ourselves over to laughter. We'd barely been able to contain ourselves. Tears had streamed down our faces; we'd been on the verge of having to urinate, folded over, giggling in heaves between breaths, everything rushing out of us in one mad delirious stream. Had we been crying then? Crying together through our laughter, articulating side by side our profound sense of loss and loneliness? Had we been asking the universe not to turn its back on us? Had we been asking God to kneel down as our witness?

## 7

BY THE TIME I GOT to the building entrance, the fog had lifted. I'd wiped my face, calmed myself down. I looked up at the sky. A few clouds hung above the sun's round bright face; their bellies glowed with a refracted copper light. It was going to be a sweltering day. The air was humid, heavy. It clung to my skin. I felt clammy, weighed down from the brackish waters that had dried into a white flake on my skin and from walking through air that felt like a bowl of tepid water, from sobbing like an inconsolable child. I couldn't wait to change my clothes, to dry off. I needed to restart the day.

When I walked in, Ellie was sitting on a towel on the floor. She was leaning against the couch, her legs stretched out under the coffee table. She was eating dates, and there was a pile of pits growing next to her coffee mug. There were pillow marks on her cheek, and her hair was wispy, the curls loose. I could tell she'd slept in. She was wearing a wrinkled black romper and one sock that had the face of a cat on it. She was licking her fingers free of the sticky meat of the dates, staring blissfully at the blue sky beyond the window, at the palms leaning against the sun-washed walls hemming in the old city. In that light, the walls were the color of wheat.

I stared at Ellie as she absentmindedly cleaned her hands. I remembered that she used to have a lip piercing, that she'd had a habit of rotating it with her tongue, tugging at it with her fingers. Her bottom lip was often moist with spittle. I'd once told her that it wasn't the most flattering of habits, that she should be careful not to do it while she was conducting a reading or teaching a class. It was a nervous tic, if slightly erotic at the same time.

She'd just looked at me with a wide smile and, in the most earnest voice, asked: "It really bothers you?"

"It really does," I'd said, and she laughed like it was the funniest thing in the world, as if I was the one with the quirk. I never brought it up again.

That was years ago, I thought. Back then, in Amherst, Ellie lived with Sam and their respective partners, partners who tended to come and go, who, despite being queer, couldn't always grasp Sam and Ellie's arrangement, a kind of unromantic marriage that required financial, psychological, and emotional commitment from each of them but none of the joys of physical intimacy; it was an arrangement into which Sahar and I also had entered, and for a while, it had felt as if the four of us were all married to one another. The arrangement required that we either live together or next door to one another, a setup that fell so far outside of normal social structures that it required a complete suspension of the rules we'd been raised with, rules informed by the religions of our families of origin, that dictated a nuclear life of heteronormativity and children rather than a life of devoted companionship with friends, exes, and pets. Among us, I realized, we formed a holy triune: Ellie had been raised in an Orthodox Jewish family in Jerusalem and New York City; I in a progressive but culturally Muslim family in Iran, Spain, America; Sahar in a conservative one in Bil'in and Chicago; and Sam, who would later transition, in a Catholic family from the deep South, a family from which he had emancipated himself by moving north to New York City, where he'd met Ellie. We were able, because of the lines that ran through our lives — the homes we'd abandoned, the oppressive surveillance we'd fled — to build a home together, to become reoriented alongside one another. We'd all risked departure from what we had known; we were all curious to learn what would become available to us if we pursued our alleged deviances, perversions, side steps. And it had felt incredible to find one another. We filled one another's lives with a sense of elation and surrender.

I'd been standing there for a good three minutes and Ellie still hadn't turned to greet me. She was so lost in her thoughts that she hadn't noticed me walk in.

"Where's your other sock?" I asked.

"Oh," she said smiling softly. "I didn't hear you." She gathered her thoughts quietly for a moment then, removing the one sock she had on and pinching it between her fingers for me to see, said, "I couldn't find the other one. Have you seen it?"

It was a custom-ordered sock, and the cat's face, I now realized, was her cat Olive's face. It was a gift, she told me, from her girlfriend, a woman who lived in London, whom I had yet to meet.

I told her I hadn't seen it, but given her habit of pouring the contents of her suitcase out and spreading her scent all over the apartment, it seemed likely that it had rolled under the bed or was tied up in the sleeve of one of her shirts or in the hem of her pants. I loved nothing more than to tease her. It was an exercise that restored me.

She turned to face the window again and set to work on another date. She was, it seemed, operating in slow motion. I remembered how I'd thought she was as high as a kite when I first met her. But I knew her too well by now, knew that when she transitioned into this kind of stop-motion gear it was evidence of unacknowledged stress. I wondered if she'd also had ugly dreams. If the walls of the apartment had assaulted her with their vengeful nature while she was asleep, her defenses down, unable to protect herself. I considered the geography of her mood: it was terraced, a stratified frame of mind that made her remote, inaccessible. At first glance it seemed like she'd entered a state of deep pleasure, detached and impermeable, when in fact she was feeling overwhelmed; there was a front of artificial calm that only revealed its false appearance to those who cared to stay the course. I recognized the signs. She would turn her head slowly, look fixedly at objects, or whomever was standing before her, as if she were searching their eyes for some secret knowledge; and she would take her time responding in conversation, with a delay that only she could manage to make seem fashionable. Despite not always making a great first impression, Ellie had at her disposal such a deep well of charm that she could quickly clear the air of any tension. People fell for her in ways they hadn't expected, hadn't initially deemed possible, and that early error of judgment functioned to her advantage. The fact that her interlocutors were unable to see the extent to which she would casually seduce them into loving her only served to increase her hold over them.

What exactly she was feeling overwhelmed by now, I did not know, but I knew enough to know that this was not the moment to ask and that more than likely her stress had to do with the fact that she'd left Oxford while the semester was still ongoing, when the reasonable thing to do would have been to stay behind marking papers twelve hours a day. But she was stern in her conviction that it was her responsibility as my dearest friend to come to Marbella with me and so had convinced herself that the beach was a perfectly reasonable place for grading forty-five twenty-page student papers.

I told her not to worry, that I was sure her sock would reappear.

She stared at me for a while, then said, "This apartment is far more unassuming than I'd anticipated. I thought it would be slightly more luxurious. It's so small, so basic, but somehow still so imposing."

I told her that I'd felt the same way about her parents' apartment in Jerusalem.

"But the light!" she said.

There was a terrific Mediterranean light, a thickly honeyed auburn light that flooded the rooms of their Jerusalem apartment, a light so bold and decided that it was capable of submerging all darkness. That light, I remembered, announced itself at the windows by noon and fell in geometric patterns on the floors, patterns that shrank ever so imperceptibly over the course of the afternoon; by evening, they'd left me with the impression that the apartment was a spaceship on the cusp of levitation.

Ellie lifted the mug to her mouth and gulped down what was left of her coffee. I went into the kitchen and poured myself a cup. She'd washed a few mugs and spoons, and set out the milk and sugar. When I returned to the living room, I was in the mood to tease her, to have a laugh, to distance myself from that terrible fit of crying. What had she thought? I wondered, giggling to myself. That my wayward father had bought his wife a hilltop castle with floor-to-ceiling windows and marble floors? Decorated the front entrance with Orientalist fountains and figures? I told her not to worry. I told her that there was a very fancy yacht with palatial furniture and silver cutlery moored in Puerto Banús, courtesy of my father—a double-decker named *La Perla* with panoramic views of Gibraltar that we could move into as soon as she washed her face.

"Porto what?" she asked, giggling.

"Puerto Banús," I repeated.

I explained to her that it was where the rich and famous go to eye one another, to buy Louis Vuitton and Prada in shops with floor-to-ceiling windows, that their million-dollar yachts are visible through the glass; that way, not only could shoppers touch the clothes, examine their delicately worked fabrics, they could also imagine what they'd look like wearing them in the lap of luxury, draped across the white leather cushions of a yacht, staring out at the trail of brackish foam produced by the engine as it cut across the blue half-moon of the sea. I told her it was a sinister place, a place of extremes, a strip of earth crawling with society's wealthiest and its most dejected. The Vegas of the Mediterranean, which is to say that it was a little more exclusive and a little less visibly vulgar. It was where I'd first gone dancing with Omar. I told her that the first time he'd come to the apartment with the money my father had sent he'd invited me to go to a virgin beach with him. We both laughed. It was only now, with the force of hindsight, that I could see the irony in the fact that Omar had taken me to a virgin beach, a pure stretch of unharmed sand and straw and dunes and grassy knolls that led to turquoise waters hardly anyone knows about.

I'd agreed to go, I told her, reluctantly at first, but the longer I'd looked at his figure leaning against the fridge in the mercurial light of the kitchen, the more something inside of me shifted. I'd felt an inevitable gravitational pull between us, a pull that had led me to say yes. And as soon as I'd said that word—*yes*—the air pressure in the room had changed. I felt an ache between my legs I'd never felt before, and for a moment, as I stood there staring at him, taking in his muscular, powerful figure; his sweet smile; his gray-green eyes and long lashes that gave him the most distinctive feminine softness, a gentleness and beauty that balanced his rugged masculinity to perfection; I felt my loins grow moist and hot. I suddenly worried that my period had arrived, that blood was running down my thighs.

No one, I told Ellie, had had that effect on me before. I told her that I'd been terrified, not just because I thought I was bleeding and was too embarrassed to bend down and look between my legs for proof, but also because, just by being near him, I'd felt as if I'd stepped out on a ledge, that his influence over me was so grand and so unfamiliar, I'd lost my words.

"So what happened?" she asked.

"He took the lead," I said. "He told me to be ready at two the next day, that he'd be waiting for me on the street with his motorcycle."

She wanted to know where he'd taken me, but I couldn't remember the name of the beach or the roads he'd taken to get there. All I could remember was getting off his bike in the heat and standing on a stark, empty, sandy sliver of land that was punctuated by rocky cliffs at either end. I could see through the rows of the gold-dusted dunes a strip of the greenest, most reflective water, an emerald runway lit up by a brilliant Mediterranean sun.

I told her that I'd struggled to pull my helmet off and that he'd leaned forward to unclasp it. He'd pulled the helmet off for me with such a coquettish smile you'd think he was pulling off my bra. He'd smelled like musk, I told her; his scent returned to take its place among my memories. I told her that we'd walked bare-foot through the dunes toward the sea. We were virtually run-ning because the sand was so hot, it was burning our feet. As soon as we'd put our stuff down, using the helmets as weights to keep the towel pinned to the beach, he'd grabbed my hand, pulled me along to the cliffs, and begun climbing them. He en-couraged me to follow him because, he kept saying, I wouldn't believe the view that awaited me at the top or the feeling of free-dom that I was about to experience. "We're going to leap off of these rocks into the sea," he'd said.

I could still remember how, in his company, I had fearlessly laid claim to the land, its streets and dunes and cliffs and blue sea. I felt as though I belonged to the world, that I was made of it, that my flesh and blood and bones were composed of earthly matter. Omar behaved as though nature belonged to him, and he took such vain pleasure in it that the sentiment became con-tagious. I didn't feel remote from the earth then. I wasn't saddled with the sense that the world was synthetic, that it was a stage on which my role had been cast long before I'd arrived at my body. Everything was possibility, plausible. He'd made me hungry for life again. And yet, I told Ellie, beneath that wildness, that rush of untethered, expansive emotions, I'd felt considerable apprehen-sion, an inkling that this freedom was temporary, an eerie calm before a turbulent storm; it was only now that I could identify that premonition as an internal alarm telling me to stay away.

"So," I said, picking up the original thread of the story. "I followed him up the cliff. I climbed the sharp rocks to the top and stared down at the water, and he counted to three and we jumped in, feet first, holding hands."

It turned out, I told her, that he was right: as my body ripped through the air and broke the surface of the water, as I sunk like a rock to the bottom, I felt lighter than I ever had in the seventeen years I'd been alive on this earth. In that fleeting moment, before all my weight returned to me, it had seemed to me that as long as I could remember the feeling of standing on a rock at the end of the earth overlooking the water, utterly unrestrained, I could do anything, go anywhere, be anyone I wanted. It was as if, for that one singular moment, I was a child of the universe. It occurred to me that that's how my father must have felt at sea, that he had both wanted a family and resented our needs, which, in his view, restricted his rights to roam the world on a ship, wild and free. My mother, my father, my brother, all of their tyranny and pain and overprotection and neglect dissolved the moment I took the leap; it no longer belonged to me, nor was my fate answerable to theirs. That very evening, as we rode his Ducati back in the orange glow of the descending sun, our skin crusted with salt, darker than when we'd arrived, both of us bronzed and glowing, he took me to Puerto Banús.

"And then what happened?" Ellie asked, getting up to go to the bathroom but leaving the door open so I could continue to talk to her.

"I had a couple of cranberry vodkas, and we danced late into the night to the songs of summer. Remember that song 'Blue'?"

She said she did, then, as an aside, she opined through the open door that the bathroom was disgusting, that despite having cleaned it and taken a shower herself there were still hairs stuck to the edges of the porcelain tub, grime on the rusted fixtures, stains all over the floor. I heard her open the doors of the cabinet beneath the sink. She let out a loud shriek.

"What is it?" I asked.

"I think there's a dead animal in there," she offered, her voice trembling.

I rushed to the bathroom to inspect the situation. For a moment, I thought I saw the shadow of that wild boar sliding against the wall, looking up at me with her pitiful eyes, emitting her simpering groans, her warning siren, tensing the sharp blades of her shoulders on that thick striped torso. But she was nowhere to be found. I felt an intense sadness, a grief tinged with insurmountable guilt. Why had I not freed her?

I looked at Ellie. She was sitting sideways on the toilet, her underwear at her ankles, her knees squeezed together to make room for me to look under the sink. The cabinet was full of old shampoo bottles (all empty), a bottle of bleach (also empty), a stiff black sponge, and a large pile of rags that looked like they'd been dipped in black oil and tossed aside. Or were they covered in blood? I couldn't be sure. I went into my room and grabbed a wire hanger, bent it in half, and returned to the bathroom. Ellie was standing there, hands on her hips.

"Aren't you going to flush the toilet?" I asked.

She stared at me in shock. I flushed the toilet. It made a loud noise, as if the pipes were straining to flex their joints within the confines of the walls. I dragged the towels out of the cupboard with the end of the wire hanger. They were indeed covered in what appeared to be blood. I remembered having seen blood gathering against the seams of the walls, along the window frames. I wondered if it was the apartment itself that was bleeding. I felt my body go cold. There were red crusty patches all over the towels, which had an odd sculptural quality to them; they'd dried into strange geometric shapes.

"It's not a dead animal," I said, drawing in a breath of relief that it wasn't the wild boar. We both stared at each other in confusion while the bloody rags hung stiffly off the end of the wire hanger between us.

Ellie looked pale under the yellow light coming from the dusty bulb overhead; I assumed my complexion also looked like bile. I had no idea whose blood was on the towels or who had stashed them away under the sink. Was it my blood? Had I run out of Tampax, wiped my sex and my loins with a kitchen rag, then dumped the towels in the cabinet? I couldn't remember. Was it Omar's blood? Why would his blood be there? Did the blood belong to that wild boar whose life had barely begun when Omar had laid his hands on her? Had he killed her in the tub in the middle of the night while I was asleep? No, I thought. She would have shrieked. I would have woken up. I didn't remember either Omar or I being cut or injured, and we certainly hadn't ever drawn blood from each other. He'd always been a very civil predator; there had been a few instances when the tone of his voice had shifted to deliver an order, a command that did not allow for a reply, but mostly he'd conducted his business politely, even tenderly, lovingly.

Ellie and I walked out of the bathroom in a tense silence. She sat back down on the floor and raised her mug to her lips, drank her coffee quietly, picked up another date, chewed it, spat the pit in the palm of her hand.

"We'll clean the place," I said to console her as I walked into the kitchen and dumped the bloodied rags into the garbage. I felt an intense sadness. My chest hurt, it stung. My lungs were heavy with grief. I returned to the bathroom and looked in the mirror. I didn't recognize my face. A vertiginous sensation took hold of me. There she was, that other future version of me—her features wounded and disfigured, her skin stretched, sagging, the light in her eyes spent, her mouth cracked open—staring back at me from the reflective surface of the mirror. I grew increasingly claustrophobic in that yellowed narrow windowless bathroom. I felt the walls leaning in. I heard the deep echoing rumble of the sea, its quiet susurrus that threatened to swallow me whole. I put my hand over my face in the mirror. I didn't want to recall that disfigured face—my own—staring back at me from the tree of my dream.

"Okay," Ellie said. "Tonight?" she asked, coming back around.

"Yes, I'll clean tonight," I said.

I didn't want to think about the bloodied rags again. I told her that there was a euro store down the street and that while we were there buying cleaning products we could buy some sunscreen and a few fresh towels and slippers to wear around the house until we'd bleached the floors a few times. I told her that buffing the floors would require a few passes, that you can't clean an apartment that's been boarded up for years in one evening.

"But we're only here for a few days," she protested.

"I'll do it," I said. "You can just help me tonight, and I'll take care of the rest."

She seemed relieved at the thought of mopping the floors. A moment later, as if nothing strange had transpired in the previous five minutes, she said, "The song you were talking about just came back to me. 'I'm a blue man in a blue world.'"

"That's the one," I said, sealing the garbage bag, lifting it out of the bin, and putting it by the door. I wanted those towels as far away from us as possible.

"Eiffel 65!" Ellie said cheerfully.

That song had been on the radio incessantly the summer I'd spent with Omar. It was 1999. "That song was playing when Omar first kissed me," I told Ellie. "He put his hand around the back of my neck and pulled me toward him, then leaned in and planted his lips on mine. I could taste the salt from his sweat and heard him groan with pleasure, then"—I paused for a moment because even the retelling filled me with disbelief—"he put his hand, the same hand he'd just hooked around my neck, against my chest like he was stopping me. 'What are you doing trying to kiss me?' he said. I was so confused, I didn't know what to say. I just stared at him in shock. I was so hurt, but I should have been enraged. He was a strategist and had begun, of this I am certain, to lay out his plan of attack before he'd even reached the apartment door to meet me."

Ellie put her mug on the floor and started pinching her lips with her fingers, as if her piercing were still there, a ring she could spin to speed along all her uncomfortable thoughts. A horrified expression had taken hold of her face, an expression that simultaneously revealed the deep terror that stirs in most, if not all, women's hearts when we're reminded that we're regarded as prey in this world. She dropped her hand from her lips. "Isn't it strange," she said, "that as women we all learn that there are predators loitering at the margins of our lives, that other people are the ones who will decide what shape our lives will take?"

The problem, I told her, is that predators are so pervasive, people hardly acknowledge their presence. I, for one, had never been taught that I had agency over my own pleasure, that I was my body's keeper, its rightful owner. I had learned that sex was the man's domain, that the only surefire way to avoid conflict or violence was to oblige men's desires politely. But had anyone taught me that explicitly? No. No one had come to me and said that my body is not mine, that it has only been loaned to me, that one day a man will appear as its master and I will repay my debt without protest. Put that way, all of our heads would spin. Instead, I was made to understand these brutal facts by means of other laws governing social interactions between genders: don't speak up too often, it's not feminine; sit with your arms and legs crossed in order to appear small and frail, in need of a protector (this, we are told, is the best way to attract a strong mate); be successful but not too ambitious and certainly not more successful than your husband. The list was long. These rules, I told Ellie, were articulated silently, yet their effect was violent, oppressive. It was a twisted paradox, the thought of which left me feeling ill.

"How could that be?" I said to Ellie.

"It's like the song," she said. "A totally upbeat song about wanting to die."

I told her that if I'd known then that she would become my greatest, most brilliant friend, a friend I would refer to as my wife, I would never have wasted my time on someone like Omar. "I would have happily waited the years out alone," I said. It was true. My friendship with her and with Sam, and, however briefly, with Sahar, had restored my sense of dignity.

Ellie's face now mirrored what I could only recognize as my agony, an old, stale ache that I was trying to dislodge from my past by returning to Marbella to retrace the sour events that had caused it in the first place. I could feel a profound love radiating from Ellie's eyes, a love I often felt between myself and Xavi, a love so pure that it could break through the barrier of time and reach our former selves, the people we'd been before our lives intertwined.

I continued my story. I told Ellie that over the years, I'd become aware of how Omar had manipulated the narrative of our kiss, quite literally reversing the flow of action so I would believe that I'd been the one who set into motion what would soon become our terrible affair.

I glanced over at the garbage bag by the door and thought about the bloody rags. I thought to myself, What if the blood on the rags belonged to her? That other future version of *me*? What if she'd lived on, trapped in this savage apartment, alone, afraid, hungry for years? I felt myself split in so many directions, dissected, each part neatly severed from the other. I heard my mother's voice in the cavern of my mind. *Where are you?* she asked, at first patiently, then desperately. I felt the hot, aching pangs of guilt as her trembling voice rose to the surface of my mind, her voice, which I'd let sink into the deep, cold waters of the wide ocean that stretched between us, heaving and icy. The remorseless force of the madness I'd courted came on suddenly. I felt hollow, vacuous, unreal, inhuman. I had the strange sensation that I was standing on the edge of a sinkhole, that if we didn't leave soon we never would; the apartment wouldn't let us go. It took a leonine strength to push the image out, out, out until the thoughts that came with it left me and I could breathe easily again.

I was, I told Ellie, returning to the thread of our conversation about my first day with Omar, unaware of being a pawn in Omar's story, a captive animal in a focused hunt executed by him with military precision. My lack of awareness, I told her, was hard to come to terms with. It had made me question my own judgment for years. I'd been deeply suspicious of myself for so long—sometimes I still was—as though I were composed of more than one person. Parts of me, I thought, were ruthless, dead set on deceiving the parts of me that had hope, that clung to innocence, that wanted to give a great big yes to life. I'd been remorseless toward myself, toward that wild boar. I thought to myself, and also said out loud to Ellie, that Omar had kept the wild boar in the bathroom, in my bathroom first then in his own, and that when the shrieking had gotten to him he'd put the wild boar on his terrace, where he also kept birds in cages, birds he caught in the mountains and sold at the market, or to his friends, or to anyone who wanted one.

Then I remembered that, according to Omar, the wild boar had committed suicide. The details of that story, which he'd delivered perfunctorily, suddenly aligned in my mind. She'd crawled onto a fruit cart he'd left in the corner of the terrace and leapt off of the balcony. I wasn't there when it happened. Omar had told me the story one afternoon while we were lying in bed, the sheets moist from our sweat, the sun filtering through the curtains in his room. It was all coming back to me. We were adrift between wakefulness and sleep, but I remembered distinctly feeling that Omar was lying to me. Perhaps he'd killed the wild boar in my tub after all and sold off her flesh and bones; perhaps he'd wiped the wild boar's spilled blood with those towels and stuck them in his backpack and brought them here to deposit. It was a crime to steal wild boars, to hunt them for game. Was he trying to hide the evidence of his crime?

I walked to the door, opened it, put the garbage back outside, and shut the door again. I couldn't stand being in the same room with those rags anymore.

Ellie grunted. She mumbled something I couldn't quite hear but that sounded to me like a gesture of agreement, a kind of *Yes, we've finally put some distance between ourselves and those bloody rags.*

"It's only now," I said to her, returning to my earlier point, "after so many years of being a writer in the world, that I can see clearly that I was a character in a prefabricated plot, a powerless agent caught in a tightly manicured story designed by Omar."

Perhaps, I reflected out loud, it was because of this experience that in all of my years of writing I hadn't once been able to produce an outline or a novel that was distinctly plot driven. The word itself—*plot*—seemed problematic to me, artificial. On the one hand, it rang of secrecy, conspiracy, a desire to dupe the reader with its tropes of realism, putting forth a manageable version of reality, a legible reality composed of epiphanies, conclusions, conflicts with clear boundaries, events that administer exacting lessons to the characters, forcing them either to grow or become more calloused versions of who they already were.

On the other hand, that word—*plot*—also signified a piece of land, a territory with distinct boundaries, with a frontier designed to contain the story rather than mark the site of a potential transgression. The literature I craved was untethered, mysterious, atmospheric. It was boundary crossing. I couldn't, having lived an itinerant life, produce anything else and still be honest, honest before the page in the privacy of my own home and honest with readers, whoever they turned out to be.

I told Ellie that what I wanted was to feel the words being plucked out of the deep reservoirs of human life and brought into a feeble light while I looked on with trembling adoration. That I wanted to capture the feeling of uncertainty, to transcribe the vertiginous quality of being alive onto the page, to honor through my writing the pleasures and the dangers of not knowing how one's life will unfold, what it will amount to. "Enduring uncertainty, embracing doubt," I said to her, "is a sacred practice tantamount to religious devotion. But instead of praying, I write. Like friendship, sentences can have a devotional quality to them; they can be full of reach and yearning and interrupted longings."

"Yes," she said. "Yes. I know exactly what you mean. Sentences that are prophetic and that remind us of our long wrestle with the divine."

"Exactly," I said.

As we spoke, I kept thinking about Omar's strategic nature. I imagined him sitting in a dark cockpit gliding a plane over a vast sea veiled by clouds and mist. He was driving the plane toward a ribbon of orange light that sliced the sky in half; I could see from his relaxed posture that he was confident of what lay on the other side. He would navigate that plane over the horizon and bring it gently down to taxi on a distant runway. He made it seem effortless, easy.

"So what happened after he told you to stop kissing him?" Ellie asked.

"I barely spoke to him the rest of the night. I just kept drinking and smoking until he was ready to take me home."

I told her that when I got home I hadn't bothered to turn the lights on. I just walked through the unlit hall to my bedroom, somewhat drunkenly, a little nauseated from having smoked so excessively, and planted myself in bed. It had been raining. The rain had been slow at first, a warm summer shower, but by the middle of the night, it had turned torrential. I could hear the rain pounding the pavement. The drops were incessant. They were falling like beads on the hoods of the cars and making hollow drumming sounds against the lush foliage of the trees. The rain was playing the world like an organ. It was a symphonic storm. Cars, café sidewalk tables, the asphalt, roofs, garbage cans — they were all being battered and worked.

I sat on the edge of my bed and listened, as if Vivaldi or Bach were directly outside my window delivering a private concert meant exclusively for me. I could see the distant headlights of passing cars below, an illuminated window or two glazed with rain. All of my senses were muted except for my sense of hearing, which seemed to be at its peak. My body was numb, my mind empty. Whatever thoughts were there had been pushed out by the disco music, the strobe lights, the deep thump of the base that traveled in electric waves through the floors and walls. It wasn't long before the rain began to subside.

Once it did, I told Ellie, my feelings flooded back. I felt as though someone were reaching through my chest and pinching my heart. A malevolent air settled in the room. My lips were burning. I kept feeling the weight of Omar's mouth against mine. Every time I closed my eyes to try to get some sleep, I heard his voice repeating those same words—*What are you doing trying to kiss me?*—worried that I wouldn't see him again, that he wouldn't be next to me long enough for me to kiss him a second time.

It was all very strange, I explained, the feeling that one could be desired and rejected within a span of seconds or that a lie could be formed so quickly, a false narrative spun out of thin air seconds after the events that it referred to had passed. Not even seconds. The lie had been concomitant with the event, overlapping, simultaneous. What had Omar thought, that I had the memory of a goldfish? That I was so dumb, so utterly undeserving of a covert strategy? Perhaps I was. Or perhaps Omar was just normalizing his own bad behavior, sanitizing it; perhaps he had recognized in me a deep distaste for covertness and so had done everything openly, overtly, as if to signal to me that there was nothing to hide, nothing shameful in his advances, in my desire, no matter what he'd claimed. And I had desired him; of course I had. But I hadn't been the one to act on that desire. I wouldn't have known how. At first, I hadn't even known to recognize my desire as desire. I'd thought that the warmth I felt between my legs was my period.

I recalled that I had, in fact, felt furious that night, that I'd been smoking out of rage. The sense of indignation had come in waves. I'd wanted to charge into him like a wounded bull. But, simultaneous with the anger, I'd felt an even more powerful emotion: longing. I'd longed for Omar, longed for an adult who understood the world far more easily than I did—someone I could rely on. Who could translate the world for me. That was the longing that Omar recognized in me, and he'd distorted it to meet his own needs. I'd turned my back on my mother; my father was entirely absent. I was parentless, alone, scared even if I didn't recognize my fear as such.

I remembered that my mother had tried to call me the next day. She'd called me frantically, every hour, and I'd ignored her calls. When I finally did pick up, late in the evening, sleepy from having napped on and off through the day's heat, I told her that I was fine, that there was nothing to worry about, that my father had left only for a day or two on business, that he'd be back by morning. All lies. But I didn't share much with anyone back then. I bottled up a lot of things, mostly because there was no one around to consult or complain to but also because I was always afraid that my mother would overreact; she'd become so terribly overprotective. Who could blame her? She was a mother. She'd licked our eyes clean, fed us with her own body. I wasn't a great comfort to her, no. But I tried as much as I could not to worry her.

"I suppose it's my character," I said to Ellie, who sat there listening attentively. "I don't like to go around vomiting my feelings; I like to analyze them privately, thoughtfully, without the interference of well-meaning outsiders. An old habit," I said, reaching for my cigarettes, "like smoking."

Ellie asked if I would sit next to her; she wanted to do a tarot reading for me. She needed to practice her hand, and my uncertain fate made for perfect material. "Your struggle is focused," she said. "It lends itself well to this kind of thing."

I lit my cigarette and asked Ellie if I could use her mug, which was empty, as an ashtray.

"Sure," she said, somewhat reluctantly.

She'd quit smoking years before I'd met her though she occasionally shared a cigarette with me. We'd pass it back and forth between us, taking two drags at a time. I offered her the one I'd just lit.

"Not on an empty stomach," she said, pushing my hand away. We decided that after she was done with the tarot reading we would go out to eat and buy cleaning products, and that we'd reward ourselves afterward by going down to the beach to watch the moon rise in the opal sky above the sea. I'd gone on and on about the sky in the Costa del Sol; about how, at times, it appeared so thin as to be translucent only to shift abruptly into an opaque gunmetal, thick with fog. When the fog dissipated, I'd told her, the sky would turn an intense blue again, darkening and lightening in shades, eventually turning lilac, then a regal purple, and, at twilight, navy blue, before going black altogether; the moon, silver and mercurial, would hang dead at its center, a bright flame that would burn until dawn. I was already dreaming of staring at that moon, of seeing it reflected on the surface of the water, which took on the texture of hard plastic at night, thick, solid, impenetrable. And as I thought about that round, sleepless moon, Lorca's lines returned to take their place on the stage of my mind, the curves and eddies of his words lit up by that metallic light: *The moon holds out her arms, her metal breasts are bare.* It was my favorite thing—to daydream about words.

I ate the remaining dates in between drags, spat my pits in the mug, then piled in the rest, which Ellie had stacked into a tower. They looked like the exoskeletons of cockroaches.

Ellie wiped her hands on the towel, tucked a few loose strands of curls behind her ears, and shuffled the deck. The cards were beautiful, as glossy as silk. I'd seen them before, in Sam's apartment in Lefferts Gardens, which he shared with his girlfriend. It was the Next World Tarot deck. All of the cards featured the artist's friends and acquaintances, one of whom happened to be Sam's girlfriend. The deck represented minorities, differently abled bodies, women in hijabs, gay and trans couples. It was a deck that sung its tune proudly and professed a kind of transgressive, revolutionary love.

When Ellie was done shuffling the cards, she placed the deck on the coffee table and told me to divide the deck three times thoughtfully, holding in my mind's eye a clear vision of my predicament. "Then," she said, "take deep breaths, connecting your mind to your heart and your heart to your hands, and restack the deck."

I did as I was told. I envisioned Omar as I'd seen him just a few hours earlier on the beach and tried to locate him in the larger complex of my past. I'd been trying for so long to understand my own cravings. To understand the shape of whatever longing I'd foolishly believed he could fulfill, a longing he'd clearly detected and was eager to string around my neck like a noose. I felt my belly grow warmer with every breath. I cut the stack in two. It was the heat of rage, of an old repressed fury, a feeling I couldn't sustain for long; it made me want to hurt myself. It was an unwieldy, dangerous energy, an energy that I recognized as a consequence of having been branded with Omar's appetite, his lack of control. In other words, what I was feeling, I told myself as I cut the deck a third time, was *his* rage. By sleeping with me, by manipulating and controlling the contours of my life as an adolescent, Omar had unloaded his anger onto me. His frustration with his own life. His shame. His toxic secret of grooming young girls. And I was left to hold the hot coals of his dark longings for the rest of my life.

"Relax your face," Ellie said.

She put her hand on my back. My muscles relaxed with her touch. For a brief moment, the room filled with the silence of a wake.

Eventually, Ellie whispered in a hypnotic tone: "Each of us is spurred on by a private mystery, a secret that escapes our notice despite being deeply familiar to us." Then she instructed me to open my eyes and select one card from the deck, which she'd spread out across the table in such a way so as to make the edge of every card visible.

Laid out like that, the deck looked like a staircase rising in gentle gradations to a purer, more transcendent space. I felt time folding and unfolding itself like a dream. I studied the cards. I moved my hand over the length of the deck and tried to feel the vibration coming from each card. It was strange, the way some of them stood out to me and others faded into the background, signaling that they had nothing to offer. For a moment, with my hand gliding over the cards, I heard the sound of my own laughter, an unrestrained laugh that had come out in fits and bursts that summer. I saw Omar chasing me around a food shack on the beach at sunset. The sand was firm and wet underfoot. The sun was an orange ball of fire, a perfect radiant globe hovering over the black band of the horizon. The sea, in that fading light, appeared moss green, a dark half-moon with a gelatinous surface. The water had been rough that day. The lifeguards had raised red flags on the poles that dotted the coast, signaling to swimmers that they should take caution.

When Omar finally caught me, short of breath, I was standing by a flagpole. He wrapped his arms around me from behind and said the most pathetic thing in the world. "Age," he whispered in my ear, "is irrelevant when it comes to love."

I said nothing. Or perhaps I said something about the seagulls circling like vultures overhead. I remembered that I was cold, that the wind was picking up, that my feet were clammy from being wet.

I examined the deck one last time. My hand was on fire. I pulled a card and turned it around. It was the Five of Wands.

Ellie concentrated on the card. She was studying it and examining the position of my body in relation to it. She moved a penetrating gaze over my face and hands.

As she contemplated the message, which I had presumably

called forth from the deck, I scanned the sky through the window, lost in thought. I was stuck in the same mental loop I'd been stuck in for years, a loop that felt oppressive to me but that I didn't seem capable of exiting. I was lost in the mental maze that I'd constructed over the years, built with the most primitive thoughts. I was fundamentally in agreement with Omar. I believed and had experienced firsthand love's capacity to transgress and challenge social norms, love's radical inappropriateness, and I felt thankful for it. I'd been deeply accepting of relationships in which one partner is significantly older than the other, irrespective of sex or gender, so long as both parties were consenting adults. I wasn't the kind to raise an eyebrow or wince at other people's relationships.

Besides, I took issue with the laws governing and dictating the terms of adulthood. These laws were unstable, mutable; it is impossible to separate our understanding of sexual politics from our notions of cultural progress, of time itself. Who is an adult? Who determines which people are of mature age and which aren't? It all seemed so deeply arbitrary to me, so confounding; the fact that others so willingly swallowed the rules of decorum without demonstrating even an inkling of doubt or resistance only increased my confusion. Surely, the laws governing adulthood had resulted from a debate or in response to some tragic incident. But who were the people who'd had a seat at that table when they were written, and where were those people now? Were there women at the table, lesbians, bisexuals, gay and transgender citizens, children and teenagers who had been abused, or adults who had been abused as children? Why were these laws, which so carefully police our bodies and the exchange of fluids among them, being shaped predominantly by middle-aged white men who were, in all likelihood, either straight or at least pretended as much? Why weren't these laws continually subject to the scrutiny of time? I considered, as I had considered countless times before, that I had been raised in countries that had laws and social rules that practically repelled one another and that, at their extremes, went so far as to demonize one another for being too restrictive or too lenient or both, a combination that seemed impossible but somehow wasn't. The moral codes I had internalized were deeply contradictory.

I saw a seagull approach the terrace and land on the railing with a steely grip and a grace that left me dumbfounded. Its eyes looked red in the sun, as if sparks of fire were about to leap out of them. I elbowed Ellie to look at the bird, and she turned silently, gently, so as neither to scare the bird off or lose her own train of thought, her intuition of what the card held in store for me. As soon as she turned back to the card, the seagull took off toward a set of razor-thin clouds. Soon it was out of view.

I returned to my thoughts. Once I was in the maze, I had to complete the circuit. This, too, was an old habit, a kind of compulsive mental attitude I'd developed as an adolescent, likely due to the fact that I'd had to leap from language to language, from Farsi to Spanish and English and back, like a toad between ponds; I was always in the process of examining my understanding of a culture through one diametrically opposed to it: I viewed the East from the perspective of the West and vice versa. I was trapped between these supposedly antagonistic forces. These absolute hemispheres, the lines that had been drawn across maps, that severed my body, my being, sawed it in half. It was too much. My life required of me an almost inhumane level of cognitive flexibility, an openness that left me unprotected; I had to let every bit of cultural subtext in, then sort through it later once I'd had time to measure any new information against the knowledge I'd acquired previously in another land. It required a herculean effort made more exhausting by the fact that each of these lands policed my body, my female body, differently. In Spain, I reviewed mentally, the age of consent is sixteen when only years earlier it had been fourteen. And then there's Iran, I thought, where a woman is considered an adult at the age of nine. And what about the United States where I'd spent the majority of my adult life? I had come to understand there that adulthood is the age at which one finishes high school. Out of the nest at eighteen, I thought — a luxury, really, when there isn't enough space or capital in most of the rest of the world to accommodate such desires. Taking all that into account, how was I supposed to conclude anything? I was caught in that triangle — Spain, the United States, Iran — in the most arbitrary triangle of all, that space where culture's prejudices and its laws coincide to draw boundaries around the lives of its citizens.

I was on the cusp of realizing something that had evaded me for years. What had given me pause when Omar had indirectly professed his love to me on the beach, I realized, was that I hadn't believed him. I hadn't believed that he loved me. Rather, I had knowingly tricked myself into believing it. He had insinuated his love through a statement of fact, and I knew enough to know that love, true love, consumes a person, makes them uncertain, causes their voice to tremble, and there was, I realized—because it was as though I could hear his voice at my ear again now just as I'd heard it that evening—no sign of trepidation in his voice, no quivering, no emotion. But I'd wanted to believe that he loved me—or worse, I'd needed to believe it, and that need was stronger than my analytical powers; it had intercepted my ability to listen and respond to my own body, which had gone, under the weight of those words, stiff with grief and confusion, as rigid as the flagpole I was leaning against. I had overridden my body, cut myself off from its innate wisdom, and in that moment, I had lost contact with myself. I had lost all communication with my intuition. A corpse—uninhabited, cast off, a waste of space.

I felt tears gathering in my eyes. I felt something toxic and solid caught in my throat. I put out my cigarette and looked down to avoid Ellie's gaze. She didn't notice, or if she did, she sensed that I didn't want her to comment on my pain, to let on that she could see me holding back a flood of tears.

She began to speak, her eyes still fixed on the wands. She traced their lines with her finger, and said, "This card signals conflict and change. The conflict you experienced is deep and continuous with an ongoing conflict that existed and still exists outside of you, a cultural conflict between East and West, earth and water, masculine and feminine, the psychic and the material —you were caught at their fault lines."

She sounded like she was reading from a text that had been transcribed in the gossamer of the universe. She was a conduit, reciting the message that I'd called forth by allowing my hand to hover over the cards, my body to direct my choices. I was shocked by the continuity between my thoughts and her words.

"In order to resolve this conflict," she said, finally looking at me and searching my eyes for a response, "you'll have to draw on all of your psychic and emotional resources. The resolution may be subtle, the path toward its achievement equally so, composed of nearly imperceptible shifts in consciousness that ultimately will integrate all of the many differing opinions that you carry within you." She added that true integration didn't mean eliminating contradiction but rather aligning the inconsistencies inherent in my intellectual and physical life with the high ideals of the heavens, not the heaven we've constructed from our limited position on earth, from our religious perspectives, but a heaven beyond the paradise we've been taught to imagine, a space that is abundant, wide open, that allows opposing realities to exist side by side without judgment—a complex space where we are invited to let go of our constant need to know or understand everything, where we are no longer measured by our supposed purity.

I couldn't hold back my tears any longer. They dropped out of my eyes, though I no longer felt the need to cry. I was astonished by the correspondence between Ellie's rhetoric and my private thoughts; the deck of cards appeared, in light of the exchange, to have an infinite dimensionality to them, to contain worlds that willingly lent themselves to a variety of interpretations. I did exist on a fault line and that fault line was not something I could resolve. My not-quite-white skin, the fact that I was the abandoned child of a British sailor and an Iranian mother.

I barely knew my father. I'd seen him only sporadically throughout my childhood, and when I did, his presence was so disorienting to me, it disturbed me more than his absence had. Most of the time I forgot he even existed in the first place. I'd been raised in Tehran, speaking Farsi. It was my mother's language, the language she'd nursed me with, the language she'd used to soothe me when I'd cried as an infant. And yet my features and the color of my skin bore a resemblance to both my parents; my face was ethnically ambiguous, a face onto which all manner of fantasies and political narratives could be projected.

I was a hybrid child. I was Omar's hybrid teenage lover. And Omar was a hybrid, too, by virtue of having migrated to Spain, a Lebanese man from the upper echelons of Beirut society, a man who spoke French and Arabic and Spanish and English with seductive ease, a man who'd internalized the colonial logic under which he'd been raised, who'd been conditioned to desire a girl like me, half West, half East. I was a physical manifestation of his psyche. To him, I finally understood, I was a fantasy. My body contradicted the very notion of the invented self. Who has that privilege? I wondered broodily. Not I; much like Omar, I'd been branded by someone else's power long before I'd had the chance to find my own sense of self. The magnetic field directing our internal compasses, I realized, was blocked forever by the force of colonialism. The card I was holding seemed to insinuate this split nature of mine, the fact that my subjectivity was implicated on both sides of the divide.

"Ready?" Ellie asked. She told me to draw a final card.

I lifted my right hand and let it hover over the spread again. Perhaps, I considered, as I moved my hand back and forth across the fanned stack, Omar had believed that I wouldn't be able to transition into womanhood without his direction, just as the West believed the East incapable of transitioning into modernity without its "benevolent" imperialism, its narrative of conquest as salvation. There were, I admitted to myself, feeling an attraction to a card toward the end of the spread, ways in which my relationship with Omar had rescued me: he had shocked me back into life, taught me that it can be full of adventure and pleasure, laughter and good food, and the joys of wilderness. Our relationship had healed and destroyed me in one swift blow. What had been balm for my younger self had cast a dark shadow over my future self, the self I had become, the self who was sitting on a dirty floor in an old, abandoned apartment about to pluck a card from a deck in order to understand her fate. Aware that my younger self had taken a loan out on my life.

I flipped the card over. It was the card of Temperance. The card featured a young woman with brown skin kneeling next to a river and pouring water from one cup into a lower vessel. "This card," Ellie said, "is about rising from a lower plane to a higher one. The woman in this card is protected by natural law. She is able to resist abuse because she feels deeply that she has a right to her humanity."

She paused thoughtfully, then reached for the interpretive book. She looked for the page that offered information about the card of Temperance. It read: *she tempers the whimsical flight of the fool, she mixes hot water with cold, she has one foot in the water and one foot on dry land.*

"She is reversing the flow of the water, which means, I believe, that subconscious elements may be rising to the surface for you. Think of her as your ancestor. Do you remember that line from Benjamin?" Ellie asked.

Benjamin was far from my mind even though I'd spent years thinking about his work, communing with his sentences.

"We exert," Ellie said, "a weak messianic power over our ancestors." What this means, she went on to say, is that time flows in more than one direction; it moves simultaneously forward and back, sideways, even in elliptical, spiraling loops; we can heal the wounds of our ancestors by making space in the flow of time for our bodies, which have been persecuted since time immemorial, subject to erasure, extermination, restricted mobility. We carry their scars, their genes, their languages or the ghosts of their languages; but we, too, have an effect on them. We, the living, can influence the dead by changing the arc of history; by restoring justice, we also reinstate their sense of dignity.

We both drew in deep breaths.

The seagull returned. It was the same bird. It landed with the same power and grace, looked at us through the window, then turned around and leapt into the sky, cutting the air with its wide wings. It flew in oblong circles, then vanished into the white horizon. Into the future. In that bird's labyrinthine flight, Lorca's lines came back to me: *In Spain the dead are more alive than the dead in any other country in the world.*

# 8

THE NEXT MORNING I AWOKE to an agonizing cry. I sat bolt upright in bed, my heart beating with fright. The apartment was abusing me again. It was unleashing its darkness; its twisted grief was seeping through the walls. I heard trotting noises. I heard the muffled sounds of a struggle, the hollow echo of an animal pawing gravel. I heard the clip-clop of the wild boar's hooves falling against the floors followed by tiny whimpering cries. A thin yolky light was coming through the window. It fell like a spotlight on the opposite wall, a yellow ring resolved to track the animal. The wild boar's shadow slid against the wall. I traced her long ears, her muscular body, the tips of her coarse hairs, all standing upright. She was agitated, fearful. A deep ache spread across my heart as if I'd been punched in the chest. The surface of the wall turned liquid, as though it were a silk curtain or a rumbling waterfall. The room turned into a whirlpool, its vortex drawing me into its cruel embrace. The eerie susurrus of the waves returned. I could hear them crashing breathlessly against the apartment walls, a tsunami of water longing to crush me under its pressure. The wild boar's face emerged, her round snout and deep-set eyes turned toward me. I was seized by a terrible anguish. She was so large. She, too, had grown in this apartment.

"I'm so sorry," I whispered, my lips trembling. "I'm so sorry for what I did to you."

The wild boar's eyes were as black as tar. They shone with an unbearable light; her eyes were ablaze with rage from the injustices she had endured. I thought she was going to charge at me; she was staring at me the way that Omar had in our parting moment, as he crouched like a tiger on his Ducati, glaring at me through the rear windshield of my father's rusted Mercedes, his eyes aflame, murderous. He'd looked like a man with an unquenchable appetite for carnage, destruction, hatred, evil. I heard the booming sound of his motorcycle. In my mind's eye, I saw him speeding toward a sunlit horizon beneath a blue sky, the surrounding landscape shamelessly beautiful, a spine of rugged earth covered in aloe and palms, their fronds splayed open toward the sky with earnest expectation. Omar tore through them, severed the terrain, sliced it this way and that with no thought of who would mend the wounds.

Now the wild boar simpered. Her stiff legs struck the ground. Her face retreated into the rippled waters that seemed to be falling from the heavens like a great flood. She looked down. She sniffed. Her image dissolved. The wall closed over her again. And those waves, too, retreated.

All was silence: a cold, stunned quiet that left me raw. I thought to myself that we had both been so young, yet what we knew of this world was despair, confusion, fear, an unimaginable loneliness that had struck us dumb.

I sat in bed and let out a long repressed cry. I cried quietly, silently. I held the blanket against my mouth. I was afraid of belting out my pain, afraid that woven into the fabric of my grief was the violence and cruelty of my relationship with Omar, what had happened between us, and all of the people—family, strangers, animals—who had cleared the path for us to meet. The last thing I wanted to do was unleash that cruelty back out into the world. I'd taught myself to regard my pain as my greatest asset, productive, instructive, generative; but only if I could figure out how to hold it kindly, gently. There was something transcendent in that pain. And for that reason, I'd wanted to avoid unleashing its unfiltered storms and dark shadows on another. I'd thought that if I held on to my suffering long enough I'd be able to metabolize it; it would dissolve and never again be recycled back into the currents of the world. But no. I'd been eclipsed by Omar. The injustices he'd assailed against me—against that wild boar and the birds he kept in cages, and who knows what other beings—could not be contained in a single temporal dimension. That's violence's greatest asset, I thought; the ability to make time itself servile to the deviousness of its will. We are left to manage the discrepancy between the scale of the event, its limited temporal duration, and its boundless posthumous influence over our hearts and minds.

I heard Ellie call out to me. I wiped my face on the sheets. I tied my hair up. I drew in a few deep breaths.

"Are you up?" she asked through the door.

I told her I was, that I would be out in a moment. I steadied my voice before I answered. I didn't want her to know that I'd been crying; admitting it would only make me powerless to the impulse to sob still more, an impulse that had taken hold of me so intensely the day before.

"I'm cleaning," Ellie said.

So, I thought, calming myself, I'd heard the sounds of Ellie cleaning the house. I got up and walked down the hall. She'd thrown open all the windows, was carrying a bucket of steaming hot water from the kitchen to the living room. She dipped a frothed sponge into the water, knelt down, and scrubbed the tiles clean.

"The mop won't do. Vulgar, scummy apartment," she said. "How'd you sleep?"

A warm vinegary light was coming through the window in broad shafts. Another hot day, I thought. It was, in fact, the perfect morning for lying on the beach, tanning in the scorching sun, drinking without restraint. I needed desperately to change the channel.

I shrugged my shoulders in response. I didn't want to speak. I was afraid that if I opened my mouth I'd start sobbing again, so I just stood there as mute as a rock.

"Shocked?" she replied, cocking her head to one side and

smiling somewhat whimsically. I must have had an afflicted look on my face still.

"Don't be silly," I managed to say.

I had never seen her clean without being begged to do so, though once she got going, her efforts were always earnest, always thorough. Perhaps, I thought, the apartment's filthy, vile nature had claimed her, too; it had shifted her disposition, drawn her toward itself. The gashes, cuts, wounds, the ravaged flesh hidden beneath the blistering paint, the sour smell of rot, the cracked walls with their globs of brown stains were demanding her care, laying claim to her attention, bending her will to their darkness. I wondered if she'd fallen victim to the apartment's vindictive, spiteful nature. She was, quite literally, on her knees at its service. The thought disoriented me. I'd expected to wake up to her painting her toes, chatting with her girlfriend on WhatsApp.

"Is there coffee?" I asked.

She gave a regal bow and pointed at the kitchen with the wet sponge. I had no idea what had gotten into her. I wondered how long she'd been up, cleaning. I wondered if she'd heard Omar's motorcycle rip through the apartment walls, the wild boar stab the ground with her hooves. But she couldn't have. She looked happy, carefree. Her cheeks were flushed, rosy. She seemed steady, calm, as she kneeled back down to scrub the floors. We'd been out drinking the night before. Perhaps she was still drunk, I thought, inebriated and happy. We'd eaten octopus salad and liver pâté and drank rioja. We'd dipped our bread in salted olive oil and peeled grilled langoustines until our fingers were raw from the shells and the lemon juice that had been brushed onto them. We'd stumbled home, laughing and drunk, dragging the cleaning products we'd purchased up and down the steep cobblestone streets: a mop and bucket, bleach, sponges, trash bags, baking soda for the greased surfaces, vinegar to disinfect the floors. I remembered I'd promised her I would clean, but now I wanted to be as far away from the rancid surfaces of the apartment as possible.

"I had to force some of the windows open." Ellie beamed from the living room as I poured my coffee.

It tasted bitter; it was undrinkable, as black as tar. I added some sugar and milk to cut the acid and searched for my cigarettes. She'd put them in a small straw basket along with my lighter and a note that read, *Stop smoking!*

"Funny!" I said. Then I walked over to the sink, turned the tap on, and washed my face in its weak stream. It was lukewarm and smelled like sewage, so I held my breath. I turned the tap off and caught my reflection in the water that had pooled in the sink. I lifted the end of my shirt to my face and rubbed it dry, then looked into the sink again, that pit of dirt, and watched my image dissolve. I drew a cigarette out of the box and lit it. I stood there smoking it, inhaling its warmth as I took in the narrow rectangular kitchen. Despite having been cleaned, it was still dull, no light or shine. The air smelled of mold and dampness.

The atmosphere of the apartment was permanently heavy, its surfaces forever soiled from disuse, the energy cluttered.

I took a sip of my coffee and grabbed a second cup to use as an ashtray.

I was not in the mood to clean. The thought of touching the apartment, of caring for it, filled me with disgust. I told Ellie not to bother, that I'd changed my mind, that it wasn't worth restoring the apartment or making it habitable again, that no matter what we did we'd be unable to rip it back from death's grip; we'd never be able to expel the ghosts trapped in its floorboards and walls. No matter what we do, the apartment will revert back to its hermetic life, greedily drawing dust to itself, shutting out fresh oxygen and light. I told her that I planned to abandon the apartment to the elements, to the dust of the universe. That the longer we stayed, the likelier it was that it would pull us into its entrails and turn us into ghosts for its own entertainment.

She stared at me in disbelief. "You'll change your mind," she said. I felt furious with her but I said nothing. "Did you try on the underwear we bought?" she asked, gently guiding the conversation away from the walls and windows.

"What underwear?" I asked. Then I remembered that we'd stopped at a Calzedonia store the night before and that I'd drunkenly complained that I never had enough underwear and that I'd never bought myself a swimsuit, not since the purple two-piece Speedo she'd discovered in the closet. Ellie had encouraged me to take care of myself, to shop, to buy underwear, lacy underwear that I could show off to Xavi, that I would adore every time I looked between my legs, and also a swimsuit, a bright-green bikini that she swore would complement my skin once I'd spent a day on the beach. That's all it takes for my body to completely transform, I thought, regaining my equilibrium; six or seven hours in the sun and I turn a deep olive, the color of my grandfather's skin.

I put out my cigarette, waving the smoke out of my face, and went to help her. I'd promised I would clean. *I'd given her my word*, I repeated to myself in a punitive tone. I started on the bathroom. I got on the floor and leaned over the edge of the tub. There they were: the short black hairs—pubes—scattered along the sides. Whose pubic hairs were they? I remembered again how cold and stiff Omar had become when I'd asked him to pet my smooth legs, how I'd learned not to express agency, to let him direct me as if I were a doll. It took all of my strength not to chastise myself for having been stupid, so irremediably foolish. But I couldn't stop myself for long.

"An idiot; a desperate, lonely teenager," I said to myself sotto voce as I poured baking soda into the tub, opened the tap, and let the hot water run. The water had an orange hue to it. The pipes had rusted. I scrubbed the grease, the scum, the pubes, and watched it all run down the tub into the drain. Then I put the stopper in and let the tub fill with water. I added vinegar and let it sit, eroding the filth. I scrubbed the walls, the sink, the toilet. I was sweating profusely.

A house is meant to be cleaned, adored, decorated. This was

not a home; it was a catacomb. A lifeless, repulsive enclosure marked with danger, betrayal, and annihilation. Had I sought the danger out? Had the house manipulated me into craving what had then seemed to me unparalleled bliss but which I now recognized had come with staggering losses that would be paid out like dividends for the rest of my life? I would never be done grieving what had happened between Omar and me. I would never be able to fully account for it, to make sense of it, order it into a digestible sequence of events with consequences that had clear boundaries. No. The consequences seemed to multiply and acquire fresh dimensions with each new phase of my life. The damage he'd caused was alive. It had a mercurial disposition that never failed to surprise me.

I felt dizzy, nauseated from the pungent smell of the vinegar. I could hear Ellie's heavy footfalls in the living room. She, too, was working against the grime with a fierce and diligent hand, a concentrated attitude. The bathroom walls and floor were wet. Black puddles pooled at my feet. The dirt had layers. I caught my reflection in the mirror. It was divided in half by tracks of water. I observed myself dispassionately. I could see in one half of my face the desire to run away, to shut this place out of my memory, and in the other half, I perceived a mature resistance to that same impulse. It was time to confront the ghosts of my past. I was sick of their covert operations. I felt an intense strength blossom in my gut. I was resolute. I stood there and stared at myself until that other face came forward again, the lineaments of my battered future self, her wounded eyes, her gaunt cheeks, her brittle hair crusted with blood. I saw her mouth move in the mirror. *Let me out*, she seemed to be saying. *Take me away from here.* Her lips moved continuously as she repeated the phrase. I winced with shame, with disgust, but I refused to look away. The image flickered, then I saw her sitting inside the trunk of a tree, that same tree I'd seen in my dream. The sequence reversed with delirious speed. I saw the bark seal up again, and her figure disappeared from view. I felt my lungs release, my stomach relax, my shoulders drop. I felt relief, momentary but powerful, as transcendent as that warm light that poured into this hellish pit each morning. All that was left was my own face staring back at me in astonishment. I sprayed the mirror with the bottle of Windex and watched my reflection turn diffuse and pixelated. I was covered in sweat. I worked harder. I wiped the mirror clean; it seemed to shatter every time I looked at it. I threw a few towels on the floor to absorb the muddy water, carried them quickly into the kitchen, and deposited them into a trash bag. Ellie was buffing the tiles in the living room. She smiled at me. She was in a terribly cheerful mood.

"You're going to wear that swimsuit and we're going to the beach!" she announced.

I agreed. I told her that I was coming undone. That I was losing my mind. That I needed to leave the apartment. That we needed to reward ourselves by spending the whole day at the beach, tanning, giving in to our base desires, hiring the women, who were often from different parts of Asia, China mostly, and who hustled up and down the coast selling massages in the heat. A laborious job, dangerous not only because of the extreme temperatures but also because of the police who monitored their every move. I told her we'd hire them to cover us in oil and make us as slippery as fish. That we'd pay them twice what they'd ask for so we could be sure they were pocketing some of the money in case they had to hand their cash over to a ringleader, more than likely a man, at the end of the working day. "I'm going to order us a huge platter of grilled seafood," I said, "and those ridiculous pineapples filled to the brim with cocktails. I don't care how much they cost."

She laughed with ease. "I can't wait," she said.

I felt slightly better, slightly freer. I hurried up and finished the bathroom. I drained the tub. Then I opened the tap and let the water run for a long time before I undressed and got under it. The water was tepid. I was overheated from cleaning and it felt cool against my skin. I soaped myself. I reached for Ellie's razor, which she'd set on the edge of the tub, and shaved my legs. I marveled at the ease with which the hairs came away, at the clean tracks on my calf and shin as I worked in sections around one leg, then the other. I worked my way carefully over my knees, behind them, around my ankles. I was gentle, careful not to cut my skin. It wasn't easy. Halfway through, I felt the pressure in my hand increase as if another, larger hand had lain over it, its fingers longer, thicker, more masculine, its grip stronger. It was Omar's hand. "Like this," he kept saying, guiding my hand up my legs toward my inner thigh. "Good," he kept saying. "Right there." He pressed the razor against my loins, between my legs, and removed strip after strip of hair until my vagina was exposed and raw, its purplish lips like the squashed petals of an orchid. He had curated a clean surface for his pleasure.

The room was thick with steam. The water had turned hot. In that heat, I felt his breath against my neck and heard the words, "I want you naked as the day you were born. You," he said, "will be mine. Don't you see that I'll have you forever?" A shiver traveled down my spine. I looked at my legs.

"My legs," I said, "are mine." I played my voice over his. I said the words again, firmly: "My legs."

It was a proclamation, the articulation of a deep and boundless truth. It felt incredible to regard my legs, to know that they belonged to me. They were mine to enjoy, to touch and kneel and walk with and spread. I remembered that Omar had once pushed me in front of him on an evening stroll along the beach so he could watch other men turn their heads to take me in. He'd pawed at me like an animal. I could still feel the force of his hand on my back. I stumbled in front of him, then regained my footing. It was as if his hand had gone through me, cut through my spine.

"Don't you know how attractive you are?" he'd said. "Your long legs, your hair." He was always whimpering with pleasure, on the cusp of an orgasm, all of his fluids spilling forth. I heard him laughing behind me. It was as if he experienced each man's gaze as an applause intended for him, a reward that enhanced his self-esteem and robbed me of mine. Once he was satisfied, he caught up with me and ran his hands through my hair.

I opened my mouth and let it fill with water. It tasted terrible, so I spat it back out.

"I need to shave, too," Ellie called through the door. "And then we can get going."

"Okay," I said, and turned the tap off.

"Enough cleaning," she said, opening the door and stepping into the humid air. "This is as good as it's going to get."

I moved the shower curtain aside and looked at her. "Not a hair in sight!" I said.

She was wearing her reading glasses; the lenses had fogged over. "I can't see a thing!" She giggled.

I reached for the towels and wrapped one around my body and another around my head like a turban. I told her that it was likely that, by the time we returned from the beach in the evening, the apartment would have again covered its surfaces with every particle of dust that floated through.

We both laughed. It sounded terrible to be trapped in a living apartment, a house that had a consciousness of its own — and a dark one at that — but the truth is, we all learn to dislike the company of others when we've been left to our own devices for long enough. The apartment's conduct was heinous, terrifying, brazen, but I knew the source of its pain: it was as empty and dry as an abandoned well. All it had for company were ghosts and it clung to them desperately. It's hard to restore an abandoned home, to reverse its willful self-destruction, I thought. And I neither cared enough nor was innocent enough to try. After all, what did I owe these walls? Nothing, I thought, and got out of the way so Ellie could shower. The best thing I could do was remain steadfast in my conviction that some piece of who I'd been would be restored to me as a result of having returned to reacquaint myself with who I had been, perhaps even to reclaim some part of that previous version of myself.

I went into my bedroom and saw the Calzedonia bags I'd abandoned the night before. I emptied the contents onto the bed. I smoothed out the green bikini. I folded the underwear. I went over to my suitcase and pulled out a dress: a simple black linen dress, sleeveless, with a row of delicate pearl-white buttons running right down the middle. I'd gotten it in New York City between book events. I'd seen it on a mannequin in the shop window and had immediately been drawn to its simplicity, its air of effortless elegance. I'd enjoyed going shopping after or before a long reading or a live interview. It reminded me of my body, that I wasn't just a floating head, a mind charging through life with its sword of reason.

I put on the green bikini and pulled the dress over it. I regarded myself in the mirror. I pressed my hand against the wrinkles, but there was no getting rid of them. I'd have to get it dry-cleaned. But I liked the way it fell on my body. I admired its straight lines. I thought about how Xavi would encourage me to wear a belt over the dress to accentuate my waist. But he would do it lovingly, tenderly; he was always careful to say that what mattered most was how I felt wearing the dress, that it looked beautiful either way. I missed him intensely for a moment.

I unwrapped the towel from my hair and used it to soak up the water. I'd cut my hair right up to my shoulders. I liked it that way. It was easy to maintain, easy to style if I ever felt like it.

I walked around to the window and listened for a moment to the sound of distant traffic, to the children at play in the park up the road, the frenetic chatter coming from the café patios. I heard a clanking in the distance; it sounded like someone pounding metal. Then I heard the engine of a scooter as it labored up the hill, followed by the harsher, sharper sound of a motorcycle being revved to its limit and a propeller plane flying overhead. Up above, I saw a kite floating in the sky. It was shaped like a bird and flapped about uncontrollably. There was a warm wind coming off the ocean. I reached to close the window, and heard Omar's voice.

"You should never offer to give a blow job," he said.

The air smelled of musk. I was afraid to turn around, afraid he'd walked out of the walls and now was standing behind me, monitoring my every move, asking me to rehearse my words, to use my body in ways that pleased him.

"I thought I was your whore," I said.

"What?" It was Ellie's voice. She was knocking on my door, ready to go.

"Nothing," I said. "I'm ready."

I grabbed the oversize straw purse shaped like a basket that

Xavi had bought for me as a reminder to have fun, to take it easy, to enjoy the beach. I put my towel in it and my sunglasses and notebook, strapped my sandals to my feet, and before I knew it, we were reclining on the cushioned beds under the coconut umbrellas, listening to summer hits, sipping our drinks, watching the waves crash onto the shore and retreat.

## 9

THE SUN HOVERED OVER THE COAST. Our waiter, Salim, was a bronzed muscular man in his thirties. His shirtsleeves were rolled up to expose his large biceps, and he had a bandanna wrapped around his head to keep his curls out of his face, which was covered in stubble; it all served to give him an air of cool indifference. He set a chilled bottle of rosé on a small plastic table between our sun beds then swung impatiently away toward a triumvirate of topless women who were lounging in the front row. They'd arrived already drunk and were now chattering away loudly, pinching one another's nipples.

Ellie opened one eye and turned to me. "Remember Yaakov?"

"Yaakov!" I sighed. "Can I please put the tip in? Just the tip!" I said to Ellie jokingly.

She shook her head and giggled uncomfortably.

She'd spent an evening with Yaakov in our hut by the Dead Sea. That was years ago, back when we still regularly spoke to Sahar, before she'd disappeared from our lives. Yaakov had fallen for Ellie. The second he'd seen her, he'd pulled me aside and told me that he'd dreamt of her the night before, his princess; he couldn't believe that she was standing before him in flesh and bone. The fact of having manifested in life the woman who'd appeared to him in his sleep had left him dumbfounded. He spoke like a child relaying to an adult their first experience of an incredible coincidence: open-mouthed, wide-eyed, forgetting to breathe or swallow, picking expectantly at his nails.

"Please," he begged me. "Tell her that I am her prince."

He must have thought that those words, as charming as they were odd, would somehow be more persuasive if they were delivered by me. What did he expect me to say to her: *Princess Ellie, meet your prince, Yaakov?* I couldn't remember how I'd delivered the message, but I could remember Ellie's face contorting in response, taking on an unsettled expression that revealed her incredulity. She was in her thirties and not once had a man approached her claiming to have dreamt her up the night before. Yaakov's childlike rhetoric and sweet demeanor had piqued her interest enough for her to concede to a make-out session.

"He really begged," Ellie said, winking at the blinding sun. "We were just lying there, making out, and he took his dick out, and whined: 'Can I put the tip in? Can I put the tip in? Just the tip!' He wouldn't stop. It was like his gears had gotten stuck. I thought he'd never say anything else again. Eventually I just got bored and asked him to leave!"

She hadn't found Yaakov to be intimidating. There had been

no hint of aggression in his voice, only desperation, a child's begging.

During our days at the Dead Sea, we'd gone to bed each evening in laughter. We'd spent the days asking each other at every turn if we could dip the tip of this or that into this or that other thing. We were still laughing about it now. We would likely go to our graves laughing about the evening Ellie had spent with Yaakov being harangued about the tip of his penis near the shore of the Dead Sea. Surely, he seemed to suggest, she could kindly step aside while he dipped his penis into her. What did he think? we wondered. That he was merely asking to dunk his croissant into her morning coffee?

A shift of bodies in the front row brought me back to the present. One of the women, the most petite of the three, stood up and checked herself out in her friend's tinted lenses. She smoothed her eyebrows and smiled at herself, then brought her hands to her waist and said something inaudible to Salim. It was hard to hear her voice over the breaking waves.

"What are they doing?" Ellie asked, sitting up and looking straight at Salim, who'd walked over to one of the women. He'd begun to do squats in front of her. He squeezed his biceps and reached down and swiftly lifted her sun bed, tilting her backward.

"Ready?" he asked, pumping his arms. We realized that he was going to wheel her down to the water but first intended to do a hundred squats with her in tow.

Her two friends were giggling wildly, and saying, "Oh, Salim, Salim!" It was as if they were having an orgy.

I poured myself some rosé. "Cheers," I said, lifting my glass. "To all the truly great men in the world, like Xavi."

I lit a cigarette and reclined. In the distance, a flock of birds was gliding down toward the water. I could hear dance music coming from the bars up the coast and, periodically, the sound of a jet ski engine sawing through the water. Nearby, a group of quieter women were getting massaged by two Chinese women in sun hats, striped shirts, and chinos. I wondered who'd established their uniform. Their faces were powder white, ghostly, covered with huge dollops of sunscreen. They were working away at the women's feet, diligently pressing their thumbs into their toes, oiling their calves. One of the masseuses looked up at me and smiled, aware that I'd been observing them. Her smile, I thought, was gorgeous. She was tall, slender, and her eyes revealed a focused intelligence, a sharp wit.

"You next?" she asked.

I nodded yes, and pointed to Ellie to indicate her, too; the woman's smile broadened.

Salim was grinning triumphantly as if he were an actor in a well-rehearsed play. He was still doing his squats. The woman in the sun bed was squinting up at him and smiling coquettishly. She was holding her sun hat down with one hand and her breasts were bouncing around. She was having a grand time, they all were, until he lost his footing. Her arm swung overhead as the bed faltered, knocking their wine bottle onto the ground. Several long, tense seconds elapsed. They all stared at one another, then down at the wine, which was spilling out, staining the sand. I looked at the women, their pursed lips and drawn faces, their stony gazes. Salim's spectacular failure, it seemed, had caused their mood to shift from extreme carelessness to mundane fastidiousness almost immediately. They were distressed over their lost wine, wine they'd paid for, and Salim, aware of their discontent, took care to smile through his embarrassment; he promised them a replacement bottle and left to fetch one before they could make a move to dismiss him.

He soon returned with a fresh bottle of wine for the women. He neglected us. Instead of asking for our order, he evaded us and ran swiftly back into the kitchen. We wanted a platter of grilled fish. I could already feel the wine going to my head. Ellie, I remembered, had woken up hungry; she'd been saving her appetite for the exquisite seafood I'd promised. We called on Salim several times. At first, we asked gently if he wouldn't mind coming around to take our order, then we asked again with a hint of irritation that seemed only to exaggerate his apparent distaste for us.

"In a minute," he snapped, and he disappeared into the back of the restaurant.

The beach was momentarily quiet. In that respite, I thought again of Yaakov and the long weekend we'd spent in the dizzying heat of the Dead Sea. Everything about that weekend had been strange, almost surreal. The landscape had seemed warped to me. There was an inconstant quality to the thick desert air, the silky camel-colored sand, the briny dense water of the Dead

Sea. It all seemed tenuously attached to the earth, on the cusp of disappearing. I remembered wondering if we would vanish with it, if the landscape would peel away from the ground and lift off into the sky while we bathed in that thick bowl of salty water. I had the distinct sensation of having hallucinated the place myself: the dry white earth, the palm trees that shot out of the roads, the brush and bramble on the gray hills, the Dead Sea's unmoving surface—no waves, no wind—the blood-blue oily surface of the water, the white ruffle of salt that skirted the sea, that winked and flashed in the harsh rays of the sun. It had appeared almost surreal to me. The landscape was so ancient, so beautiful, so barren. I had often returned to it in my mind just for the pleasure of revisiting the wide stark sky and the flat salty disk of that sea.

I could still remember Ellie turning to me on the bus on the way there to ask: "Don't you think it's strange that we're traveling to the lowest point on earth just to float?"

We'd taken the bus from Jerusalem in the high-noon heat. The bus, I remembered, was old; its stench of body odor and cheap cologne made me queasy. The engine choked as the driver settled into second gear; he was trying to hold the bus back as he drove it downhill. It was a dizzying drop, as if the bus were spiraling down to the hollowed center of the world. The sun glowed with a blinding golden light; my vision skipped like a rock across the flat surface of the water.

"Maybe," I remembered having said, "it's about a journey to the interior of one's self."

I turned to look at Ellie, but the sun, which was coming through the window as if with a design to blind and dehydrate, obfuscated her features. I saw her eyes—round and unblinking—and her mouth moving, but the rest of her face had atomized.

"Arezu," she said. "Not everything is an allegory."

Her face came back into focus. We were almost at Ein Gedi. We just had to go past the checkpoint to reach the first stop.

"Lots of things feel good," I said to her in protest. "But to come all the way here to float is a strange obsession. People must experience it on a deeper, more metaphysical level, no? An ancient healing ritual?"

Maybe, she'd conceded, people have found it difficult to bear their own weight since time immemorial and have come to the Dead Sea to float and lighten their load a bit. She'd laughed freely, animatedly, as we'd been laughing now, reclined on our sun beds, waiting to eat seafood, to get our feet massaged to the sound of the breaking waves.

Salim finally surfaced. He stood towering over us, sulking. He was in a foul mood. "What do you want?" he asked rudely.

We put in our order, but before he could turn to leave, I asked him what his name was. I already knew the answer because I'd heard him introduce himself to the women—he was half Egyptian, half Austrian, he'd told them, but like me, he had not seen his father, the Austrian, in more than a decade—but I thought we deserved the same courtesy.

"Why do you want to know?" he asked, looking over at the women scuffling about, raising their voices as if the beach were theirs alone, caressing their breasts, throwing their heads back, playing with their loosened hair. All of their movements seemed rehearsed. I told him that I'd overheard him offer his name to the others and that it seemed odd that he'd be so wary of introducing himself to us.

Ellie glanced at me in disbelief then moved her astonished gaze over to him.

"Salim," he said bitterly, taking in Ellie's expectant smile.

The water level appeared to be rising. We were approaching the afternoon and the light was softening. In the waning heat, the wine we were drinking went down more easily. The three women, I observed, were onto their third or fourth bottle.

I told Salim to bring another our way, then there was a moment's pause when we all stared at the women in the front row. Their capacity to draw attention to themselves seemed boundless. They'd flagged down a British man with a potbelly and a white head of hair. They'd dragged their sun beds together and made them into a makeshift bed. He was sitting on the edge, his floral shirt unbuttoned, his belly distended and hanging over his thighs.

"Clifford," he said, introducing himself.

"Oh, Clifford, Clifford!" I joked.

"No," Ellie said, drawing out her words for emphasis. "Get it right: his name is *Clifforis*."

I laughed, and Salim joined in despite his mood. He let out a dry giggle, a little puff of air, and his posture relaxed. The sky was taking on a pinkish hue, and the music we'd heard in the distance grew louder.

"Do you party much?" Ellie asked Salim, observing that there didn't seem to be much else to do here but tan, drink, and dance until dawn.

"Sometimes," he said. "It depends on how long my shifts are."

I took advantage of this moment of earnestness to ask him why we put him in such a dark mood when the other women seemed to do exactly the opposite.

"I can tell you're from the Middle East," he said, turning to glance at his former playmates, who were now busily pawing at Clifford's hair. Salim laughed sourly. "You see that?" he asked. "He's going to pay to get them drunk because he thinks at least one of them will go to bed with him, but at the end of the day, he'll end up at the club alone, sticking euros in a stripper's underwear. I see this kind of thing all of the time."

He seemed blissfully unaware of the fact that a moment earlier he'd been in Clifford's position, humiliating himself in exchange for whatever might be left over at the end of a long day's drinking. The women were having fun. That was clear. And there were three of them. They seemed to know their own limits; they were watching out for one another. I never once got the feeling that they were in danger. They were looking for a distraction, for a wild weekend, a fling; and they had every right to. They had every right to drink themselves under the table, every right to go looking for an easy lay without having to worry about who might take advantage of them. If I had a bone to pick, it was with Salim, not because he'd been so easily persuaded by the women or because he'd recognized in them a desire he was more than willing to fulfill even if in doing so he had to act the part of a clown. No, he'd projected waves of animosity at us for precisely the reason that I'd suspected: because we were from the Middle East like he was, and our common codes of behavior required us to be, at least in public, extremely reserved with one another. We —Ellie and I—were required to be chaste, virtuous, to differentiate ourselves from the supposedly licentious vixens of the West even if to their men we were exotic goods, commodities who showed no restraint in bed. This strange paradox demolished us all, dispossessed us of our sexuality, our ability to give and receive pleasure. We were always worried about seeming too free, seeming too invested in ourselves, too unguarded, loose, disposable; to do so would be to invite danger into our lives, a danger the consequences of which we deserved. Any exhibition of sexual pleasure on our part was an opening for men to treat us with disrespect. That's what Salim had been taught, and that, too, was how Ellie and I had been raised.

Ellie asked Salim if he'd moved to Marbella after the Arab Spring had erupted in Egypt; he said he worked the season on the coast from May to September then returned to Cairo for the rest of the year.

He'd grown animated again, gesticulating fiercely as he railed against the Egyptian government and the conduct of the Egyptians themselves. He was shaking his head vigorously; we understood from his reaction that he was well-aware that his flirtation with the topless women was a way of reclaiming some of the power he'd been disabused of as a brown man from the Middle East. And we, it seemed—Ellie and I—with our notebooks and reading glasses and our more reserved body language (arms by our sides, feet close together), our formal way of engaging a stranger, had been a wrench in Salim's day. He was not free, he told us, to consume and be consumed without guilt while we were there watching him.

I told him that I thought he had a point. "But that's exactly the issue here, don't you think? That you can channel your sexual energy toward them more freely than you can toward us?" It sounded as though I was envious of his attention, but I was more than willing to imply as much in order to advance the conversation.

The circles under Salim's eyes darkened. Clifford was still sitting with the women, letting them have their way with him. They'd taken his shirt off and wrapped it like a turban around his head. I heard one of them say, "You only have a few hairs left. Your scalp will burn, Clifford!"

There was a great deal of whispering in his ear. He was nodding along, smiling, his eyes electric, his loins likely swollen.

"Well, ladies," he said, and got up to leave. They agreed to meet at such-and-such bar once the night had matured, and they blew kisses at him as he walked up the beach.

"What do you think of what I said, Salim?" I asked, turning to look at him.

"You know how we've been raised," he said. "I can't be free with you; I am not free"—and here he paused as if searching for the right word—"to misbehave."

"Right," I said, considering his words. It seemed that Salim could not express his sexual desire freely with us, nor could he expect us to express our sexual desire freely with him—or anyone else, for that matter—at least not as freely as the white women, which was, I thought, a dangerous line of thought that left us all open to being treated like a heap of meat: the white women for being regarded as wanting sexual objects and us for being stripped of our sexual agency. It was all terribly imbalanced and insulting.

His belief system was so flawed, it was insulting even to him; it implied that his misguided advances were an attempt to avoid shame, the shame he anticipated being subjected to were he to make an inappropriate remark to one of us. Paradoxically, it was his inability to negotiate shame that might cause him, or another man like him, to charge at women like us behind closed doors, to pounce on us with his sexual energy when there was no one there to judge. Did he not think we were human? People with agency, needs, desires, and wants of our own? People with a right to like or dislike? Were we always, in his view, on the receiving end? Is that where he thought we belonged?

I felt terrible. I couldn't help but think that on this occasion the women in the front row had protected us; they had, unbeknownst to them, acted as a buffer between us and Salim, us and the likes of Clifford. In an effort to avoid feeling shame, we had all subconsciously agreed to a set of transactional interactions that left us vulnerable to violence, to finding ourselves quite suddenly, and without knowledge of how it was we'd arrived there, in a situation that could spiral quickly out of control. By damming yourself up, by acting out of shame, you're only ensuring that the eventual explosion will be all the more dangerous.

I felt a sharp pain in my chest, a pain that left me restless, eager to spring to my feet, to walk into the water. My skin was burning; I hadn't worn any sunscreen.

Ellie was taking in the even beat of the crashing waves, the purring and gurgling noise of the sea as it tenderly combed its sand and stones. She leaned her head back, drew in a deep breath, and closed her eyes.

"I'm so ready for that platter," she said with a neutral tone designed to conceal her disappointment. Our collective mood had plummeted, and there wasn't much Ellie or Salim or I could add that would restore our spirits.

He left to go put in our order; no sooner had he gone than Ellie reached into her bag for the papers she had to grade. I was parched. My lips ached. I thought again of the briny bowl of the Dead Sea.

I got up and walked to the water. I waded in. It was salty, warm, and burned and tickled my bronzed skin. A few seagulls dashed through the sky, and caught a gust of air, and glided inland again. I dipped my head underwater and let the sea wash over me. I thought of my mother. I wondered what it was she was escaping from in marrying my father. Her mother had refused to speak to her for a year for marrying a European man, a man who was not Iranian, who could not understand the family customs, manners, traditions. Had she been rejecting her identity? Had she married him as a means for leaving Iran during the revolution? For a moment, I had the strange sensation of swimming in a lake of blood. I heard my mother's voice, heard it sink into that sea of blood. She was calling me to her. *Your body,* she kept saying, *was my home. Why did you leave me? My heart is filled with fear at the thought of never seeing you again.* I came up for air. The sky was pale. A single seagull dove into the water; its beady eyes had a razor-sharp focus. I watched it break the surface of the water and reemerge with its prey. I remembered how the birds had looked like missiles as they'd flown across the checkpoint at Ein Gedi, how the land of Israel and Palestine, in all of its variations, had drifted across my mind as I'd watched those birds dash across the desert.

"The Judean Desert," I mumbled to myself.

Palestine? Israel? A land without a people for a people without a land? What a strange and false saying! I listed the names of the territories as I'd listed them during that bus ride to the Dead Sea, as Ellie and Sahar had listed them as they'd drawn maps of Israel and Palestine under the dim light of the kitchen in our home in Amherst so many years ago.

"The Upper Galilee, Haifa, the Negev," I said, splashing water on my face.

My voice caught in my throat. I thought about the Jordan River emptying out into the Dead Sea. Then I remembered that there were, in fact, three Dead Seas: the half that belongs to Jordan, and the remaining half divided again—one portion of its deadness to the West Bank and the remainder to Israel. The landscape is always forced to bear our wounds. We purge it of certain people while we populate it with others; we draw artificial lines to protect ourselves from our supposed predators; we spend our lives policing those boundaries, going to war for them.

When we'd arrived in Ein Gedi, a soldier wearing a bulletproof vest, his hand casually coiled around his gun barrel, had walked down the aisle of the bus examining our passports and belongings. He was the paradigm of manhood, the perfect representation of the health and vigor of the state. We were close to the water. We could see the white sand of the sea sparkling like diamonds through the windows. A curtain of mist hovered above the water, and the Jordanian mountains looked pink through the vaporous air.

The soldier returned our passports to us without saying a word. As American citizens, we benefited from unrestricted mobility while Palestinians, who were born and raised on this land, were trapped without citizenship in a few arid square miles. "Maybe," Ellie said, tracing the soldier's gun with her eyes, "this is why they called it the Sea of Death."

The sky was yellow; it was bright. The Sea of Death, I thought, a sea separated from its source water in the Jordan River—dams had been built, irrigation projects initiated—a sea in a desert, exposed to constant heat that sucked up the water and churned it into vapor. The heat was so intense, it had compromised our senses. We'd spent hours languishing by the sea, floating on the water, talking about the ways in which the gaps in the story of the land had wrenched the gaps within us open still more, about how so often the gaps between external narratives of race and gender and nationhood and our private sense of self are unaccounted for.

That, I considered, turning on my back and floating on the water, staring at the diminishing sun, drowning out the frenetic chatter on the beach, the chatter of the women in the front row who grew rowdier by the second, is what I was trying to do. I was trying to account for the gap between the narratives that I, as a survivor of rape, was asked to perform and the reality of my experience, which was forever in the process of morphing, full of contradictory feelings that I had learned were best kept to myself.

Except with Ellie. Ellie, who understood the pain of knowing that our bodies had experienced pleasure even in the midst of undeniable violence. As if our bodies did not belong to us, as if they were divorced from our psyches, our consciousness. How else could we feel physical pleasure while being psychically annihilated? We had desired our own deaths. Ellie could barely stand being in Israel, and she had dealt with her feelings by running headlong into a toxic relationship with an abusive man. She had felt the power of the unacknowledged violence in Israel and Palestine, the violence that was invisible in Israel as it raged on against the Palestinians who were continually invaded and dispossessed of their homes. She had wanted a physical manifestation of the violence; she had wanted to engage in an activity that would cause her pain that she could account for, a pain with a concrete source. Sleeping with her boyfriend and all of his friends had been, she'd said to me, the equivalent of cutting oneself in response to a traumatic event that is not being acknowledged by the community in meaningful ways. Those runaway years had led to years of insomnia. She complained of feeling trapped and alone in a culture that had experienced extreme torture, that was now engaging in the destruction of an innocent people as a way of purging themselves of their inherited pain. Even after she found the strength to leave her boyfriend, she hadn't returned home. She'd fallen in love with a Palestinian woman and moved in with her. Which is to say she'd been to the other side, where children waited with folded arms and legs under the burning sun. Where the water ran dry. Where the olive trees shrank. Where bodies withered. Where infrastructure—roads, electricity, water—were built for Israeli settlers while being denied to the Palestinians. There were the shelled-out buildings, the black water tanks on the roofs, the burning piles of garbage, the bullet holes in the walls of houses. All of the things that continued to unfold on the other side of the separation wall.

Months later, when she finally saw her parents again, they called her a traitor. "Once a traitor, always a traitor," they said. She had been shunned. They had sent her back to America. They'd been afraid of the judgment of the Orthodox community to which they belonged. And yet, after years of living in Israel against her will, Ellie had been transformed by it; she no longer belonged squarely in America either. She was lost and alone; she was left without guidance, without anyone to speak with in Hebrew.

We had both experienced the bitter pain of exile, of being banished by the people we loved, from the nurturing nest of our native language. Where does a story begin? I wondered. What are a story's origins? Because the more I considered the arc of my life, the more I had to contend with the glaring truth that my story with Omar had begun long before I'd met him. I had been primed—through my culture, my family dynamics, my own unbending character—to fall prey to him, to believe that I'd been the one to seek him out. I needed to believe that in order to persist, in order to live. I needed to believe that I'd had some agency in the matter however minor that agency had been in comparison to his. After all, I didn't feel I could heal without acknowledging that I had participated in my oppression by giving him permission to be my oppressor. I needed to account for the fact that I had taken steps toward him myself even if I'd misjudged what it was that I was stepping toward. I'd underestimated his capacity to outinjure me.

I turned and dove under the water. I kept my eyes open. There wasn't a fish in sight. The water was nebulous, gray in bits, green in patches. It was composed of a range of hues melting and blending together just like in the sky. I could still hold my breath underwater for the better part of a minute. I came up for air. I kept my back to Ellie, the women in the front row, Salim, the whole lot of them. I looked out at the horizon. The water stretched out as far as the eye could see. I thought of my father as a young man at sea. What a lonely life my father had led. What a troubled life. I felt my body grow soft under the weight of that thought.

What was I doing there? I suddenly wondered. What had I been doing here? The sand hollowed out beneath my feet. I heard Ellie calling after me. I turned to look for her. She was standing ankle deep in the water, her hands on her hips.

"Food's here," she said.

I felt the water rush off my limbs as I emerged from the sea.

Salim was bringing us two glasses, another bottle of wine, a bottle of water, some napkins.

I felt as though I were floating—up, up—as if all of the heaviness within me had sunk down like an anchor. I was drunk. I was hungry and thirsty and craving a cigarette. I saw the masseuses come out from behind the wall. I wanted to rush toward them. I wanted someone to rub my feet, to massage my legs, to push their hands into the nape of my neck. But the women in the front row beat me to it. They ran across the beach to them and grabbed them by the hands. The masseuses were laughing, laughing wholeheartedly. The women dragged them to their beds, forced them to lie down. They took their shoes off and started to massage their feet, their scalps, their hands. I laughed, too. We all laughed. It was the most delightful thing I'd seen them do. I sat down next to Ellie and we ate our hearts out.

"Look at this squid," Ellie exclaimed.

The masseuses were laughing. They were rolling on their

backs, bringing their hands to their faces in disbelief. They lingered for a short while, enjoying the view alongside us. There we were, each of us misunderstood in her own way, watching the sun go down together.

"And the octopus," I said, lifting one up by its maroon tentacle and dangling it in the air.

Ellie grunted with pleasure. "Orgasmic!" she said.

And it was. It was the best thing I had ever tasted. In the distance, the seagulls cawed. They were eyeing our plates, their squeals overlapping, calling, "Go, go, go!" I watched the sun dip beneath the horizon. A shimmering copper blaze emerged from the sea. From that heaving pit of darkness, a golden tunnel of light shot up toward the heavens; I stared at it for so long that I forgot myself.

## 10

WHEN WE GOT BACK FROM THE BEACH, the apartment was pitch black. Its mute walls towered over us in the darkness. The lines and angles of the floors, the curve of the sofa, the seams in the tiles, it all appeared ominous to Ellie and me. We had arrived full and drunk and pleased with our day, pleased with what the day had revealed to us, only to find ourselves in an apartment prepared to pounce. I wondered if the apartment was rejecting us, punishing us for having taken a cloth to its dust, having rubbed its surfaces raw with vinegar. Ellie leaned against my arm. We were standing in the foyer, trying switch after switch.

"It hadn't occurred to me until now," she said, pulling like a child at the hem of my dress, "that it was strange for the electricity to have been on when no one's been here for twenty years."

I made my way cautiously across the living room, Ellie in tow, and opened the shutters. The silver glow of the moon spilled in; it leaked through the curtains and reflected off the polished floors, giving us enough light to see by. I felt a hand at my back. It was Ellie's, but for a moment, I feared it was Omar pushing me into the halo of moonlight so he could regard me from behind, examine my adult body for the curves of my youth. My legs went stiff, my arms numb. My heart beat furiously. It sounded to my ears like a galloping horse treading a cracked thirsty earth; I heard a *thud-thud, thud-thud thud-thud* across that barren land.

"Arezu," Ellie whispered, placing her hand tenderly between my shoulders. "Arezu, maybe we should get out of here." We had four days left in our trip.

She had a point. Standing in the feeble moonlight that had pooled at my feet, I felt stripped of understanding, stupid—a silly, wayward girl with no control over the hours of her life. What had I been thinking? That overcoming who I'd been was as simple as returning to this apartment? That word—*overcome* —I turned it over in my mouth and thought, What a laughable word. I said it to myself with derision—*overcome.* What did I think, that I could lift myself out of my own wretchedness, the murky, war-torn, blood-soaked landscapes that had made and unmade me? I wanted to laugh, to laugh like I'd laughed all day, to laugh at how stupid it all was. How false it all felt. How utterly ridiculous my life had been. I looked at the spilled moonlight that was spreading across the floors, following me from room to room like quicksilver. This apartment, I concluded, is diseased, irremediably savage, attached to its darkness, to its psychological games. How had I ever survived a summer alone in this place? I heard the sound of my own strained breathing as Omar closed his hand around my neck. While I'd been lost in the fantasy of love, of pleasure, he had almost killed me.

Ellie's voice came at me from behind. "Didn't we buy candles at the euro mart?"

"Yeah, we did," I said, weakly pushing my thoughts aside. There was a part of me that wanted to give in to that darkness, to crouch down and let it rule me. I was exhausted from the struggle, the daily strain of staying alive. Ellie tugged at my arm and I floated through the apartment alongside her. "Those candles," she kept saying, willing them to appear before us.

We walked down the corridor, an interminable hallway, its walls seemingly capable of compressing our bodies between their cold stones. I felt my heart harden, felt the walls grind it down. We made our way to her room.

"They're in here somewhere," she said, and stepped carefully around her scattered belongings toward the window, then opened the shutters to let in the light.

The arabesque windows of the old city, lit up like little fires, were visible in the distance. I could see the gigantic frames of the trees leaning their shadows against the solitary hill. I could hear the tender laughter of the children who had spilled onto the street to play while their parents took a stroll. Farther away, there was the sound of gypsy music, a guttural cry accompanied by the soft strokes of a guitar. It sounded primordial, as though it were coming from a buried heart, a fierce heart that had been treated gravely but that recognized pain as the first intimations of joy.

"Do you smell that?" I asked Ellie, who was still searching through her bags.

"It's amazing," she said.

The night air was punctuated by the smell of jasmine, frankincense, basil, tobacco, bergamot. It smelled lush and sweet, so perfectly unlike the apartment's stench of mold and rust and rot. The evening air was calling us away from the apartment to greener pastures, somewhere we could lie together in safety and listen to the quiet susurrus of the universe. The breeze, as it traveled down from the mountains toward the sea, was stirring an awakening in us. "Get away from here," it seemed to say.

"Aha!" Ellie said, and lifted a candle out of a plastic bag, holding it between us like a sword. "I found it." She was pleased with herself.

I didn't have my lighter on me. I'd left it in my bag by the door. As we retraced our footsteps through the house, I felt a shift come on: a latent anger stirred in my heart, an anger that set my limbs on fire, my limbs, which had felt so heavy and immobile just a moment ago. I recognized the feeling. It was an anger that I reserved exclusively for my father. I had barely spoken to him since that summer long ago. But we had communicated recently about the apartment in Marbella, a brief, formal exchange. He'd promised that he'd paid someone to reconnect the water and electricity. He was always quick to pay someone to take care of his chores. It was the one favor I'd asked of him in years. The keys and the deed he'd mailed to me without a card or a note, without any hint of sorrow. I'd asked him more than once to make sure there was light, make sure there was water. And he'd promised he would. He'd said to himself, *Let there be light when she arrives to that reckless pit of her painful past*, then he'd washed his hands clean of it all by gifting me this wreck of a place, a place that I had no money to fix up or maintain, a place I would never again inhabit. No, not for long. The apartment, he had known, was a burden. A wound passed from hand to hand. A scar no one knew what to do with. And yet here I was, trying to come to grips with life in this apartment that rejected it, that resisted even the electricity coursing through its walls. *The lights have gone out. The lights have gone out*, I kept saying to myself, astonished at how alive those walls were, how overpowering.

The moon rose higher in the sky and more light leaked into the living room. I again considered the possibility that my father had paid Omar to run his errands. My father, Omar's patron. Perhaps the man on the motorcycle that first evening had been Omar after all. I listened carefully for the sound of its engine revving but heard only the sweet song of the children and the gypsy music gliding in through the windows. For a brief moment, I was thankful that the rear half of the apartment was veiled in darkness. I wanted to hide in the penumbra, in the shadows; I wanted to conceal my grief even from myself.

I searched for my lighter and found it. Ellie leaned the wick of the candle toward me. I lit it and its small flame oscillated in the breeze that was circulating through the apartment. I retrieved the candleholder that I'd bought from Rosario's son. We set the candleholder on the coffee table and collapsed onto the sofa. We were exhausted from the sun, from the conversation we'd had with Salim, from all the wine we'd drunk. I was drained from the ancient hold the apartment had on me. I wondered again if Omar had been the one to reconnect the utilities, if my father had told him that I'd be arriving soon. Assuming, I reconsidered, that he was still alive.

I thought again of those bloodied rags. It occurred to me that the blood could have belonged to Omar. Had he tried to kill himself? The idea of his death—of this spinning earth no longer containing his human form—had crossed my mind in a tangible way only once before, when I'd heard about his accident, the accident that had nearly killed him. I'd felt aggrieved and relieved by the news, quarreling sensations that were quickly followed by an antiseptic wave of numbness. He'd lost control of his motorcycle on the highway. It had skidded out from under him and dragged him across three lanes of traffic. His leg was pinned under the weight of the motorcycle as it sailed across the hot tarmac. Cars and trucks swerved to avoid him. He was lucky. He'd kept his life but had lost his skin in the process. The road had shredded the skin right off his body. It had peeled him raw. It had left his musculature seared, uncovered, and exposed. He was in danger of contracting an infection for months. He was hospitalized for a long time. He'd spent weeks screaming for help, had felt as though he were caught in an interminable fire, a fire that had the capacity to burn him without turning him to ash, without melting the flesh off his bones. He was alive, trapped in a scalding body that stung without relief. He'd lived that way for months. My heart, I'd told Ellie, had ached for months once the initial shock of hearing the news had passed. "How come?" she had asked me. Because I could feel his pain, I told her, because it was the same pain he'd inflicted on me. We'd both been left raw and unprotected; what he had done unto me, he'd also done unto himself.

I'd told her before, and was telling her again now, that after Omar I'd felt dispossessed of my life, as if my life, the very energy that coursed through my body, no longer belonged to me. Perhaps it never had. That lesson had been drilled into me early and often so by the time I was a young woman—my breasts growing, my hips widening for the birthing of children, my thighs filling out, becoming lean and muscular—I fully believed that I existed for the taking, an edible woman with an expiration date. I told her that until the moment I'd heard the news—delivered to me by my stepmother in an email, a bitter and accusatory email that suggested that I'd brought the accident onto him through the ill feelings I harbored toward him, through my *evil eye*, she'd written—until that moment, I'd felt as though I were completely alone, left to spend the rest of my life uncovering the stratified layers of his crime while he walked away without consequence. That accident, I told her, became, in my mind, the end of our physical story together. The consequences of our enmeshment were captured in that image: me, raw, hollowed out, and him with his skin scraped off, denuded.

But he'd recovered. He'd come back from the dead. I told Ellie that being here, in the apartment, walking the same streets I'd walked with him, surrounded by the mountains he'd taken me to, I'd realized that in some ways I was more afraid of him dying than I was of seeing him alive.

"Who's to say he won't appear at my back wherever I go, wherever I happen to be once he's been liberated from his body?" I said. His ghost could hover over me undetected, could torture me without consequences; there would be no tangible evidence of his ability to manipulate and distort me from beyond the grave just as I had no physical wounds—no scars that were visible to the naked eye—to prove that I'd been raped. His fantasy, I told Ellie, would once again be my demise.

"It's just a feeling," she said.

"A feeling that stings," I said. "But that, too, shall pass."

I told her that I considered myself lucky that my relationship with Omar was not the only violent event I'd lived through or witnessed. The scope of my pain was far greater than my relationship with Omar; and that, I realized, was a kindness on the part of the world. There had been other chapters; other hands had penned the lines of suffering in my book. And what that meant was that, while there were moments when I wanted to annihilate myself because of the shame and repulsion he'd made me feel, I would never hurt myself; I'd already encountered, and would encounter again, life's vindictive nature. The evil this world harvests had come to seem normal to me, par for the course, part of everyday life. That knowledge had hardened me, yes, had removed me from myself for many years, a rift I would always be negotiating, but it had also made me resilient. It had awoken me to the full power of love, the expansiveness and radiance I'd cultivated with my queer family, my chosen people; with Ellie, with Sam, and briefly with Sahar, I felt like a peaceful warrior. We grieved and laughed together. We restored our lives in one another's company. We built ground under our feet and put roofs over our heads; our individual homes were always shared.

A long interval of silence passed. Ellie and I listened to the gypsy music.

"It's beautiful," she finally said. "It's so full of grief and pleasure. It's the bravest music I've ever heard."

It was. I told her that it was the most complete music, the song of the heart, of the flesh and the earth. I thought of Lorca's gypsy ballads, of the lines I'd memorized. I recited a few verses and Ellie listened with her eyes closed. I felt so much stronger. I felt held by those words, nurtured by the forward moving energy of those lines.

Ellie rubbed aloe into her skin. "I must be so red," she said. Her voice was calm, tender. She, too, had breathed in those words. She'd devoured them and was happy now, satiated.

I picked up the candleholder and scanned her body in its light. "You are!" I helped her put the aloe on her back.

I went into the bathroom, soaked a few towels in the tub, and brought them over for her to lay on her skin. After that, I smoked a cigarette.

"Are you going to reconnect the electricity?" she asked.

"No," I said.

I told her that I didn't want to give any more than I already had to this place.

"So we're going to live in darkness, by candlelight?" Ellie asked, her voice trembling. "How am I going to finish grading?" I'd forgotten about the papers she'd lugged with her from Oxford.

"I'll find us a place," I said, "in Granada."

I felt something stir in me, a voice, an intuition, that seemed to say, *Get away from here before it's too late. There's nothing more to see. Take who you used to be far, far away from here.* I told her that there was one last thing I needed to do, to go to Puerto Banús where my story with Omar had begun, where I suspected, if he was still alive, he'd be. I needed to know that I was stronger than those streets where we'd first kissed. I told her I would go there in the morning, that we would spend one last night here and take off the next day, that we would get out of here.

"One more night after this," I said. "And then we'll go to the heart of that music, to the caves in the hills of Granada." I got up and went to bed. I lay there for a long time staring emptily at the ceiling. I was hot. My skin was damp. The moon was hovering in the sky, yolk colored. I saw Omar standing before me. A mildewy yellow light spilled through the window. I felt my breath catch in my throat. He was mumbling something.

"You are a ghost," I said to him.

I drew the covers over my face, but I could hear him breathing, struggling, and I understood that he was trying to confess something to me. The line between memory and madness is razor-thin. What's the difference, I thought, between a recon-struction and a hallucination? I couldn't make out what he was trying to say. I heard sirens blasting in the distance. I pulled the cover off my face. Broad shafts of light were coming through the window. A searchlight. There were helicopters chopping the sky overhead.

"I want you naked as the day you were born," I heard. There was a violence in his voice I hadn't heard before. As if he were holding a knife out of view, a knife he was prepared to nick me with, that had been there all along though I hadn't seen it. "Now," he said.

I stripped off my clothes. I was weak, confused. We'd been so tender with each other until then. He got down on his knees and pulled my underwear off.

"Lift your legs," he commanded, and I lifted them one at a time.

He slipped my underwear off and walked me to the bath-room. He had me put one leg up on the edge of the tub, the same tub where that poor wild boar had cried with its squealing tones. He shaved me completely on one side then had me turn around and put my opposite leg on the edge of the tub. He shaved the other half of my vagina then kissed the surface and grunted with pleasure.

"That's how I like it," he said. Then he laid me down on the bed.

That I'd merely been compliant, and in no way participatory, had not dissuaded him. I don't remember what happened after that. All I see is darkness. A black square exists where the memory of the rape should be. A black impenetrable square. But I do remember coming to after he was finished. I was lying there, on my side, in the fetal position, limp and lifeless, watching the curtains float in and out of the window in the breeze.

That had been the first time we'd had sex. A month into what I had considered to be our relationship. Once that terrible day had passed, sex became normal, just as it had become normal to hang around the deserted lakes, to eat at odd hours in the loneliest of Chinese restaurants, to search together for distant beaches hardly anyone ever went to. I had gone back for more. We'd had sex almost daily after that. He would tell me what to do and I would do it. My relationship with Omar was a lesson in obedience. And I felt pleasure; I felt a pleasure that was born in pain. The violent event, I had come to learn, becomes a non-event through repetition.

The night felt interminable. I felt pinned to the bed as if a wild animal—that wild boar—were sitting on my chest, forbidding me to move. I had to get through the night. I had to bear the weight of my own past. No one else could hold this story for me. Not my mother, not my father, not Omar.

Dawn broke. I had lain awake the whole night, chain-smoking, drinking water, getting up to pee. The sirens waned. Omar was gone. The apartment was silent. Ellie was still asleep. I got up. In the light of morning, I could see that we'd done a good job cleaning the place, that we had, if nothing else, removed the stale dust. In the limpid light of morning, I could see that the candles we'd lit were a radical act of defiance against the darkness of the apartment. We'd relit the flame of my life. We'd created warmth where the arctic chill of death reigned supreme. There was no going back.

## 11

THE DAY TURNED OUT TO BE OVERCAST. I rushed through the gray streets early in the morning. I walked past women with narrow eyes sunken into yellowed skin, past young girls in bright dresses and expressions of tragic boredom, older men with faces as lined as the sharply angled streets of the city, streets laid in rough slabs of stone. I felt as though the city's houses, squatting side by side, their stunted, square facades overlooking the passersby, were leaning over me, ready to come crashing down at any moment.

At the bus stop, I bought a ticket to Puerto Banús from the driver, a man with eyes that bulged out of their sockets, a man possessed by a forbidding, indisposed air. I stood in the back of the bus where the crowd was thickest. The air on the bus was heavy with the smell of salt and body odor, and I struggled to move each time the crowd parted to let another passenger through. I felt nauseated.

The bus made its way down a gently sloped street and picked

up speed as it left town. The buildings grew more severe, practical and unadorned, at the edges of town. There was a long interlude of silence on the bus as we were transported along the highway, a flat two-lane road carved into the arid hillside punctuated with cacti, a lone aloe, the pale curved trunks of palm trees, which looked to me like the fingers of corpses pointing at the ashen sky above. I felt light-headed. I was in a strange state of mind, hungover from lack of sleep and strung out with anxiety at the thought of returning to Puerto Banús. I knew I would find him there, not necessarily in flesh and blood, but I would be able to sense him lurking about or see his apparition as I had so many times before; yes, I would see him, feel him, smell his skin moist with sweat as it had been on that interminable evening we'd spent dancing and drinking vodka. I could hardly believe that twenty years had passed. I could hear my blood roaring, my heart pulsing in my ears, as if I were deaf to all sounds beyond my own: my organs working, my heart receiving and pumping blood, my skin holding my tissues and bones and ligaments together.

I hated that feeling, the old feeling of terror washing over me. To distract myself, I looked between the passengers' pressed bodies at the road. We exited the highway and made a few turns; the bus leaned to one side, then the other. We went past an El Corte Inglés. I gazed at the rectangular concrete building; its austere facade was adorned only with the refined green sign hanging over the door. I remembered shopping at an El Corte Inglés in another Spanish town as a child, my mother holding me by the hand and leading me down the long corridors of clothes. That's where we'd lived during my childhood years in the aftermath of the Iranian Revolution. Spain had been—through chance and the random assaults of history—our temporary home. And what a strange, liminal space it had turned out to be, I thought, on the margins of Europe, its Arab and Sephardic roots still so visible in the present day; it was, will always be, a contested space I couldn't leave behind. Spain haunts me, just as Omar does; it shows up in my dreams, tortures me with false pangs of nostalgia. My mother. Forced to care for us in foreign lands! I remembered how soft her hand was, how lovingly she'd held mine. I remembered her stopping at a wooden table to admire a stack of neatly folded sweaters.

"What if we got matching ones? A mother-daughter set!" she'd exclaimed enthusiastically.

She'd been a devoted mother. I wondered if in that moment she'd had any premonitions about how our lives would turn out: my brother's attack, our moves around the world, my adolescence marked by all manner of violence. She'd done her best, I thought, which was a lot given my father's negligence, his laissez-faire attitude. I missed her deeply. I wished for nothing more than to put my head in her lap and weep, to feel her warm breath on my cheek as she stroked my hair. She'd sensed I was in danger even when I'd fled home, living as if in a fugue state far from her gaze; her gaze had seemed so oppressive then, but in truth, it stemmed from a kind of punitive vigilance for which, I considered, she could hardly be blamed. She was punishing herself, and me by extension, for not having been able to protect my brother.

I felt my anxiety give way to a deep, aching sadness. The bus came to an abrupt stop. I immediately recognized the port, its restaurants and bars and nightclubs, the roundabout that led to the walkway along the docks where people moored their yachts. I made my way off the bus with the rest of the passengers in single file, our heads lowered, all of us watching our step with what seemed to me a funereal air. I saw Omar in my mind's eye lazily leaning against his silver motorcycle at the curb, his head tilted back, his mouth open to reveal his teeth, the light shining off his peppered hair. I was so sure he would be there, but when I got off the bus and breathed in the fresh maritime air, all I saw were two teenage girls taking selfies, pressing their faces together, pursing their lips as if they were blowing kisses at the camera. Their cheeks were full of color and their eyes shone with an attitude of joy. I smiled at them and wished Ellie had come along with me.

I stood there on the curb and watched the girls shift their postures before the camera. They leaned back-to-back and crossed their arms. They looked at the camera with a hardened gaze. When they were done, they giggled and admired themselves in the shiny screen of their phones.

As I made my way toward the port, across the road and past the roundabout, I realized that there were no images of me from the summer I'd spent here. No photographs. No evidence. I had no way to prove what had happened. I was a ghost in my own past. I had only the memories I'd stored away, but they increasingly came to me like old paper left too long in an orphaned desk, yellowed at the edges, ink smudged. It had been twenty years since that summer; twenty years had passed before I'd been able to confront what had been done to me, before I could sink into my own guilt and shame, my sense of complicity. Who would believe me now? I'd researched the law. There was nothing I could do. The statute of limitations had passed, and the law in Spain, a law largely developed in the dark shadows of Catholicism, was not on the side of any victim of sexual abuse. I looked at all of the teenage girls as I walked toward the port, their cut shorts and cropped tops and white sneakers. The tides of fashion had turned backward, and these girls looked just like I had two decades before. I wondered if they had parents or guardians who spoke to them frankly, plainly, calmly about their rights.

At least they had each other. What had I been doing walking around this place all alone at such a tender age? I felt as though I'd been punched in the gut. I began to recoil from the vast gulf that separated me from who I'd been as a teenager. I looked around, and in my mind's eye I saw myself walking down the port in my Dr. Martens and my jean shorts, my sunglasses on, a T-shirt pulled over my two-piece purple Speedo, my thin, tanned body. And there was Omar, tall, elegant, extraordinarily fit, towering over me as we weaved in and out of the bars. I wondered what had happened to my boots. I wished for a moment that Ellie had found them in the dusty cabinets of the apartment. I would have had them resoled. I would have walked in them again. I wanted so desperately to bridge the gap between who I had been then and who I had become. I wanted to seal the chasm. I wanted to take the girl I had been away from this place for good. But the process of doing so was terrible, so deeply terrifying, that it required an all-consuming bravery. I was exhausted most of the time, and yet I knew that I had to fan the flames of my courage if I was going to cross that twenty-year ravine.

I walked to the edge of the jetty and stared at the oily waves lapping gently against the hulls of the moored yachts. The water was opaque, and yet I could see through its teal surface to the murky shapes of the carp swimming about, gurgling the water in their whiskered mouths. There were Ferraris and Lamborghinis parked on the jetty. I could hear techno music booming in the distance, coming up through the ground. There was money spilling down from the sky. Everywhere I turned there was flesh on display. It was a place that promoted addiction and all of the promises of relief that come with it.

I wondered for a moment what it would be like to disappear again into this world. How easy it would be for me to walk on board one of these yachts and blend in, to have my glass filled by a suitor, to lean my head against another woman's breasts for the pleasure of others. I could spend the afternoon popping olives into my mouth and getting stroked by the rich hands of strangers. I wanted a coffee, a glass of water, but I hesitated to walk into one of the bars; I didn't want to speak to anyone or have to excuse myself, weave my way through the velvet patio furniture draped with lovers. There were people moving down the jetty in droves, stopping here and there to take pictures. I thought again about how I didn't have any photographs of my time with Omar. About how I didn't have any tangible evidence that our lives had ever collided. I heard the loud giggle of a group of adolescent girls and searched for them in the crowd. They were sitting on the jetty with their legs dangling over the water, their blond hair slick with sunlight, their faces hidden behind oversize glasses. They looked happy.

The closer I came to the edge of the jetty, the closer I felt to the adolescent I had been. I felt as though my Lorca books, my Dr. Martens, my cut jeans, my trinkets were with me still. I felt as though they were floating around me, as if they'd dissolved into the air of Marbella, their essence absorbed in the particles I was breathing that were blowing down from the mountains toward the sea. Here I was, I thought, in this strange environment, trying to recover a time in my life without any concrete leads, unaware if Omar was dead or alive.

I sat down on one of the rocks. I could see Morocco and the Strait of Gibraltar in the distance. How remote those lands seemed! I could feel some understanding sliding into place, a memory rising in me, a freeze-frame that had, for years, remained static. I saw myself standing with Omar under a blistering, unforgiving sun amid an endless sea of dunes. I had no idea where we were. Even as I looked back at the image, with all the perspective of time and age, I couldn't see beyond the frame that my mind had cast around the event. I saw dune after dune after dune and the hot sun setting the golden granules of sand aflame.

Omar was standing near his Ducati. His helmet was at his feet. He was restless, agitated, ill at ease. I remembered wondering for one single moment, a moment that had severed me from myself, if he was planning on murdering me. There wasn't another person in sight.

"What are we doing here?" I'd asked him, my voice weak and trembling.

He'd just looked at me, and said, "Relax," with a twisted smirk on his face.

After a while, I heard the low roar of a second motorcycle and saw a man approaching on his bike in the cleft between two steep dunes. The man parked his bike next to Omar's and got off. He, too, seemed simultaneously nervous and elated. He walked around me and examined me from all sides. I wasn't sure what was happening. When he was done, the two of them walked together and talked in a low whisper. After that, Omar returned and told me to put my helmet on and we drove away.

We went back to the city and he dropped me off at the apartment. I had no idea what had happened. I'd spent years not understanding what had occurred that day, revisiting the scene on the rare occasions I could access the memory only to remain dumbfounded, uncomfortable, astonished; and yet, I ended up repeating to myself: *Nothing happened! Nothing happened! It was an innocent meeting between friends!* But something was stirring wide awake inside of me, an understanding that I knew would take me the rest of my life to digest. Omar, I realized, had been showing me to another man, discussing the possibility that I could be this other man's youthful lover, too. It had been, quite simply, a meeting of like-minded men. In that scenario, Omar was the one procuring the girls and I, I suddenly realized, was one among many being groomed and packaged to be moved down the assembly line of pussy-hungry men. If to them I was a nymph, then to me they were murderous apes.

I felt a fire light up in my belly. There was so much heat spreading through my limbs. The walls of my stomach were lit and burning. It was as if I had swallowed gasoline; the fire was roaring, choking me from the inside with its smoke and heat. I could barely stand the pain. I doubled over and tried to take in deep breaths. What would have happened to me if I hadn't left Marbella? I tried to center myself. I was trembling, overheated. I thought again of the bloodied and bloated face of that other future version of me. I winced at the thought of her. At the thought that she represented a life I'd nearly lived, a life so racked with pain and guilt and isolation that I could hardly sustain the thought of her. How on earth would I have borne the weight of being her?

I walked back to the bus station. I passed the Virgin Mary weeping in her enclosure, and for a moment, I had the impression that time was standing still. The Virgin Mary weeping. What a tired image, what a worn-out image. The image of the dark night of the soul! I wondered, Was Omar conscious of his power? A power that had near fantastical proportions? Had he spent years, as I had, contemplating the residual aftereffects of his crime? His delinquent nature? The sinister conspiracy he'd subjected me to? Or did he lack the capacity for self-appraisal? Even now, I thought, hidden under the hardened filth, the bitter repulsion, was a mild happiness. A burgeoning will to hold the hand of the girl I'd been, to make room for her in the woman I'd become. I walked under the gunmetal sky and let myself be cleansed by a warm, sweet gale.

It dawned on me that by returning to Marbella, this eternal landscape of sunshine and guile, I had plunged my body back into the past—the tortured chapters of my adolescence—and that doing so had delivered a terrible shock; but I needed that shock to carry on. I could sense an incredible burst of energy ahead of me, a limpid energy born of hope. I thought about the fragility of all living beings, of the planet itself. Our resilience, I thought, is born in our vulnerability. That much was clear to me. It's not easy to honor our fragility, to care for it, to acknowledge it in the first place. It's not for the faint of heart. But it would be worth it, because tenderness and fragility, like kindness and love, are expansive, elastic, impossible to exhaust. I felt my chest widen, my heart expand; my body was making space for the girl I had been. My body, which was her eternal home. It wouldn't be long now. We would escape together soon. Our heads held high. Fire in our eyes. Discerning, vigilant, open, free.

# 12

ON THE WAY BACK, I got off the bus a few stops early. The leaves on the trees lining the road looked greener to me now. The sky, which had been thick with fog, appeared lighter, more forgiving. A mild sunlight was breaking through the heavy mist. It streamed down through the gaps in the leaves and brightened the grass and the asphalt. I caught sight of the sea every time there was a break in the row of southern buildings. The ocean looked varnished in that shy mustard light. As I made my way toward the apartment, it seemed to me that the earth was calling life back to itself, that the sun, having been absent all morning, had come forth to spend the last hours of the afternoon warming the roads and hills and stones of the city, heating up the waters that lapped along its shores.

I was excited to return home to Ellie. I couldn't wait to burst through the door and tell her that I'd survived my trip to Puerto Banús, that I'd gone to Puerto Banús and returned unharmed even if I'd felt shredded by terror, my guts minced. I stopped at a flower shop to admire its potted succulents, its young potted cacti nursing in the sidewalk sun, and thought about how, as all-encompassing as Omar's presence was, I hadn't seen him. No. We hadn't run into each other. I walked through the florist's door. There, in the dimly lit interior, in a corner, resting on a carved wooden stool, I spotted a crystal vase full of irises. They were beautiful. I walked over and stroked their fresh petals.

I heard a woman's voice at my back. "I can make you a gorgeous bouquet," she said. I turned around. "I just got some angel's breath in this morning."

She was a middle-aged woman with dark skin, bright black eyes shaped like almonds, and coarse hair she'd braided to one side. She took in a deep breath.

"Don't you just love the aroma of the flowers?" she asked tenderly. Her smile was full of patience and warmth.

"I wouldn't know what to do with the flowers," I said. "I'm leaving tomorrow for Granada."

"That's where I'm from," she said. "There's no place in the world like it."

I turned back around to glance at the irises. They'd been my favorite flower through my twenties. I remembered that my boyfriend, the chef, had gifted them to me early on in our relationship when we still spoke to each other at length and pined for each other during our long work shifts. He'd given me the irises for my birthday along with a box of handmade chocolates he'd flavored especially for me: dark cherry truffles decorated with gold leaves; eucalyptus-infused white chocolates dusted with

Himalayan salt; red peppercorn and whiskey bonbons. They were delicious. My mouth watered at the memory of them.

A moment later, the shopkeeper came up from behind me and plucked three irises out of the vase. "I'm going to wrap these for you as a gift. Take the bouquet with you to Granada. Consider it my offering to the city of my youth!"

She wrapped the flowers in brown paper and tied them with a ribbon she quickly twisted into a bow. As she put the finishing touches on the bouquet, spraying the flowers with fresh water, she told me that as a child she'd lived in the caves in the mountains overlooking the river, that every night she'd walked to the edge of the road to admire the Alhambra.

"It sits on a hill like a crown jewel." She sighed. "There isn't a day that goes by that I don't miss that view."

I told her I believed her. That I'd seen the palace once long ago and had never been able to forget it. That every time I thought of it I felt chills run down my spine, chills of disbelief, because it seemed impossibly beautiful to me, so extraordinary that I couldn't shake the idea that I'd dreamt it.

"Exactly," she said, and handed the bouquet to me. "For you!"

I thanked her and left, dipping my nose in the flowers. I loved their subtle, herby smell. The day was taking a wide, unexpected turn toward grace. I felt an electric energy course through my veins. I smiled to myself, oblivious to the passersby, as I considered the fact that I was going to seal the door to the apartment for the last time. I was going to abandon it to the elements. Sure, I thought, the apartment will live in my mind forever. I was sure, too, that what had transpired inside its walls would transform over the years; it would change as I, too, would.

I walked up the road and made my way to the apartment. Our bus would leave early in the morning. We had a few hours of daylight left to pack our suitcases. I couldn't wait to leave. We'd spend one last night in the apartment's unlit interior, navigating our way by candlelight. I was feeling light, positive, spacious. I was nearly there, on the cusp of freedom, finally about to exit my relationship with Omar that had been sinking me like a stone as long as I'd been denying its existence. I'd touched bottom. The only place left to go from there was up. It occurred to me, as I saw my future on the horizon, that Marbella had been my open-air prison. That I'd felt restricted, monitored, controlled by Omar's moods. I made my way to the building, through its heavy glass doors, up the stairs with firm footfalls. As soon as I walked in, I met Ellie's gaze.

"I'm so happy to see you," I said.

It was incredible to open the door and be greeted by her face, her adoring smile, her humor. She was sitting on her suitcase in the foyer, using her weight to seal it.

"It won't close!" she said with a giggle.

"You probably just arranged things differently," I said.

I could see her throwing her clothes and books and shoes into her suitcase impatiently. She, too, I considered, couldn't wait to get out of the apartment, to be as far away from its darkness as possible.

"You bought flowers?" she asked, looking up as she turned to kneel on the suitcase. She was on all fours, and she still couldn't close it.

I went into the kitchen and placed the flowers on the counter. I told her about the florist and how she'd punctuated my day with color.

"That's so sweet," she yelled breathlessly in my direction.

By the time I returned from the kitchen, she'd given up; she'd opened her suitcase and was busy pulling out her shoes and clothes. I still had to pack myself, and despite my eagerness to leave, I suddenly felt a pinch in my chest, an unexpected tightening of my heart. I paused in the threshold and observed Ellie. I told her that I thought she'd have an easier time if she rolled her shirts rather than folding and stacking them.

"You think?" she asked, and got to it, picking up a dress and rolling it against her thighs.

I got down on the floor to help her. I picked up her shoes and lined the edges of the suitcase with them, leaving a rectangle in the middle where she could deposit her clothes, which, once rolled, looked like rods and pipes. It was a very efficient affair, a method I'd learned and perfected over the course of my itinerant life. Packing, leaving, departures . . . they'd always been easy for me. But as we packed Ellie's belongings, I noticed that the pressure in my chest was worsening. The buoyant feelings hadn't lasted long. I feared the apartment would take me hostage; that we would leave, yes, and I would be free, yes, but I wouldn't know how to lay claim to my freed self. That challenge lay squarely ahead of me. It was a challenge that didn't offer prizes, that resisted mastery. But beneath that fear ran a deeper, darker one: that by leaving, I'd be discarding my past self—that lost adolescent girl—to the bowels of this behemoth to be devoured out of sight. I tried to breathe through the panic.

"What are you doing?" Ellie asked. I realized that my face must have looked contorted.

"I think I'm afraid to leave," I said.

She stared at me with a vacuous gaze that betrayed her lack of comprehension.

Even I could not understand what I was feeling. I had barely wanted to come to Marbella, and once we'd arrived, I'd wanted to leave at every turn. But now that our hour of departure was approaching, I was feeling reluctant, fearful, ambivalent. I explained to Ellie that I was breathing through a difficult feeling.

"What feeling?" she asked, tilting her head to one side and softening her gaze.

"I don't know," I said. "I'm afraid of abandoning the life I led here, the person I was back then."

"You're not abandoning anything," she said.

I explained to her that the thought of leaving my former self, the ghost of the girl I'd been, alone again in this dreadful apartment, this apartment that seemed capable of mauling everyone and everything, frightened me; it left me riddled with guilt. That I had realized while walking around Puerto Banús that I would have to find a way to take my teenage self away from here. That I couldn't leave her here to be consumed by the ashes of history, to erode with time.

Ellie listened quietly. Then she said, "I can help you pack as soon as we're done with this. Maybe it will help if we do it together."

I told her that I wasn't sure what would help.

We sat there quietly for a moment, crestfallen. Then she leaned over and put her hand on mine and reminded me that we'd purchased tickets to Granada, that our bus was scheduled to depart first thing in the morning. I looked at her, and for a brief second, a millisecond, I saw my own teenage face come forward in hers. She had a pleading look in her eyes. She looked terrified, and yet she was calm, resigned to her fate and speechless. I remembered how quiet I'd been as a teenager. How utterly alone. I could feel my lips trembling. I could feel tears rising up in my throat. I tried to swallow, but it hurt. Ellie squeezed my hand.

"How about I take care of this and you go pack," she said. She added that she thought it might do me good to walk through the apartment alone knowing that she was there sitting quietly on the living-room floor.

I felt my mind catch on the word *pack*. It was as if the fabric of my thoughts had snagged on that consonant-heavy syllable — *pack* — that word that made the sound of a punch or a tear, that frayed the fabric of my thoughts. I inhaled and exhaled slowly, deliberately. I kept thinking that I have to remove the person I used to be from this bereft, miserable place. Then I thought that I am still that person. She is a part of the person I have become. It occurred to me that perhaps, unbeknownst to me, I had returned to Marbella to gather myself, to take myself — her — out of here, to salvage what was left of her, to lift her out of this savage place. I wasn't afraid of what would happen to *me* once I left the apartment. No. I would be free of its walls, of its crushing weight. But I was afraid of leaving her alone in this greedy enclosure. I felt as if I were forsaking her to the darkness once again, but this time as an adult, with all of the insight I'd gleaned in the passing years, and that was unforgivable. What would she do here, trapped in these brutal walls? I took in the harrowing hallway that led to the bedrooms, which would soon be as dark as a tomb because the electricity had been shut off, likely forever. My thoughts turned and spun. Stay here and do what? I considered. Keep vigil over the ghost of Omar, the ghost of the person I'd been as his lover?

I felt the pressure give way to an intense sadness, a sadness that I found almost soothing; it was a feeling that had evaded me for years. I'd never felt sad for the girl I'd been. I'd never felt the scope of her loneliness. I'd only felt her stubborn defiance, her arrogance, her self-destructive nature. Her claim to freedom and untethered wildness. The feral bent of her character. She'd mocked me in the mirror. And now, on the cusp of my departure, she was showing me a softer side: her vulnerability, her pain, her exhaustion. So my presence had been helpful after all, I thought. I felt my strength slowly return to my limbs. I lifted the last few items and placed them neatly in Ellie's suitcase.

"I'll help you finish this first," I said.

She nodded, and we got off the floor in silence, a silence that felt almost sacred, and we closed the suitcase and zipped it shut.

"At last!" Ellie exclaimed, and stared adoringly at her sealed suitcase for a long moment.

I asked if she wouldn't mind walking through the apartment, closing all the windows and lowering the shutters, drawing the curtains, folding the towels and placing them back on the rack, removing the trash, emptying what little food we had in the refrigerator so I could take a moment to gather myself, all of my parts, and all of the possessions that belonged to those parts. We wouldn't have time to close up the apartment in the morning. She agreed.

I made my way to my bedroom and sat for a moment on the edge of my bed. I heard a whooshing in my ear, a hollow drumming sound; I remembered the symphonic rain that had poured throughout the night the first time Omar had kissed me. "He had kissed *me*," I murmured to myself. He knows the truth, I thought inwardly, and he knows that I know it, too. There are no fools left in this story, I thought, and got up as if on autopilot.

I walked toward the closet and reached for my ruined two-piece purple Speedo. Every time I touched the elastic — salt-eaten and exposed by the holes in the fabric — it cracked some more. I lifted it gently, carefully, and brought it to my nose. I smelled it like I'd smelled the flowers. They were the same color: a deep, joyous purple. I opened my luggage, which was still half-packed, and placed the swimsuit in a silk bag that I'd used to carry a few of my earrings and necklaces (accessories I'd forgotten to wear) and returned it to my suitcase. I reached for my sunglasses, my old red sunglasses, and placed them on my head.

The window was open in my room. I suddenly felt a cold breeze rush through it, an icy draft that caught me off guard. I walked to the window and stuck my hand out into the open air. It was warm, even balmy. When I stepped back again, I felt the draft, a cold spot hovering over my suitcase. I reached down and lifted the silk bag out of it. The bag was cold, almost icy, as if it contained the submerged memory of a corpse. I was taking the girl I had been away from everything she knew. I'd gathered her things; I'd packed them alongside my own. Perhaps, I thought, she'd gone cold in response. Even if she'd known nothing but cruelty here, it would be impossible for her not to cling to her darkness; we're all attached to our pain and the circumstances that have brought it about. We become tethered to our oppressed selves; we learn to identify with our servitude, to the ways in which we've become habituated to sacrifice ourselves to the needs of the powerful.

I wished desperately that there was something more I could do for my former self, the version of me that *I* had left behind — that everyone had left behind. I wished it with my whole being, more than I'd ever wished for anything. Then I heard a whisper, a suggestion so subtle I couldn't be sure if it was coming from within me or beyond.

"I am just a ghost," the voice said.

I had uttered those words to Omar. I had told him, "You are just a ghost."

And he was. As was I. But now my ghost needed to come with me. I needed her to leave the apartment.

"This," I told her, "is Omar's domain." I could feel her listening intently. "This is his lair." I told her that she no longer needed to live in the feeble light of this ruin. I told her that she had nothing to feel ashamed about. She had nothing to fear.

She listened warily.

I placed the swimsuit in the suitcase again. This time the temperature remained steady, so I walked over to my closet and grabbed my linen dress, my dirty underwear, the sweater I'd lent to Ellie. Who knew what had become of my jeans, I thought, my Dr. Martens, my T-shirt, my copy of Lorca's ballads, my toothbrush, all the other items I'd used that summer.

When I was done packing, I walked to the window and stared one last time at the view, at the church tower extending out of the hill and piercing the sky, at the Roman and Arab and Visigoth ruins, at the palms and aloes resting against the old stone walls. I felt as though I'd become two different people. As if I were staring out at the city with the eyes of the girl I'd been and the eyes of the woman I'd become. My vision felt doubly powerful. Her heart was beating alongside mine. It was trembling, fearful, unsure of itself, but also eager to leave. I could feel her resolve rising to match mine.

"I haven't left this apartment in twenty years," she confessed.

I told her that I understood her reluctance. And I added that I'd been out there all along; I had a pretty good read on the situation. She laughed, and I laughed with her. Then I closed the window. I lowered the shades and sealed the curtains. The room went dark, like a stage at the end of a play. I walked out with my suitcase in tow. I felt the room slide off of me. I felt its weight remain anchored in place. It didn't follow me, didn't wrap its black tentacles around my ankles and draw me back into its hysterical folds.

"Done?" I asked Ellie.

She was sitting on the couch.

"Done," she echoed.

I walked into the kitchen to grab a glass of water. The flowers were still on the counter, but they didn't look the same. They had gone limp and wrinkly. I stared at them, astonished.

"They wilted," Ellie said in a bewildered tone. "I don't know how they could have wilted so fast, but I felt a sudden cold that left me shivering; it was like an icy wind had moved through the apartment. It was just for a second. It was so strange, I thought it was just my imagination. But then I walked into the kitchen to put the flowers in a vase and noticed that the leaves had hardened. They'd almost crystallized, as if they were frostbitten. When I picked them up, the petals collapsed. They drooped down. I'm sorry, I don't know what I did wrong." Ellie was apologizing as if she'd stirred the cold gale that had entered the house.

"This place is hideous," I said. "It's not you." I told her that I was sure the flowers would regain their vitality the second we left the apartment. I observed the irises. They were limp, lifeless. I let out a little laugh. The symbolism was too simple; it aligned too easily with my circumstances. There was nothing left to read between the lines. I laughed again. Then I placed the flowers in the vase.

Ellie came up behind me. "What's so funny?" she asked.

We both peered down at the wilted flowers. And then she laughed, too. She saw what I had seen: the lack of irony, the sincerity and simplicity of death, the facility with which the vital energy of life wavers and becomes diffuse in the face of evil. Then, as if a long corridor stretched between my birth and the present moment, a corridor through which I could walk back and forth, that contained within it all of the stages of my personality, all of the episodes of my life, season after season, I remembered a certain man, much older than I was and famous, a man of a certain social standing, a documentary filmmaker. I remembered his hot, heavy breath as he leaned into my ear and said: "If you don't use that flower of yours, it's going to wilt."

We'd been in Jenin in Palestine. Ellie hadn't been with me. She'd cut her trip to Israel short and returned to America. She could handle being in Jerusalem only in short doses. Jerusalem was a site of pain for her, a living wound, just as Marbella was mine. I'd driven to Jenin with the filmmaker and another man, a young Israeli antioccupation activist. They'd pretended to be Israeli settlers every time we got to a checkpoint, putting kippahs on their heads and removing a Star of David necklace from the dashboard to hang on the rearview mirror, a performance that had made me extremely uncomfortable mostly because it had given us access to the Jewish-only highways in the occupied West Bank; we were actually headed to the Freedom Theatre, which recruited young men and women who had been training as suicide bombers in order to help them reestablish their relationship to life through acting. I'd spent the evening in an empty mansion on a lone hill overlooking the refugee camp in Jenin, a mansion I later found out belonged to a high-profile Palestinian leader who'd been on the IDF's most-wanted list for years. Late into that evening, the filmmaker had crawled into my sleeping bag, pulled out his cell phone, and shown me a video of two of his ex-girlfriends fucking. The women kept grunting as they screamed out his name, and I could see the edge of his hairy distended stomach in the video. He was the one recording the event, the sex being performed in his honor.

At first, I'd frozen. I hadn't known what to do. It was dark and we were on a remote hill, miles from the city center. Then it occurred to me that the best thing I could do was exit the situation politely, to leave so respectfully that he'd have the impression that everything was fine, that I would be right back so we could pick up where we'd left off. So I said nothing. I watched the video with sangfroid then told him I had to go to the restroom, that I would be right back.

I left the room and searched for an exit. There were other people — musicians, activists, lost youth — sleeping in the hallways, on the couches and the floors. I stepped over them as quietly as I could. I opened the door and walked up the stairs to the roof. It was cold. The air was crisp; a harsh wind whipped me in the face. Dawn was on the cusp of breaking. In the mild yolky light, I saw machine guns and empty cartridges abandoned on the roof. I stepped over them cautiously. There was a plastic chair in the corner. I sat in it and watched the sun rise over the green hills and the deformed houses of the refugee camp. All those lives, I thought, stacked one on top of the other. A literal open-air prison. There was nothing metaphorical about it. A ghetto, the infrastructure of ethnic cleansing in the works. I felt a deep ache radiate across my chest. The suffering of Palestinians was palpable, could be denied only from afar. An hour later, I heard the sound of a terrible explosion, as if the sky were being ripped from the earth. Israeli warplanes were flying overhead toward Lebanon, and the sound of the explosion repeated every time a new plane broke the sound barrier. I could hear that bang as clearly as if it were happening now, as if it were happening above the clearing Marbella sky.

"It's getting dark," Ellie said. "I'm going to rest. Try to get some sleep. We have to wake up at dawn," she said.

"Okay," I said.

It was late. For a second, I saw myself walking the long lonely miles to the center of Jenin and the bus station. What a strange world we live in, I thought, as I walked down the corridor one last time to my bedroom. A world where love and forgiveness and freedom, such expansive, ephemeral ideals, are so difficult to attain, impossible to hold or gift. That, I thought, is the strangest mystery of all: the propensity toward evil when love costs us so much less. It was a simple thought, perhaps even simplistic, but its execution required a level of empathy and self-assessment few of us can ever achieve.

The next morning, we lugged our suitcases and the wilted flowers up the road and passed the roundabout to the bus station. By the time we got there, we were covered in sweat; we were exhausted. We handed our suitcases to the driver, got on the bus, and sat quietly down. We leaned our heads together.

"Look," I said. "The flowers are coming back to life." It was true. The petals were firmer, the flowers perkier, the stems brighter.

Ellie smiled. "Unbelievable."

"I know!" I exclaimed, deliriously happy at the sight of their color returning.

I put my old sunglasses on. The harsh early morning light of Marbella appeared dim through the lenses. I felt so strong. As strong as a bull. My two hearts—my present heart and the heart of the girl I'd been—were pounding as one. As the bus pulled out of the station, backing up slowly and beeping to warn the people walking across the street, I felt a deep sense of relief wash over me. I told Ellie how much I loved her. I thanked her for having come with me. I told her that I loved the girl she'd been during those lonely years she'd spent living on the streets of Israel, trying to break free from her family, from the oppression of a strict religious life she didn't feel belonged to her. She told me that she loved the girl I'd been as well. That it was the wildly lonely parts of each of us that had brought us together. We called each other by all of our names: *sugarplum, potato, sour plum, pumpkin.* "I love you," we said. That was all we could say. That was all that was left to say as we left Marbella. We couldn't wait to walk through the streets of Granada. To bask in its warm southern light. To smell the orange blossoms, the basil, the jasmine bush.

We couldn't wait to greet our common ancestors, the Jews and the Muslims who had lived there, who had built it up in all of its grandeur and beauty then been persecuted, cast out, banished from their homes. We felt it was still our home, our land, a place where understanding awaited us; it was as if our ancestors had buried our truth in the earth for safekeeping so we would discover it centuries later as mature adults.

Granada, I thought quietly to myself, city of gardens, city of fountains, city of light and water, city of lush fields of pomegranates growing under a wide blue sky. I couldn't wait to be there. I couldn't wait to return there with the girl I had been; I could feel her excitement beneath my own, her old sense of adventure, her appetite for life, her gentle understanding of pleasure. I was happy. I was so happy.

# 13

THE GENTLEMAN WHO OPENED the pension door stared at us. He had one freckled hand on the door, the other wrapped around a wooden cane, and glanced at our faces with an empty gaze. He was wearing a wool cardigan over a checkered button-down, slacks, house slippers lined with fleece.

It was terribly hot outside. We'd arrived in the high heat of late morning, and were parched and tired. I asked if we could be let in; I explained to him that we had a reservation for a room with a private bathroom and two single beds, and I immediately heard an unsettling of chairs in the back of the house followed by whispers directing him to let us in.

As we stepped across the threshold into the cool interior, he returned to the living room with strained movements and turned the television off. He worked his way back into his armchair and, once there, hung his head and stared at a half-eaten apple and a bowl of shelled pistachios that had been, we presumed, placed on the table for him by the woman who'd told him to bring us inside. The woman was wearing her house clothes: a blue floral cotton dress and a white apron stained with grease, tomatoes, turmeric, saffron.

"*Aquí tienes las llaves,*" she said, handing me the keys and pointing up a spiral staircase to the second floor. "*Puerta* 2C."

We had already paid. The room had cost us only thirty-two dollars for the night, so we knew not to expect much by way of service. All we wanted were clean sheets and a corner to shower in.

"This place is so strange," Ellie said, as I unlocked the door to our room.

"Stranger than the apartment?" I asked.

Ellie rolled her eyes with complicity then sighed in relief.

"I can hardly believe we escaped," I said.

She laughed tenderly.

I thought the pension was charming. It was familiar to me, legible, as were the ambivalent manners of its elderly keepers, who were mainly concerned with balancing their books. I'd spent the night at a place just like this all those many years ago and remembered that even then I'd marveled at the careful construction of Spanish homes, their cold walls and buffed marble floors, their wooden floor-to-ceiling shutters and narrow terraces wrapped in delicate ironwork; these homes were so intelligent—so what if their keepers seemed indifferent to the world, shut out of life as if by a great and lasting shock. The buildings were designed to keep the heat out in summer when temperatures could reach more than a hundred degrees. We were in the high nineties that day, the heat dry and persistent enough to whittle our veins and shrink our appetites even late into the afternoon. Ellie's face was flushed.

She collapsed onto the bed closest to the door, and said, "Do you care if I take this one?"

I told her I didn't. "Don't you know that I prefer sleeping next to the bathroom?" I teased, as I removed my sandals and stared down at my swollen feet. "The heat!" I said, peeling my damp clothes off my limbs. "It's unbearable."

"I don't think I can move," she said. "Can we start the day over again in a few hours?"

"Yes, please!" I exclaimed, observing that my bare legs were covered in red patches from having sat in the window seat on the bus. The sun had been unrelenting.

We agreed to wait out the worst hours and sleep until the late afternoon. We'd both learned early in life to reset the day with a long nap, to take a break from reality so we could gather the strength to enter its harsh gates again.

Ellie got under the blankets and rubbed her face. "What's wrong with me?" she said in an aching tone. "I'm so tired!"

I wondered if our days at the apartment had introduced us to a new register of disorientation, a disorientation that had pierced through our calloused skin, left us raw and exposed in ways we hadn't fully experienced since our adolescence. I told her that perhaps being exposed to so much grief in our youth had numbed us; we were still in the process of recovering, tragically exhausted from carrying the burden of our pasts, but at least now our lives were pleasurable to inhabit and buttressed by the support of friends who had become, as we were to each other, family.

"Remember that saying we had?" I asked, as I got under the sheets and rested my head on the worn pillow. "Because there are no fixed points in the desert, it is not possible to get one's bearings."

"Yeah," she said, looking up at me in delight. When we'd lived in Amherst, we'd gotten into the habit of speaking to each other in maxims whenever one of us was down, and this particular refrain was one of our all-time favorites.

I told her that I felt as though the apartment in Marbella was a kind of desert, a decentered, shifting landscape where death was imminent, where it was impossible to let one's guard down. Her exhaustion would pass, I was sure, at a pace in keeping with our growing distance from that wretched nonhome.

She said that she wasn't so sure her fatigue stemmed exclusively from the apartment, that she'd been feeling this way on and off for months ever since she'd moved to England to take the job at Oxford. She told me that being one of the only Middle Eastern faculty members and one of the only women who specialized in reading the concealed archives of Middle Eastern history — the contents of which had been lost or displaced due to war and colonization and the annihilating logic of empire — left her feeling perpetually alone and exhausted.

She could hardly keep her eyes open. She reached for her shirt, which she'd taken off in a desperate attempt to lower her body temperature, and spread it on her face to avoid the light coming through the window.

"Sleep tight," I said. "I'll nap in a second."

I lit a cigarette and took in a deep drag. The bitter taste of the tobacco, the warmth it spread down my throat into my chest, was the sweetest feeling in the world to me. I got up and went to the window. I stared down at the street. It was empty. I traced the long rectangular shadows the buildings cast on the stone-paved road. The view was so finely geometric, all gray and yellow; the dazzling play of light and dark gave the place the appearance of a gorgeous abstract painting. The lines were so straight, the angles so sharp, the sky above so blue. It was the picture of clarity. All of the dimensionality of the space seemed to have collapsed into a single plane, an essential image that contained both surface and depth.

I thought of the deep history of these streets, how thousands of Muslims and Arab Jews secretly practiced Islam and Judaism after the Christian reconquest of Spain — performing their rituals of Sabbath, eating on the floor, carrying out the ritual slaughtering of animals, washing and burying bodies in their traditional ways, hiding Quranic writings and Torah scrolls in false walls and pillars. I thought again of the questions Ellie had been asking herself for years through her work: How can we read a history that's been erased? A history on the verge of vanishing? How do we relate to our own histories' disappeared contexts, to lifeworlds that no longer exist because the landscape was destroyed and its inhabitants banished? Al-Andalus, I considered, breathing in the dry, coarse air, is one such place, a space from which Muslims and Jews were purged. It is, I thought, glancing up and down the empty street, a place where their bodies and forms of life, their rituals and architecture and language and foods, are only apparent as a disappearance, as an end, an end that returns, that haunts with the perfumed waters of its fountains, its waterways, its lush gardens, its underground conduits, its Mudejar architecture, its leftover wall writings, its Torah scrolls found in false floors and ceilings, the Arabic and aljamia engravings in this or that arched passageway.

How, I wondered, can we bear witness to their disappearance? To all the ways, public and private, in which we are forced to lose parts of ourselves? I thought about how, on a smaller scale, I had been severed from myself by Omar's hands in that dreadful apartment, separated from the artifacts of my past, from my body and the language that belonged to that body. I considered again the fate of Muslims and Arab Jews around the world today; I considered the fact that our difference had been repeatedly turned into a deviance that called for punishment and felt my heart ache for us all, for myself and for Omar, who was, irrespective of everything that had come to pass between us, my brethren.

At that, I felt Omar's hand on the nape of my neck once more. I felt a shiver go down my spine and down the spine of the girl I'd been as a teenager. I felt an intense sexual energy course through my veins and blend my body with hers; we were indiscernible from each other; in that moment of erotic desire, we were one and the same. I wished then that I could smell Omar one last time, that I could return to his bedroom as an adult and make love to him, to the person he'd been at forty, tall, handsome, powerful, a man as decided, lithe, and ardent as he was adrift and playful. This was a familiar desire, to bend the laws of time so he and I could meet as equals, as fully embodied human animals eager to exchange pleasure, to give and take, to feed and be fed. I'd always thought that the fantasy served me; it did, after all, allow me to momentarily diminish the damage that had been done to me, at least in my head, and perhaps even dissolve some of Omar's pain, too, the shame that isolated him, that kept him moving restlessly around the globe—most likely, I thought, either to avoid being caught or to fish in fresh waters, to feed on fresh meat.

At that realization, my desire for him, soft and seductive at first, primal and bodily, transformed into a deep repulsion. I felt my heart turn heavy, its newfound density dragging me down, forcing me to lower my head in shame. It would always be like that, I thought; my feelings about Omar would always be in flux, shifting from leftover pangs of desire to pain; they were a reflection of my mutilated identity.

I was finally ready to reset the day, to leave behind the tireless march of the afternoon and start over. Ellie was breathing so deeply that I could tell it would be a few hours before she would wake. I fell asleep quickly; I felt as though my body were falling through the mattress and soon I was dreaming. I dreamt that I was back in the apartment, that Omar had laid the bloodied rags over my face. I was naked. He was penetrating me; I could hear him breathing heavily with pleasure, grunting as he pushed his own body through mine. But he couldn't see my face. I couldn't see his. I started to sob in the dream, and I could feel my tears being absorbed into the rags. The dried blood came alive; it spread over me as if the blood, like my tears, had been freshly spilled. I was drinking the blood, choking on it while Omar carried on unaware, indifferent, or perhaps even turned on by my suffering —his creation.

I woke up gasping for air. There were shafts of the late afternoon light coming through the window. I looked at the clock. We had slept for hours.

"Ellie," I called, and she stirred in her bed. "Ellie, wake up!"

She turned toward me and opened one eye.

"I had a terrible dream."

She reached her hand across the gap and I held it. I told her that I'd dreamt I was dead. She gave me a squeeze.

"Don't say that," she said. "I can't imagine being in the world without you."

We got up quietly. Once we were dressed, once we'd combed our hair and brushed our teeth, I opened the window, and we leaned our faces into the electric-blue air of twilight.

"Look," she said. "A fruit stand."

We made our way down the stairs and handed the keys to the woman who'd shown us in, stepped into the street, and made our way to the fruit vendor, who was leaning against the wall, whistling a quiet tune to himself. We bought peaches and grapes and oranges and dates and almonds, then we walked through the streets, past the cathedral and down Gran Vía de Colón, gazing open-mouthed at its elegant buildings, their reserved, dignified facades; the lush greenery that punctuated the sidewalk; the sky overhead that was acquiring the texture of silk and turning pink, a deep rose interrupted by streaks of purple and amber that dazzled us. Before we arrived in the Albaicín, we caught sight of the Alhambra. We stared at it breathlessly. It was seated regally in the bright-green foliage of the densely forested hills, and beyond it, the Sierra Nevada's sharp peaks, barely visible in the darkening sky, seemed to be keeping guard over its ancient stones.

"Ah," Ellie sighed. "I can't wait to walk its corridors and gardens. We need a palace full of light and love to cleanse ourselves of that apartment!"

I hooked my arm around hers, and we entered the Albaicín. The streets turned steep and narrow; the lanterns had already come on to buttress what little bit of light slipped through the gaps between the buildings.

"There are so many worlds inside this city!" I exclaimed.

There were tourists everywhere. We wanted mint tea. We wanted hummus with freshly baked pita bread. I wanted to eat baklava between drags of a cigarette.

"What could be better," I said, as Ellie glanced at the shops, their colorful glass lanterns hanging from the ceilings, glowing like tropical fish in the evening light, "than to balance the bitter taste of tobacco with the sweet aromas of ground nuts and phyllo dough soaked in floral honeys?"

"Nothing," she said. "Nothing could be better."

For a brief moment that left us both feeling foolish; we pretended we were home among our people, that nothing had been lost. We walked through a pair of hand-carved wooden doors into a tea shop so covered in tapestries that it smelled of camel hair and wet wool. I loved that smell. It was so familiar. It was the smell of my childhood. We sat in a wooden booth near the window and draped our bodies over embroidered pillows. There were mirrors hanging between the tapestries that reflected the passersby examining tajines, key chains with the dangling hands of Our Lady of Fatima, keffiyehs, babouche slippers, and silk scarves in the tourist shops across the steep alley.

We wondered what they were going to do with all of their souvenirs.

These people, we told each other, have no qualms about buying goods made in North Africa and sold by a new wave of Moroccan immigrants, immigrants who are essentially being commodified as stand-ins for the ghosts of Granada's waylaid past. But in all likelihood, the tourists' political attitudes toward Muslims—attitudes they would likely reclaim as soon as their vacation in Granada was over—revealed a mistrust and upheld a stereotype of Muslims as unpalatable and dangerous, as though inside each Muslim lay a terrorist waiting to be unleashed. That, we concluded, as we put in our order, was capitalism's dissociative and predatorial nature. It spared no one. Even we were active participants. There we were, after all, waiting for our order in a room full of tourists covered in Arab paraphernalia.

A few minutes later, our tea arrived, followed by our food. We ate ravenously. We barely exchanged a word. When we were done eating, we sat there and took in the darkening folds of night through the windows. Then we paid for our meal and made our way out of the Albaicín toward the city center. We found ourselves standing in front of a great stone building with carved wooden doors; at either side stood two women with long black slick hair and rosy skin. They welcomed us in, regaled us with sensuality. It was a hammam designed to recreate the illusion of Andalusia's Moorish past, another destination on the path of nostalgia tourism.

"Should we go in?" Ellie asked, her eyes wide with the anticipation of pleasure.

"We might as well," I said.

"I'm still so tired," she said. "All I want to do is soak my body in water."

We entered the hammam and were led by a second pair of women down a series of steps into a humid room that smelled of musk and rose. They handed us checkered Turkish towels and told us that we had ninety minutes to enjoy the baths, that they asked guests to speak in a low whisper. We walked through arched passageways lit with candles; the air was thick with moisture. There were trickling fountains at every turn, and dazzling tile work surrounded the pools. There were rooms lined with hot stone benches where the steam was so intense that we could only see each other's extremities. It felt incredible to bake in those rooms. To sweat. To purge ourselves of the apartment.

We eventually made it to the central pool. It was located directly beneath a domed tower that had holes shaped like stars carved into it. Through those holes, we could see the real stars in the night sky; we could see the moon in portions. We floated on our backs, staring through the openings in the dome for what felt like a long time. All I could hear was the pressure of the water against my eardrums. I felt as though I were within myself and beyond myself all at once. I felt light, supported, as if all the tension in my body was being released, dissolving in the warmth of the water.

Ellie swam up to me. "Hey," she whispered, cupping her hand under my head and lifting it so I could hear her. "I was thinking about how, in the mystical Jewish tradition, reading histories that have vanished, that have been hidden from view through time's erasure, through the systemically concealed violence against our people, is considered an approximation to nothingness, to Ein Sof, to the divine. So maybe interrogating a space like Al-Andalus, like the apartment, however wretched it was —a place where the past exists as an eternal disappearance—is like entering the void itself, the place where language feels divine because it is capable of naming that which has been made to disappear, of articulating the unspeakable. Do you think that's possible?"

I told her I did. I told her that I thought language was its own taking place, that it had its own historicity full of continuities and disruptions, and that what I'd been doing, what I'd been trying to do, was to trace the history of my relationship with Omar across time through language; to translate its annihilating effects, its mercurial shifts, its hard facts, its eternal contradictions into words so this text would exist as a context unto itself, as a second taking place that both mirrored the original event and further complicated it.

She looked at me steadily for a long time. "You know," she said. "I spent my thirties processing the years I lived alone on the street in Israel. Every time I had to work through a violent episode in therapy, I made sure you were in the room with me; the therapist would ask me to pick someone who made me feel safe and pretend that this person was there next to me. You were my safe person," she said, then she dipped her head underwater to rinse her hair and face.

So we had each received the other's story. We had acted as spillover containers for each other. I couldn't think of a deeper or more profound act of service. What else could we do but bear witness for each other? Receive each other's testimony and believe it, regard it, and preserve it lovingly? This trip, too, I thought, like the time we'd spent in Jerusalem, had become yet another thread that connected us through time and space.

In my mind's eye, I could see my teenage self—thin, tanned, my hair long, my eyes brighter, my movements more hesitant— swimming across the lake, Omar struggling to keep up, eventually pulling me back by the ankles and pressing his body against mine. It was strange, I thought, that I could remember so much about his body—the lean musculature of his legs, his wide chest, the precise shade of his skin, the taste of his mouth—but

I couldn't remember the length or girth or shape of his penis or how it had felt in my hand or against my body or inside of me. It was eternally lost to me no matter that I would spend the rest of my life haunted by it. That very forgetfulness, I thought, as we were called to exit the hammam—our ninety minutes were up—revealed my lack of experience, my innocence, my naïveté, my powerlessness against Omar. I had hidden from my fears, suppressed any awareness of my vulnerability, a strategy that had allowed me to survive all these years. For the first time, I felt gratitude toward my mind, its discernment and natural intelligence, its hardwired will; my mind had known to let some things recede into the distance, to discard what I could not, and would likely never be able to, bring myself to hold. There was a power in forgetting I hadn't been able to acknowledge before.

That night Ellie and I slept soundly without stirring or waking to use the bathroom, without remembering where we were. We slept a true sleep, a profound, transformative sleep, and woke up feeling refreshed, ready to take on the day. We had plans to get breakfast—*café con leche* and *pan rayado*—and head over to the Alhambra. We would finally walk through its glorious halls, take in all of its divine beauty.

What we didn't know but would soon discover was that most people had reserved their tickets months in advance. We weren't going to be let in. We hiked up and down the hill in the heat and asked every vendor, every guided-tour office—we even asked other tourists if they would consider selling us their tickets. Nothing. We stood at the arched gate of the Alhambra dumbfounded, in utter disbelief. Then we walked over to the mirador and looked down at Granada, at its white houses and green trees and clear-watered river. We sat there for a long time, staring out, crestfallen, shut out by our failure to grasp that the Alhambra was now the most popular tourist destination in all of Spain. "How odd," we said to each other, just as we had the previous evening, the realization so utterly absurd that it warranted repeating. "How strangely dissonant the world is. Islamophobia was rampant. It had been singing its deadly tune steadily since 9/11, and now, almost twenty years later, hatred of Arabs and Muslims the world over was so common, it was considered normal. And yet here was our civilization's ghost being celebrated."

"Let's just go," Ellie said. She was breaking into a rash from the heat.

"My pale pumpkin," I said, and leaned my head against hers.

She looked at her phone for other sites we could go to and found the Palacio de los Olvidados, the Palace of the Forgotten. We laughed heartily at our own strange fate as we made our way back down the hill and across the river to look at the recovered artifacts of Jewish families who had been tortured and banished from Spain's frontiers.

We were the only ones there. The entire museum was ours, empty; all we could hear was the gorgeous Sephardic music playing over the loudspeakers and our own distressed footfalls as we walked through the exhibition, taking in Torah scrolls, challah covers made of embroidered velvet, wine goblets, menorahs, children's clothes. We took in the framed deeds. We took in the torture devices used in the Inquisition: skull crushers, the famous *doncella de hierro*, the Judas cradle, with its pointed pyramid that ripped victims in half, knee splitters, waterboarding devices, brass bulls in which suspects were burned alive, their remains exiting the bull's nostrils as plumes of smoke. We drew sharp, purposeful breaths before a set of metal "masks of shame" that were shaped like wild boars' faces, with long metal beaks and muzzles that made it impossible to eat. Women were forced to wear them in public until they eventually starved to death. I saw that the wild boar, my wild boar—her soft animal body, which had never been given a chance to grow, her heart, like my own, unable to graze the green pastures of childhood—was omnipresent. She had always been there with her piggish face, her frightful gaze, her uncertain gait, tortured, hounded, hung upside down and denuded, skinned, hacked into pieces, and fed to men, not a being unto herself but a tool for satiating the hunger of others just as we women had been: edible, interrupted beings whose bodies were overpowered, whose lives were lives of service no matter our will.

I thought I saw the shadow of my wild boar sliding across the walls of the museum. I thought I saw her weaving her way between the artifacts. No—I did not *think*—she *was* there. We stood side by side looking at the boar masks mounted on female mannequins, our chests aching in equal measure. I breathed alongside her. I felt the rhythm of her hot, heavy breath synchronize with the beating of my heart, my two hearts. I saw myself running through time with her and knew that she would always break the laws that separate the living from the dead to pay me a visit. She would be most welcome. I would eternally salute her.

I looked one last time at the masks of shame. I thought of my mother, of all of our mothers. I thought of my father, of how his presence in our lives was made through absence. What is a father? I wondered. What is fatherhood, motherhood, brotherhood? I wanted to reach out and comb my brother's hair. To whisper in his ear, *Not everything is absence; let's hold on to this life together.* I'd been forced to bury the brother I had known while he had gone on living, a ghost of his former self. How confused I'd been. How utterly wrecked. How plainly disoriented. And yet I wouldn't change anything that had happened. What's the point of wishing for the impossible? The only way forward is to surrender to fate, the fate that had been made for me and the fate that I'd made on my own. It was all exactly as it needed to be. I was not alone. Neither was Ellie. We were bonded to each other, to our mothers and grandmothers and sisters and aunts across time, and while we could not change the wrongdoings of the past or fix the errors of others, we could hold hands and purge ourselves of the shame of our perpetrators. We weren't the ones who should be wearing those masks of shame. No. They did not belong to us. Maybe they didn't belong to anybody. Maybe we weren't meant to experience shame at all. "There's nothing to be ashamed of," Xavi had said to me in the early days of our relationship when he had intuited that I was holding back some internal darkness to protect our relationship. He, too, like Ellie, had softened me, had helped me to accept the shape of my life, to love it even. Xavi, who had learned my story, who had become my witness through it all. I missed him terribly. I needed to hear his voice. I needed his kindness. I needed to return to him and sit by his side, to feel him breathing next to me.

We walked up to the last floor of the museum. It was a partially covered terrace with a bench facing a gallows pole, a window looking out to the Alhambra. We sat down.

"Even here," Ellie said, "there's no historical context provided, no information plaques acknowledging the violence of the Spanish Inquisition, the expulsion and torture of Arabs and Jews. The hanging instrument, used to execute Jews and Muslims alike, is just sitting here, facing the Alhambra, without having been properly encased. There are no boundaries around it to imply its anachronism, which suggests it is still a tool that can be employed spontaneously."

I told her that it seemed positioned in the most sinister way, as if to suggest that our death as Muslims and Jews was and would always be imminent.

She pulled out a bag of leftover peaches from her backpack.

"You're going to eat those here?" I asked.

"I am," she said, and bit into one of the peaches. "It's delicious and I'll take my small pleasures where I can."

I remembered sitting on Sahar's roof in Bil'in, drinking tea, eating fruit, smoking hookah after hookah as we watched Israeli tanks roll through the streets, the trash being set on fire, dogs being beaten by frustrated kids. We had waited for days for the water to be turned back on. We hadn't left her house more than once in the five days we'd been there. Eventually, we'd gone down the street to buy bottled water that had been brought in from the other side of the security wall. That terrace, I thought, was Sahar's open-air prison. That was the last time we had seen her. She was no longer a part of our lives though we thought and spoke of her often. She was another vanishing point, another absence unaccounted for; we carried her memory with us even after she'd disappeared from our lives. I closed my eyes and took in a deep breath. I heard the tap-tap-tapping of the baby wild boar's feet on the tiled floors again. I could smell her. She'd smelled of earth and dirt and mud, and I thought to myself, She, too, was my witness and I would forever be hers.

Ellie spat the pit into the palm of her hand. "Look," she said, spreading her palm for me to see. "This pit is both an end and a beginning."

"It is," I said. "It truly is."

We sat there staring at the gallows pole for a long time. We sat in silence. I thought to myself that in certain respects I had been beheaded by Omar, my identity interrupted. I'd had to invent myself anew after him. And I had. I had managed to look at my death head-on. I'd tried to venture toward what was concealed from me. I had tried to trace through language the accumulated erasures to which he had subjected me. But beneath these erasures, I had found others, just as within each verse in a poem is hidden another poem. So, as it turns out, I thought, I hadn't written a book about Omar or me. I had written a book about the savage ghosts of history, about the dead whose pain continues to be recycled through this earth because we refuse to acknowledge our wrongdoings. I had created language, this language, as an offering bestowed to others, an offering of the simplest truth of all: that Omar and I and my mother, my brother, my father, his mother and father, and so on and so forth, every one of us, we are all caught up in this vortex of cruelty together; there were no victors, no victims; we were caught in a web we had woven together. We are all of us implicated, all of us responsible. That the betrayals we commit on others we first commit against ourselves. That we go down and rise up as one single organism. The undoing of one of us is the undoing of us all. How are we to contend with our fragility? We who are so reckless, so impatient, so perpetually obsessed with our unfulfilled needs? I hadn't the slightest clue. The answer, I thought, looking at the sky beyond the window, a pearly pink lifted by a wild golden glow, was beyond my reach. It was beyond grammar. Beyond language. Beyond the spoken word. And then, looking one last time at the Alhambra in all of its glory and beauty past and at the gallows pole that had been used to annihilate that past, looking at the tool of death superimposed on this architecture that so thoroughly celebrated life, I thought, isn't it possible to transform the cruelty that had connected Omar and me back again into love?

## About the author

## Read on

Insights,
Interviews
& More...

# Meet Azareen Van der Vliet Oloomi

Kayla Holdread

AZAREEN VAN DER VLIET OLOOMI is the author of the novels *Savage Tongues, Call Me Zebra,* and *Fra Keeler* and the director of the MFA program in creative writing at the University of Notre Dame. She is a National Book Foundation "5 Under 35" honoree and the winner of a 2019 PEN/Faulkner Award, a John Gardner Award, and a 2015 Whiting Award, as well as the recipient of a Fulbright Fellowship and residency fellowships from MacDowell and Ledig House. Her work has appeared in the *New York Times,* the *Paris Review, Guernica, Granta, Bomb,* and elsewhere. She lives in Chicago and is the founder of Literatures of Annihilation, Exile, and Resistance, a lecture series on the global Middle East that focuses on literature shaped by colonialism, military domination, and state-sanctioned violence. ᐁ

# An Excerpt from
## *Call Me Zebra*

Read on

If you loved *Savage Tongues,* read on for an excerpt from Azareen Van der Vliet Oloomi's *Call Me Zebra!*

ILLITERATES, ABECEDARIANS, Elitists, Rodents all — I will tell you this: I, Zebra, born Bibi Abbas Abbas Hosseini on a scorching August day in 1982, am a descendent of a long line of self-taught men who repeatedly abandoned their capital, Tehran, where blood has been washed with blood for a hundred years, to take refuge in Nowshahr, in the languid, damp regions of Mazandaran. There, hemmed in by the rugged green slopes of the Elborz Mountains and surrounded by ample fields of rice, cotton, and tea, my forebears pursued the life of the mind.

There, too, I was born and lived the early part of my life.

My father, Abbas Abbas Hosseini — multilingual translator of great and small works of literature, man with a thick mustache fashioned after Nietzsche's —

was in charge of my education. He taught me Spanish, Italian, Catalan, Hebrew, Turkish, Arabic, English, Farsi, French, German. I was taught to know the languages of the oppressed and the oppressors because, according to my father, and to my father's father, and to his father before that, the wheels of history are always turning and there is no knowing who will be run over next. I picked up languages the way some people pick up viruses. I was armed with literature.

As a family, we possess a great deal of intelligence — a kind of superintellect — but we came into this world, one after the other, during the era when Nietzsche famously said that God is dead. We believe that death is the reason why we have always been so terribly shortchanged when it comes to luck. We are ill-fated, destined to wander in perpetual exile across a world hostile to our intelligence. In fact, possessing an agile intellect with literary overtones has only served to worsen our fate. But it is what we know and have. We are convinced that ink runs through our veins instead of blood.

My father was educated by three generations of self-taught philosophers, poets, and painters: his father, Dalir Abbas Hosseini; his grandfather, Arman Abbas Hosseini; his great-grandfather, Shams Abbas Hosseini. Our family emblem, inspired by Sumerian seals of bygone days, consists of a clay cylinder engraved with three *A*s framed within a circle; the *A*s stand for our most treasured roles, listed here in order of importance: Autodidacts, Anarchists, Atheists. The following motto is engraved underneath the cylinder: *In this false world, we guard our lives with our deaths.*

The motto also appears at the bottom of a still life of a mallard hung from a noose, completed by my great-great-grandfather, Shams Abbas Hosseini, in the aftermath of Iran's failed Constitutional Revolution at the turn of the twentieth century. Upon finishing the painting, he pointed at it with his cane, nearly bludgeoning the mallard's face with its tip and, his voice simultaneously crackling with disillusionment and fuming with rage, famously declared to his son, my great-grandfather, Arman Abbas Hosseini, "Death is coming, but we literati will remain as succulent as this wild duck!"

This seemingly futile moment marked the beginning of our long journey toward nothingness, into the craggy pits of this measly universe. Generation after generation, our bodies have been coated with the dust of death. Our hearts have been extinguished, our lives leveled. We are weary, as thin as rakes, hacked into pieces. But we believe our duty is to persevere against a world hell-bent on eliminating the few who dare to sprout in the collective manure of degenerate humans. That's where I come into the picture. I — astonished and amazed at the magnitude of the darkness that surrounds us — am the last in a long line of valiant thinkers.

Upon my birth, the fifth of August 1982, and on its anniversary every year thereafter, as a rite of passage, my father, Abbas Abbas Hosseini, whispered a monologue titled "A Manifesto of Historical Time and the Corrected Philosophy of Iranian History: A Hosseini Secret" into my ear. I include it here, transcribed verbatim from memory.

Ill-omened child, I present you with the long and the short of our afflicted country, Iran: Supposed Land of the Aryans.

In 550 BC, Cyrus the Great, King of the Four Corners of the World, brave and benevolent man, set out on a military campaign from the kingdom of Anshan in Parsa near the Gulf, site of the famous ruins of Persepolis, to conquer the Medes and the Lydians and the Babylonians. Darius and Xerxes the Great, his most famous successors, continued erecting the commodious empire their father had begun through the peaceful seizing of neighboring peoples. But just as facts are overtaken by other facts, all great rulers are eclipsed by their envious competitors. Search the world east to west, north to south; nowhere will you find a shortage of tyrants, all expertly trained to sniff out weak prey. Eventually, Cyrus the Great's line of ruling progeny came to an end with Alexander the Great, virile youth whose legacy was, in turn, overshadowed by a long line of new conquerors, each of whom briefly took pleasure in the rubble of dynasties past.

Every one of us in Iran is a hybrid individual best described as a residue of a composite of fallen empires. If you were to look at us collectively, you would see a voluble and troubled nation. Imagine a person with multiple heads and a corresponding number of arms and legs. How is such a person, one body composed of so many, supposed to conduct herself? She will spend a lifetime beating her heads against one another, lifting up one pair of her arms in order to strangle the head of another.

We, the people — varied, troubled, heterogeneous — have been scrambling like cockroaches across this land for centuries without receiving so much as a nod from our diverse rulers. They have never looked at us; they have only ever looked in the mirror.

What is the consequence of such disregard? An eternal return of uprisings followed by mass murder and suffocating repression. I could not say which of the two is worse. In the words of Yevgeny Zamyatin: *Revolutions are infinite.*

By the twentieth century, the Persian empire's frontiers had been hammered so far back that the demarcating boundary of our shrunken nation was bruised; it was black and blue! Every fool knows that in order to keep surviving that which expands has to contract. Just look at the human heart. My own, reduced to a stone upon the double deaths of my father and my father's father, both murdered by our so-called leaders, is plump and fleshy again; your birth has sent fresh blood rushing through its corridors.

Hear me, child: The details of the history of our nation are nothing but a useless inventory of facts unless they are used to illuminate the wretched nature of our universal condition. The core of the matter, the point of this notable monologue, is to expose the artful manipulation of historical time through the creation of false narratives rendered as truth and exercised by the world's rulers with expert precision for hundreds of years. Think of our own leaders' lies as exhibit A. Let us shuffle through them one by one.

When the century was still young, our people attempted the Constitutional Revolution but failed. In time, that failure produced the infamous Reza Shah Pahlavi, who ruled the country with thuggery and intimidation. Years later, during the Second World War, Mr. Pahlavi was sent into exile by the British, those nosy and relentless chasers of money—those thieves, if we're being honest. And what, child, do you think happened then? Pahlavi's son, Mohammad Reza Shah Pahlavi, who was greener than a tree in summer, stepped up to the throne.

Claiming to be the metaphysical descendent of the benevolent Cyrus the Great, the visionary Mohammad Reza Shah Pahlavi anointed himself the "King of Kings" and launched the White Revolution, a chain of reforms designed to yank the country's citizens into modernity by hook or by crook.

It was just a matter of time before the people rose against the King of Kings. Revolution broke out. Mohammad Reza Shah Pahlavi spilled blood, tasted it, then, like a spineless reptile, slid up the stairs of an airplane with his bejeweled queen in tow and fled, famously declaring: "Only a dictator kills his people. I am a king."

The Islamic clergy, whose graves the king had been digging for years, hijacked the revolution, and in one swift move, the monarchy was abolished. The king's absence allowed the revolutionary religious leader Ayatollah Khomeini to return to the country after a long political exile. Khomeini, former dissident, swiftly established the Islamic Republic of Iran and positioned himself as the Supreme Leader. The Grand Ayatollah proceeded to outdo the King of Kings. His line of metaphysical communication skipped over Cyrus the Great; it pierced the heavens to arrive directly at God's ear. The Supreme Leader claimed to enjoy unparalleled divine protection.

How did he employ his blessings? By digging the graves of the secularists and the intelligentsia just as the Pahlavi kings had dug the graves of dissidents, Communists, and the clergy. With one hand, God's victors eliminated their revolutionary brothers, and with the other, they shucked pistachios, drank tea, raided their victims' closets, ate cherries picked from their gardens.

Child, we, the Hosseinis, were persecuted by both sides. The King of Kings, seeing his end in sight, made no exceptions. His men garroted the old and the infirm and the young. Mothers and children are still weeping for their lost loved ones. Your great-grandfather, Arman Abbas Hosseini, was among the executed. The ruthless pigs dragged him from his deathbed when he was eighty-nine. Two days later, your grandfather, Dalir Abbas Hosseini, had a heart attack. He could not endure the thought of his father being hanged from the rafters. Before he died, he told me that he could not stop hearing the sound of his father's brittle bones crackling under the weight of his body as it hung from the noose. Until you came into this world, my only consolation was that my father, at least, had died in his own bed. You are a flame of light in these dark woods.

Like everyone else in this trifling universe, we Iranians are a sum of our sorry parts. Put our pieces together and what emerges is not a whole, clear image. Our edges are jagged, nonconforming, incoherent. Our bloodline is so long and varied, it can be traced back to the origins of the universe. How is man to make sense of his condition when the wrangle over power between conquerors old and new herds history's stories in ever more puzzling directions?

Now that you have heard the story of our cruel fate, you are ready to listen to the Hosseini Commandments, a text that has three giant heads that you must make part of your own. Why, you might ask? Because if you know the ways of man, the various conditions of his iniquitous mind, you will not be stumped by fear, guilt, avarice, grief, or remorse, and therefore, when the time comes, you will not hesitate to plumb the depths of the abyss and send out a resounding alarm to the unthinking masses, those who are willfully blind, warning them of the advancing army of the unresolved past.

FIRST COMMANDMENT: Ecce homo: This is man, destined to suffer at the hands of two-faced brethren inclined to loot the minds and bodies of friend and foe.

Ill-fated child, trust nobody and love nothing except literature, the only magnanimous host there is in this decaying world. Seek refuge in it. It is through its missives alone that you will survive your death, preserve your inner freedom.

SECOND COMMANDMENT: Like a gored bull, history is charging through the world in search of fresh victims. Think! Does a gored bull run straight? No. It zigzags. It circles around itself. It is bleeding and half-blind. Be warned: The world's numbskull intellectuals, which form 99.9 percent of all intellectuals, will feed you lies. History, they will say, is linear, and time continuous. During Pahlavi's final years, these deluded intellectuals hoped that revolution would lead to democracy. What came of it but death? Your ancestors, the Hosseinis, paid for their leaders' ignorance with their lives. Do not be caught unawares. Spit the lie right back out. Aim for their heads.

THIRD COMMANDMENT: We Hosseinis—Autodidacts, Anarchists, Atheists—are expert connoisseurs of literature and therefore capable of taking a narrative apart and putting it back together faster than a wounded man can say "Ah!" This talent, passed on to you by your honorable ancestors, is your sword. Draw it anytime you need to strike stupidity in the face.

The depth of our knowledge, the precision of our tongues, and our capacity for detecting lies is unparalleled. We are the true intellectuals, the exception to the rule, the .1 percent. This is yet another source of our ill-fatedness.

We are the loneliest of the lonely. Our message falls on the deaf ears of the unthinking masses. Nevertheless, we are destined to wander the earth spreading the word of our forebears and our forebears' forebears, the Great Writers of the Past, who, like us, knew to retreat into literature in order to survive history's bloodshed and thus be in a position to share the truth of it with the world. For this we will always be persecuted: for pointing our fingers and asking, Is this a man?

Ill-fated child, when your time comes, you must dive headfirst into the swampy lagoons of our pitiful human circumstances and, after roving the depths, emerge with the slimy pearl of truth. Be warned: The truth is ugly,

wretched, full of craters and holes through which rise the
fumes of death. Most men, smug and cowardly, will turn
their noses away from its stench. Sooner or later, you will
have to engage with these men; you will have to persevere
despite their private delusions and collective ignorance.

Suffice it to say that in combination with the events that
unfurled during my childhood years, events charged with
everything that is futile and unspeakable in this universe,
my father's monologue transformed my consciousness. I
had not been alive long before my mother, Bibi Khanoum,
died. Her death flattened my heart into a sheet of paper. It
leveled my mind. It rubbed my nose in manure. My only
good fortune is that I realized early on that I am one of the
wretched of this earth. But this is a matter for later.

According to my father, during the long revolutionary
months prior to the establishment of the Islamic Republic
of Iran, my mother — a woman with strong legs and a
sweet disposition — would remind my father, Abbas
Abbas Hosseini, that he had been accused by the Iranian
intelligentsia of being "a passive traitor whose nose was
hooked into books while others' were being rubbed in the
blood of their brethren."

Bibi Khanoum, my father informed me, would say:
"Don't test your luck, Abbas! People don't like to be
snubbed while they're being martyred for their beliefs."

In response, my father would pace the corridor of
their Tehran apartment convulsing, his moods swinging
dramatically, while he spewed ad infinitum: "I am a
Hosseini. I would rather die than hold my tongue! Pseudo
intellectuals! Imbeciles! People have disappeared, been
arrested, executed, their bodies discarded, scattered across
the earth. And they still believe democracy is around the
corner? The revolution is going to be hijacked. Don't they
know history is full of ruptures, haphazard events, and
prone to recycling its own evil phenomena?"

The following year, an ashen sky, grayer and heavier

than a donkey's behind, settled over Iran. As my father predicted, the revolution was promptly seized by the Islamic leaders. And even worse, Saddam Hussein, that wide-eyed despot, came sniffing around the borders of our freshly assembled Islamic republic and proudly launched a brutal and tactless war on a fatigued and divided Iran.

A year after the war broke out, the few remaining intellectuals who hadn't been jailed or fled the country with false papers declared my father a clairvoyant truth teller. But my father — Autodidact, Anarchist, Atheist, whose character they had previously assassinated — refused to have his moment in the sun. Instead, he and my mother, Bibi Khanoum, ran for the hills. She was pregnant with me, and my father had suffered enough loss to last him a lifetime. It was winter. The journey was cold, and damp, and dangerous. It had felt interminable to them. But they survived it and took shelter in that stone house in Nowshahr, near the Caspian Sea, which was built as a sanctuary by my great-great-grandfather, Shams Abbas Hosseini, who referred to the house as either the Censorship Recovery Center or the Oasis of Books, depending on his mood.

I have been told by my father that halfway through their journey, in the middle of the rugged Elborz Mountains, which separate Tehran from the Caspian Sea, he stopped the car and got out. He looked over his shoulder at Mount Damavand, which hovers over our capital like the shiny white tooth of a gentle giant, and wept until the skin around his eyes was paper-thin: "That pig-headed Saddam is going to level our city!"

And level our city he did. But even in the midst of darkness, there is always a flicker of light. Months later, in 1982, I was born in the heart of the Oasis of Books, the library, which was designed in the shape of an egg and built around a date palm that shot to the sky through an opening in the roof. My mother leaned against the trunk of the tree and pushed. I — a gray-faced, black-eyed baby — slipped out of her loins into a room lined with dusty tomes, into a country seized by war. I immediately popped a date in my mouth to sweeten the blow. My parents looked down at me, grinning with hope.

I learned to crawl, walk, read, write, shit, and eat in that library. Even before I could read, I nurtured my brain by running my hands along the spines of all the old books and licking their soot off my fingers. After feeding on the dust of literature, I sat on the Persian rug and stared at *The Hung Mallard*, which was fixed to the wall. Once I was old enough to walk, I paced in concentric circles like a Sufi mystic, masticating dates and muttering the family motto to myself: *In this false world, we guard our lives with our deaths.*

The days passed. My education unfolded in the midst of the interminable war. My father read aloud to me from Nietzsche's oeuvre on a daily basis, usually in the mornings, and after lunch, he taught me about literature, culling paragraphs from books written by our ingenious forebears, the Great Writers of the Past: Johann Wolfgang von Goethe, Mawlānā (alias Rumi), Omar Khayyám, Sor Juana Inés de la Cruz, Dante Alighieri, Marie-Henri Beyle (alias Stendhal), Teresa of Ávila, Rainer Maria Rilke, Franz Kafka, Sādegh Hedāyat, Frederick Douglass, Francesco Petrarca, Miguel de Cervantes, Walter Benjamin, Sei Shōnagon. The list went on and on; it included religious thinkers, philosopher-poets, mystics, secularists, agnostics, atheists. Literature, as my father would say, is a nation without boundaries. It is infinite. There are no stations, no castes, no checkpoints.

At the end of each lesson, as bedtime neared, my father stiffly ordered: "Ill-fated child, assimilate and regurgitate!" In this way, he nurtured my mind. He taught me the long-lost skill of memorization. What is the purpose of memorization in the Hosseini tradition? It is twofold: not only does it restore the ritual function to literature — its orality — which harnesses literature's spontaneous ability to transform the listener's consciousness, but it also protects the archive of our troubled, ruinous humanity from being lost through the barbarism of war and the perpetual ignorance that binds our hands and feet. Count the times books have been burned in piles by the fearful and the infirm, men and women allergic to inquiry. Memorization is our only recourse against loss. We Hosseinis can reproduce the pantheon of literature instantly; we can retranscribe texts from the dark folds of our infinite minds. We are the scribes of the future.

While my father and I spent our days united in the realm of literature, my mother, Bibi Khanoum, spent her days in the kitchen. If she ever ventured out of the house, it was to find us food: rice, oranges, fish the local tribesmen had managed to wrench out of the sea. I didn't spend much time with her. She didn't agree with my father's methods. She considered them invasive and extreme for my age, but he, twenty years her senior, had the upper hand in all matters governing our family.

I remember my mother once walked into the oval library, where she had given birth to me, with her apron tied around her waist and her face moist from the kitchen steam, to scorn my father: "Abbas, you are raising this child to be a boy! How will she survive in the world? Who will marry her?"

My father reproached her: "These are times of war and you are worried about marriage?"

"And who do you suppose will feed her once we are dead?" she retorted. "A mother has to worry about her child's stomach!"

Confrontation ensued, but I don't remember anything after that. I have tried hard to remember my mother's face, the tone of her voice, the feel of her touch, but the details are out of reach. She would die not long after that argument, and the void left over by her death would push my father and me over the edge. He would fill the lacunae of our lives with literature. Over time, my mind, filled to the brim with sentences, would forsake her.

In the meantime, on the other side of the Elborz Mountains, that megalomaniac Saddam was spreading mustard gas across the frontier, shooting missiles at random targets, burying mines in the no-man's-land separating our two nations. What did the Supreme Leader of the Islamic Republic of Iran do? He sat on his newly established throne looking healthier than a fresh pear and ordered human wave attacks to blow up the mines that his nemesis, that bushy eyebrowed man-child, had buried at the front. Human wave attacks! As if it were the Great War!

Now, Rodents, let us ask: What is the purpose of a flicker of light in the midst of all that bloodshed? Easy. To illuminate the magnitude of the surrounding darkness.

At a certain point during the long war, my father started to wander about the perimeter of the house or along the seashore, night and day, holding me up as if I were a torch. He used my head, which shone like a beacon with all the enlightened literature he had inserted into it, to measure the scope of the encroaching abyss. Iran, he decided, was no longer a place to think. Not even the Caspian was safe. We had to flee. We had to go into exile. We departed: numb, astonished, bewildered. 〜